THE FARRIER'S SON

by

Robert D Prince

LANDING CHINESE AT COOKTOWN, QUEENSLAND

Published by Robert D Prince

robertprince67@bigpond.com

Historical fiction set in Cooktown and the Palmer River goldfield during the 1870s gold rush.

ISBN-13: 978-0-9944708-0-5

Cover art and design: Glen Holman www.glenholman.com
Editing and interior design: Philip Newey www.philipnewey.com/All-read-E

Title page image: Chinese Landing at Cooktown, Queensland, Australia: *Australasian Sketcher*, Monday, 17th May 1875 (by courtesy of the State Library of Victoria)

SOMETHING OF THE AUTHOR...

Robert Prince was raised in the tropical paradise of Mossman, North Queensland, Australia. He attended the University of New England and soon after established an accounting practice on the Atherton Tableland where he and his wife raised four children.

His roots go back to the very early days of North Queensland settlement when his great grandfather from Wales operated an engineering and foundry business on the Charters Towers goldfield and his great grandfather from Prussia overlanded supplies with pack-horses to the Russell River goldfield.

The tenacity of the north's old-timers has inspired Robert to follow in their footsteps, researching history and retracing lives. Many of their personal stories of hardship and compassion still exist but are hidden away. It is these stories he wishes to unearth and share with others and in so doing celebrate the greatness of these pioneers.

In his novel *The Farrier's Son* he writes about what he understands: the history of the gold rushes of Northern Australia and the people who opened this frontier. It is an untold story equal to the popularised American Wild West.

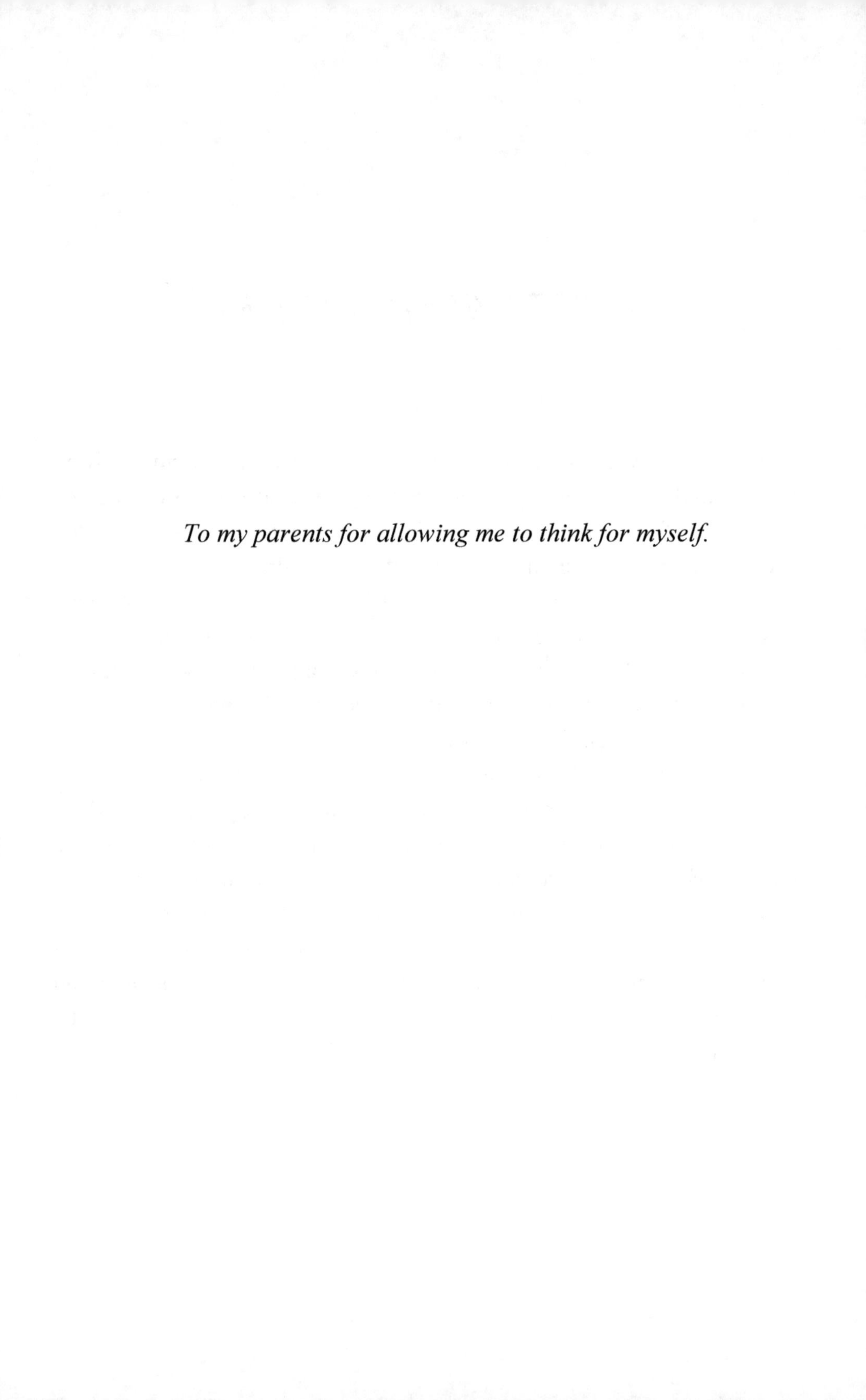

To my parents for allowing me to think for myself.

Human migration owes much to the quest for gold. Since antiquity people dazzled by its lure have sailed the seas and trekked across continents risking all to fill their pockets with the precious metal.

Australia is no exception with the gold rushes of early days drawing hungry miners from around the world. With no more than hand tools and swags they flocked to the frontier expecting to strike fortune overnight. One such strike was the Palmer River goldfield on Cape York Peninsular where alluvial gold was discovered in 1873. Thirty-five thousand men and a sprinkling of women descended upon what was hitherto a wasteland inhabited only by Aborigines. Within weeks of discovering gold the port of Cooktown was established to service the needs of those on the field. Chaotic scenes were witnessed daily as people jostled for positions on this frontier.

My parents were among those early arrivals and I was born in Cooktown on 20 January 1878.

At the age of eight I was sent to boarding school and while there began to feel distanced from my family. Though they were caring I often preferred to be alone, wandering the countryside rather than being with them. Then, later, while practicing as a solicitor in Cairns, I began to question why?

My attention turned to the family archive where I found a diary entry dated 24 June 1877. The entry read: 'I have sought the warmth of another. Only briefly but with lasting consequences. Please be accepting when the signs become apparent.' These few words cast doubt on my parentage and led me on a journey that revealed the truth and gave me a better understanding of myself.

The Farrier's Son which tells the story is based on information sourced from conversations, diaries, memoirs, letters and other historical material passed to me by family members.

In telling the story care has been taken to present a realistic portrayal of life as it was in Cooktown and on the goldfield during that time.

William O'Reilly

Life was rugged in colonial Sydney town during the 1870s. Lives were often altered in an instant and without notice.

Tom Simpson would never have guessed that his day had come, that his moment was about to arrive. As farrier for the mounted police he, as usual, was hard at work forging and fixing horseshoes at the police compound. He was alone and all was quiet apart from the tap, tap of his shoeing hammer and the crackle from the lighted forge. He paid no heed to the nasty, narrow-faced officer who left the barracks and strode his way.

How such a peaceful setting could suddenly erupt into violence, how one man could take hold of the other and upend him into the flaming forge, how this man could hold the writhing body of the other to the hot torch of the forge till death overtook, all seems incomprehensible. Yet so it happened; within a few breaths of the officer's approach, one had murdered the other.

What of the ways of man? What of conflict? What of chance? What does one man do if the other asserts, 'Very well, if my horse stays lame then it gives me more time to stain the sheets of your wife's bed!'

Thus was the situation that caused Tom Simpson to snap and murder an officer of the New South Wales Police Force and thence for him to mount the nearest horse, clear the picket fence at a gallop, clatter along the cobbled streets of Sydney town, pull the mount to a halt behind an inn, hitch the horse and dash inside.

'My God! You'll hang for this!' exclaimed Kate his sister and owner of the Bounty Inn.

She hid Tom beneath the cover of a nearby wagon, let his horse loose and then bluffed the police when they arrived.

Tom remained in hiding for a week till he boarded a sailing ship which slipped from the harbour under the cover of darkness.

CHAPTER 1

W ell! If it's not young Barney Simpson. What brings you in so late? Bit startled, by the looks.'

Edgar, the fat grimy drunk, took his weight on the bar with his forearms as he spoke. Unclean and dressed in tatters he presented himself as a distasteful oaf. Edgar was a useless drunk who had wasted most of his life. He was certainly too old, too decrepit and too poor to do business with Mrs Simpson.

Barney had just run from his mother's three-room shanty by the dockside. He now stood at the bar of the Bounty Inn puffing nervously while he listened. Drake, a man of nimble mind, was the only other company and stood easy behind the bar. The two lighted lamps cast a dingy light across the sandstone floor and their flickers ran haunting shadows across the men's faces. A peep of light beneath the closed, rear door told that Kate, Barney's paternal aunt was in the kitchen.

'Tell us,' burbled Edgar, trying to focus, 'what's your ma been up to?' Barney stayed silent. Edgar breathed heavily and then pursued his taunt. 'Well then, come on, me and Drake wants to know.'

Barney's mind was cluttered and as it was closing time he offered to close the doors to gain space. Drake was appreciative and reminded him to secure the latches. Once done he returned to the bar where Edgar resumed.

'Boy, I ain't meanin' to make offence and I don't want ya to take it that way. I'm too old for a strappin'. I's only tryin' ta help, tryin' ta be of 'sistance. Ya ma she's tradin' the best way she knows how.

5

She's been at it, well ...' he reflected, 'since she could carry a bag of potatoes. A flowerin' Bessie she was then. She's still a mighty pretty woman even though she's been worked over so much. And don't forget she's the one who's kept a roof over your head since Tom bolted. I can remember ...'

Barney's face turned ashen in the dull glow as he was told the truth about his mother's whorish ways, a truth he already knew well. He recollected the sad situation where Tom loved Bess and Bess loved other men.

'Now boy,' continued Edgar, wiping dribble from his dirty beard, 'you've grown more like your dad. You've got his farrier's build and strength and enough fight in you to take on any horse. Come here.' He beckoned with a wave. Barney stepped to within smell of Edgar's sour breath. Drake leant forward. Edgar's voice was little more than a whisper as he confided by the tint of light.

'Though, I must admit you get your good looks and interestin' personality from your ma. Kind of trim and enticin'. You just—'

'Shoosh,' Drake suddenly hissed, nipping Edgar's thought. 'Listen. Horses. There's horses running the street.'

All listened in the ghostly surrounds as the faint drumming became a distinctive clopping.

'Troopers' horses. Douse the lamps,' warned Drake while reaching for a fire poker from beneath the bar. Barney lowered the wicks and blew out the flames.

The horses were moving at a fast trot heading towards the dock. They passed the Bounty Inn, six or more, with weaponry clinking. Then, as quickly as the sound had approached, it faded, dissipating into the seaboard breeze. Drake relit a lamp.

'Filthy traps!' sneered Edgar. 'Don't you ever get on the side of the law, boy. Them that flank the Gov'nor are all mongrels. If they 'ad come in 'ere I would 'ave given 'em the Queen of England stuff. They only ...'

Barney had heard this before and wanted to disentangle himself from Edgar's blithering.

'Is Aunty in?' he asked Drake.

'Sure. Go through. Edgar and I are about to finish up here.'

'Wait,' called Edgar when Barney rounded the end of the bar. 'What happened at your ma's place tonight?'

Barney called over his shoulder, 'The Jamaican.'

'What about him?' asked Edgar.

Barney paused at the kitchen door. 'He and a trap had a donnybrook.'

Edgar's tongue tripped with curiosity. 'Maybe that's where the traps was headin'.'

'Maybe,' shrugged Barney, closing the door behind him.

Kate stood at the wood stove drawing a kettle across its hot plate. She was surprised to see Barney arrive so late in the evening.

'Hello there,' she greeted.

The homely smell of the warm kitchen was familiar to Barney. He visited often and Kate, a motherly lady, cherished his company.

'You're in luck. It's just coming to the boil.'

'Luck,' muttered Barney, taking the sugar canister from the shelf. Kate watched as he spooned sugar into the mugs. He hesitated at the third one. 'One or two for Drake,' he asked, catching her attention.

Kate poured the tea when Drake entered. He warmed his hands by the stove before being seated.

'What's the story with the Jamaican?' he then asked.

'Trouble, that's what,' growled Barney. 'That trooper, the one with the bent nose who does this beat, he and the Jamaican are fighting over Ma.'

'Oh!' prompted Drake raising his brows. 'Just words or blood to boot?'

'I'm not sure.' Barney pursed his lips and stared into his steaming mug but the silence soon pressed him further. 'Bent Nose has been calling a lot lately. He's claimed Ma as his own. Tonight he arrived in full regimental dress, cutlass and all, ready to elope. Ma said no. He tried to talk her around; promised to take her to Melbourne to buy a cottage with running water in a fancy part of the town. Said I could go too; says there's plenty of work to be had there. Ma still said no. She said she's too settled to shift. Bent Nose got really upset and kept getting up and down off his chair.' Barney fidgeted, picking at the cracked enamel on his mug while he told more. Kate unconsciously creased the drape of the table cloth. Drake listened closely until he interjected to express concern.

'I hope Bess doesn't listen to him. He's the type to leave her stranded. Then what?'

'He's got money,' said Barney. 'When Ma bailed-up he pulled out a great wad of it. Says he sold or pawned all he had. He stuffed it into her hand. He begged her to go; said he had friends in the Victorian force, that there was a chance for promotion and she could be somebody. He promised her. He wore her down and then she hugged him. I knew then; all that money—must have been fifty quid—and the chance to be somebody. I didn't want any part of it and so I said a quick goodbye and went to leave. But when I opened the back door the Jamaican's there. It was like I was struck from above. I tried to stop him but he shoved me aside and fronted Bent Nose. Bent Nose draws his steel. The Jamaican grabs a chair and Ma's screamin'. I yells to Ma to get out but she won't leave. Then I tried to drag her out but the Jamaican kicked me down the back step and told me to clear out.'

Both Kate and Drake were taken aback. Kate rapped the tabletop with her finger tips and asked, 'Why didn't you tell us earlier? She could be in all sorts of trouble.'

''Cause, Aunty, I'm never going back. Never. There's no place for me there.' Barney held a fragile grip on himself as he explained his plan. I'm going to leave Sydney. I'm going to find Father!'

This assertion spun Kate's emotions. Her words became strained.

'Barney, listen to me. There's four hundred pounds on your father's head. There's posters everywhere ... It's useless petitioning the Governor. I doubt that our petition ever reached him. There's no clemency for killing a trooper.'

Barney attempted to differ but was overruled.

'I've lost my brother but please, not you as well. If you boarded any ship the police would soon have people with their hands out selling them information. They won't rest till they get his hide. They'll hound him to the gallows. He's beaten them for two years now and the longer it goes the better his chances. You must understand. It's for the best that he's disappeared and, hard as it is for us, it's best he's gone forever.'

Barney remained adamant. 'Aunty, you won't stop me. I'll work day and night to get money to go and search. I'll … Come on, Aunty, I'm not a boy. I'll be twenty soon. When I find Father I'm going to look after him. His back's giving out from shoeing and that's all he knows. I'd recognise his shoeing anywhere. He needs me. Don't you understand?' Barney then fixed his glare on Kate. 'Where is he?'

Kate was in turmoil and to gain relief she moved to the stove. Drake, accepting Barney's stand, discussed the matter with him at length.

CHAPTER 2

The men's talk steadied the flood of Kate's concern and now the three of them stood by the stove discussing the situation. Lively tongues of flame darted from the open fire box. Barney stood nearest with shimmers of light washing over him. His hands, moulded by hard work, showed knuckle enough to be able to protect himself. More of his story was revealed by the determination smouldering in his eyes.

Suddenly, all were startled by pounding on the rear door.

'Lord,' whispered Drake, grabbing a heavy water pitcher from beside the stove. Kate put a hand to her mouth gesturing a hush. Barney stood anxious and rigid.

It came again, *thump, thump*, rattling the door bolt in its keeper.

'Let me in!' came a plea from outside. 'It's me. The Jamaican!'

Drake exchanged glances with Kate. He then moved to the door.

'What do you want?'

'Let me in. Please. You must let me in.'

'Why?'

''Cause ... 'cause I'm hurt,' he urged.

Drake opened the door, allowing the light to flood out. It was Nicholas Hart, the tall mulatto who frequented the inn. He was wounded and near to fainting.

At the sight of the blood Kate gasped, 'Mercy. Bring him in quick! Here, by the fire. Nicholas, sit here.' His body quivered beneath his blood-drenched clothes. 'Here, for God's sake. By the stove! Drake, get a sheet! Barney, more water on the stove!'

But Drake was not so sure and interrupted. 'Hold on. Where's Bess?' he quizzed.

'She's all right, I swear. I got her out before the troopers stormed the place. I took her to Molly's. That's the safest place.'

'And what about Bent Nose?'

'He's dead,' stammered Nicholas. 'Can't you see?' and he looked at the gaping gash in his shoulder.

'Were the troopers ...?'

Nicholas answered Drake's questions the best he could then leant against the wall to steady himself.

'For God's sake leave him be,' shouted Kate. 'He's bleeding to death.' She took charge and helped Nicholas to a chair then cut and pulled his shirt off, dragging away clots of blood. She pressed a poultice to the bleeding then applied another and another and so on but one artery continued to pump till she took tweezers from the stove shelf and twisted its severed end. She wanted to call a doctor but Nicholas refused so she fetched the sewing tin. Drake blackened a needle in the fire and proceeded to stitch Nicholas' shoulder. Kate then placed a maroon drape about him. With the bleeding stopped and the immediate crisis under control Kate suggested finding some place for him to hide.

'No. No way. I'm heading out,' he retorted.

'Where will you go?'

'To sea. There's no troopers at sea. Here,' and he pointed, 'in my back pocket. There's money.'

Drake took the tie from the roll and thumbed its worth. 'Twenty-eight pounds,' he said briskly. 'A bit short of Barney's estimate of fifty quid but still plenty for two passages.'

'Two passages!' blurted Nicholas.

'Yes, Nicholas, you and maybe Barney!'

'No way! By the time I get around Cape Horn it will be all gone. I know what it costs to buy that sort of way. It's hardly enough.'

Drake ignored his protest. 'For the full amount less a few pounds for yourself and Barney I may be able to arrange for you to leave on the next tide. As you said yourself it's a costly business. Risks don't come cheap.'

Drake then took Kate to one side. Barney was unable to hear their talk but imagined what they might be discussing. *Is Drake going to send me with Nicholas? Is father in Jamaica?*

After a brief exchange with Kate he again spoke to Nicholas then, when Nicholas finally agreed, Barney was told of the plan. Drake then departed for the dock.

During Drake's two hour absence Nicholas confided to Kate and Barney, 'My father was white. He was Charles Henriques, a sugar planter. He owned a large plantation in a valley behind Kingston.

'Mother was black. She was a kitchen maid in the big house and one of Charles' favourites. Six children she bore to him.

'I may have been raised in the planter's mansion, been spared floggings, had English tutors but white I am not. My kin are those who died in the slave compounds. I sought no birth rights from Charles Henriques. I took my mother's given name of Hart.'

A cautious knock marked Drake's return. He warmed his hands for a few moments then announced, 'All is set. You sail on the early tide. You'll board the *Celestial*. She's an old three-masted barque. You sail for Cooktown.'

'What! Cooktown!' choked Nicholas. 'You must think I'm crazy. There's troopers up there. It's the open sea or nothing. I swear that truly I don't want to go to Cooktown.' Drake allowed him to run on. 'I don't care whether it's steam or sail as long as it's the open sea. Sir, please be fair.'

Drake then shipwrecked Nicholas' appeal. 'It's either this ship or no ship. The arrangements have been made. He has the money, so there's no changing.' He then took the remaining notes from his pocket and shared them equally between the two—three pounds each. 'The ship's master is Captain Quill. He has a cargo of imported goods and has no time to spare. He's a handy man and knows the coast route well. Says he's heard of you, Nicholas; you're called The Cat.

Apparently you're a good man in the rigging and have done the Cape run a few times. Now, this is what you are to do ...'

Kate packed a few items into a calico bag while the detail was discussed. Barney then had his turn. 'Drake, is father in Cooktown?'

'That's where he was headed for, Barney, but where he is now nobody knows. Maybe he's on the Palmer goldfield. You can tell Nicholas the story when you're aboard.'

When it came time to leave Kate cupped Barney's cheeks in her palms and said, 'Tom's always been proud of you and I understand your loyalty to him. Be good, Barney, and don't be ashamed to use your own name. Be sure to write soon as we will be anxious to hear from you. We'll explain everything to Bess. And please ...' She paused to compose her now tearful self. 'Please come home as soon as you can. You're all we've got left. Good luck, my brave boy!' She then hugged him as though he were her own.

CHAPTER 3

They sailed 1400 nautical miles northward and reached the port of Cooktown in the young colony of Queensland. Perfect weather greeted them as, under reduced sail, they gently edged through the heads of the Endeavour River on a making tide. Mount Saunders on the north head stood as a huge copper sculpture, dwarfing the white sand dunes below. The wide river entrance before them glittered, contrasting with the hazy ranges in the far distance. The town itself lay in the shelter of Grassy Hill and its sister formations on the south bank, and as they turned behind this headland Barney felt the hot, sticky climate of the tropics.

'Heave to!' called the first mate when a row boat, manned by strong oarsmen, came close. Customs papers were exchanged then the *Celestial* berthed. Almost everything there came by sea: Europeans, Chinese, livestock, food, machinery, mining supplies, building materials and general provisions. The carriers—sail ships, steamers, Chinese junks—all cluttered the river. The wharf atmosphere was distinctively colonial with rich men dressed in white directing coolies dressed in rags. The wharf area, wedged tightly against Grassy Hill, was frantic with activity, servicing the needs of the 35,000 people manning Cooktown and the goldfields beyond. Barney saw all this and braced himself for the challenge.

The unloading of the cargo was tiresome. Winch cranes lifted cargo from the deep holds and staunch horses strained at the traces, pulling loaded trolleys along rail-lines to Heath and Sons, bond store sheds. Nicholas, who was still ill, lay in his bunk throughout the days of unloading. Quill was now ready to set sail in two days and allowed Barney to go ashore to arrange lodgings for himself and Nicholas.

The wharf decking felt good beneath Barney's feet. He breathed deeply to fully appreciate the landing as he walked along the esplanade beside the town park. The Sovereign Hotel, with its lattice and colonial style, soon commanded his view. Horse-drawn vehicles came and went at a brisk pace whirling dust along Charlotte Street, the main thoroughfare. He strode on at a man's pace passing Furneaux Street.

All about him he saw the rhythm and purpose of the town. Wide streets filled with people, their means of transport and their goods. Others bustled along the footpaths. The rich and the poor wearing everything from plumed hats to ragged trousers, attending to their needs.

The town was engineered by need: buildings and workshops, packed tightly in their dozens, varied from shanties through to the ornate. Shop fronts of the general trades and services—eating houses, butchers, grocers, confectioners, hoteliers, barbers, boot makers, general merchants and a newspaper company—were all open and trading. Sign writing was aglow, advertising city-style services: spacious accommodation and first class tables, fitted up to metropolitan style; imported embroideries; teacher of pianoforte and the art of speech. Professionals displayed smaller shingles: doctors, a dentist, chemists, accountants, auctioneers, an assayer and those of the legal profession. There were those of the transport trade: coach and wagon works, wheelwrights, livery stables, blacksmiths, saddlers, and cartage depots. He also saw other men of industry sweating in workshops: a cooper, a tanner, a bedstead and mattress maker, a tinsmith and those of the timber trade.

The Roarin' Meg Hotel, the largest hotel in Cooktown, dominated the business centre. The Roarin' Meg also had the most lucrative, if covert, gaming rooms in the north. At the far end of Charlotte Street Barney kicked at the rills in the dust then turned the corner to the Palmer Road. Cottages, built mainly of corrugated iron and with tin fences, lined the road. Horse and bullock yards could be seen at their rear. Men, returning from the Palmer goldfield, a long trek away, passed Barney with little expression on their weary faces. Local Chinese sauntered both ways carrying their sticks and baskets. Barney continued till he passed the last house. Here he rested. He sat by the road watching the gaily coloured parrots chattering in the tree tops. He enjoyed the calm of the open bushland but there was much more to see so he soon returned and entered Boundary Street then Helen Street. He explored the streets on the hillside, passing weatherboard houses with conical roofs. Eventually the waning afternoon and hunger drew him back to Charlotte Street.

He ventured into Chinatown which lay to the river side of Charlotte Street. He was cautious as he wandered through this maze of mystery. He sighted its spooky alleyways cluttered with tin, cane and calico shacks, strings of washing across bare paths and sleeping hammocks hanging from flimsy rafters. The smell of incense lingered everywhere in the evening air. With scales, abacus and keen eyes the Chinese made exchanges. Fruit, vegetables, rice, dried fish, tea, pickles and sauces; herbal remedies, clothing, hats, sandals, human hair and opium pipes were available. In their hundreds they crowded the walkways, jostling, with their pigtails, their only vanity, swinging behind. Most were celibate men with expressionless faces, seeking fortune but with unknown destinies. In the kitchens they cooked tasty food. Some men stood and others sat cross-legged as they quickly flexed chopsticks, feeding from bowls. Barney ate, scooping his rice and fish with his fingers. He then bought bananas for a penny ha'penny and as the sinewy Cantonese cut them from the bunch Barney wondered about the trader's past.

When darkness fell Barney re-entered Charlotte Street where he was attracted by the chandelier lights of the Roarin' Meg Hotel. He loitered there, on the opposite side of the street and, before long, a fat man staggered from the hotel in a rage, mounted his sulky then whipped the harness horse to a gallop. Two mounted police appeared from a side street and cantered after him with carbine butts bobbing by their sides. Tiredness overtook Barney and he headed towards the wharf. As he went an eerie spell filled the air. The night was balmy, full of intrigue, the kind of night that somebody might plot someone else's misadventure.

CHAPTER 4

Next day brought fresh promise. At first light Barney stepped ashore to find accommodation. As the early morning unfolded he drew water from the town well and washed. He later surveyed the police station and its compound. A distinctive senior officer, maybe an inspector, dressed in white and wearing a pith helmet, trotted in. Soon after, a constable arrived at the gallop and rushed inside. Almost immediately the senior officer, the messenger and others swung into their saddles and set off along Charlotte Street at a hefty pace in the return direction. Their purpose became apparent when almost an hour later the gold escort, flanked by worn men on tired horses, turned into Charlotte Street. When the escort rattled by Barney saw a trooper lying beside the trunks containing gold. The stub of a spear protruded from his back. Barney bought a copy of the *Cooktown Herald* and read while eating lunch. The few pounds in his pocket would soon be spent and he needed employment and lodgings. There was a position for a general servant and on the following page tenders were being called for rock splitting. Barney passed these over in favour of an advertisement placed by the Cavalier Hotel seeking a handy man. He threw his crusts to a hungry dog, tucked his shirt into his trousers, slicked his collar-length hair back with his fingers then stepped off along the earthen footpath towards the Cavalier.

The Cavalier Hotel, a two-storey building, stood on a spacious corner allotment with the bar room opening to both streets. The verandah provided good views of the Endeavour River. The yard at the back was enclosed by a tall, tin fence. Barney entered by a gate there, crossed the large courtyard and enquired.

Miss Prudence Swanson, the owner, took an instant liking to Barney and soon offered him the position. Accommodation was also supplied and Barney quickly accepted. They stood in the shade of a rainwater tank by the wood heap while discussing his duties. Barney was impressed with her style and attention to detail. During the interview the two young domestic helpers, Laura and Cherie, peeked through the glass panes of the kitchen window. Barney eyed the horses in the open stalls by the feed shed while Miss Swanson spoke. 'Are you sure that you and your friend will be happy sleeping in the shed with the horse feed. I may be able to—' Her speech was suddenly snipped by an outburst from over the tin fence.

'Git up there! Pull—you mongrel bastard!'

The domestics inside apparently heard because they began to giggle.

'Hornet!' Prudence called sternly.

'Yes, Ma'am,' came a surprised reply.

'That's enough trooper language.'

Shuffling came from outside the fence.

'Hornet!' she repeated loudly.

After a few moments a meek, 'Yes, Ma'am,' floated back.

Soon after, Hornet entered the gateway leading a buck goat pulling a cart piled high with firewood. He halted the goat by the wood heap. The undernourished fourteen-year-old was thin in forearm and shank. A scaly tropical sore on his knee leaked pus. His face was drawn by wasted cheeks. Threadbare clothing hung loosely from his hat-rack frame. Hornet scraped the ground with a bare foot as he spoke.

'Ma'am, how's the wood holdin' out?'

The kitchen maids were now at the rear door. Prue spoke easily again.

'We could do with some more. The *Osprey* is due in soon and it will be a full house.' She then turned and touched Barney to introduce him to Hornet Finnigan. 'Barney this is ... Hornet and his goat Billy supply the kindling wood at two shillings a load. You'll find that he is here most days buzzing about the place.'

'I got the contract for this place,' asserted Hornet, placing a hand on the trim of his cart. He prattled on outlining his cartage business, sounding as though he was the owner and master of a team of sound horses and a sturdy wagon.

The girls were anxious to meet the new help and came closer.

Prue introduced Laura and Cherie to Barney. She then suggested that they all help themselves to tea and cakes.

The boys unloaded the firewood then hitched Billy by the water trough. Hornet babbled incessantly while Barney removed his boots and washed in the basin on the wash rack.

The rich cakes and the big pot of tea on the dining table looked appetising.

'Here, have some cakes, Barney,' invited Laura.

Hornet stepped forward to grab at them first.

'Hands!' insisted Laura, hastily pulling the plate aside.

Hornet objected.

'No! Wash your hands or no cakes!' She was emphatic.

Hornet left then returned in short time wiping his hands on his dirty shirt.

From Laura's treatment of Hornet, Barney gauged her to be in charge. Though she was plump and somewhat plain in appearance the directness of her manner impressed him.

After tea the brat whom Barney now suspected was the renegade of Charlotte Street departed with his goat. Barney chatted with the girls a while longer then followed.

'You sure can cover some ground with that wagon,' puffed Barney when he came abreast of Hornet on Charlotte Street.

'Oh, Billy's good. He hates that climb to the pub but otherwise he's all right. There's money in haulage you know. Without Billy here,' and he flicked the rope, 'me and Ma would starve. Me old man died. He was a timber-getter till the Blacks killed him.' Barney listened while Hornet told of the death then when Hornet paused in reflection, Barney spoke.

'Look, eh. My mate's on board a ship down at the dock. He's too sick to walk to the pub and the ship sails tonight. What's the chances of taking him up in this? I'd pay you for it.'

Hornet tugged the lead, halting Billy. 'Could be somethin' in it I reckon. It's a big haul up that hill but there's nothin' me and Billy can't do. What do ya reckon the trip's worth?'

'That's up to you. Whatever you think is a fair thing.'

Hornet drew squiggles in the dust with a toe and squirted saliva between his front teeth while doing his sums. He considered the deal carefully then made an offer.

'Cost ya sixpence as long as you help too.'

'No worries. That's about what I thought too,' agreed Barney.

They walked behind the cart, each with a hand on it, and exchanged notes.

'Where do you come from?' quizzed Hornet.

Barney seized the chance. He told of the escape but not of its reason; of how he had steered the sailing ship; about Nicholas. And, as each scene was related, Hornet's imagination took them to greater heights.

Sailing preparations were being made when the two stepped aboard. They went directly to Nicholas' compartment where Hornet greeted him with, 'Holy, you're a mess ain't ya.' Captain Quill watched as they helped Nicholas across the wharf. He waved a goodbye once they set foot ashore.

Nicholas' concern about the rough cart was partly allayed by Hornet's assurance. 'Don't worry, mate. We'll get ya there.'

Nicholas sat side-on in the wagonette with his knees hunched upwards and an arm across the tail board. Blow flies crowded the stinking cape that clung to his back. The boys pushed arduously from behind. It was a painful journey for Nicholas, noticing little of the townsfolk who looked curiously his way. When they turned from

Charlotte Street Barney tapped him on the shoulder and pointed to the stylised lettering of the Cavalier Hotel.

Nicholas brightened a little upon entering the courtyard and when they halted at the feed shed he refused help. Instead the lads held the cart while he eased himself to the ground. The feed shed was a large, single-room dwelling with bags of corn, oats and pollard stacked to one side. Nicholas smiled meekly at Prue when entering his new home. 'Easy,' she coaxed, taking his hand in her slender fingers. He sighed, sinking on the soft kapok mattress. When Prue removed his cape it peeled away scabs, exposing his wound. While Barney, Hornet and Cherie felt sick at the sight, Prue and Laura persevered, bathing the injury with warm salty water. When it was clean they applied a temporary dressing till Eli's arrival that evening.

Much could be said about Eli the man of honours: the physician, the philosopher and the merchant trader. However Eli, for personal reasons, preferred not to be reminded of his past. Therefore, when Barney asked Prue about this man she limited her reply to explaining that Eli was an English doctor who no longer practised medicine and that currently he was in partnership with a Mr James Mulligan, operating a merchandising business known as Mulligan's Trading. Barney later learnt from Laura that Eli was Prue's companion, that he had evening meals at the hotel and often stayed the night, sharing with Prue.

When Eli arrived Prue greeted him with a kiss to his greying temple then introduced him to Barney. Barney immediately felt the aura, the glow, the understanding that this man evoked. To casual observation Eli appeared as a regular, neatly kept businessman of bachelor inclination. But on Barney's closer scrutiny he saw a man blessed with intelligence, self-assurance and a caring nature; a man able to conduct himself quietly, effectively and compassionately. The whole room was filled with his presence. No one, it seemed, escaped his influence. Even after leaving the feed room Eli's character remained foremost in Barney's mind.

Following a hot tub and dinner Barney helped in the kitchen till the girls left. He then left, alone, to scour the town.

He held some naive expectation that he might discover his father standing on a street corner and he searched several streets. He saw many people but none he knew. It became late and now there were only a few homes showing any light.

Barney returned to Charlotte Street which was partly lit by kerosene lamps. Their peeping show of light only partly illuminated the roadway. From where Barney stood the only nearby sign of life was laughter from a young couple. It grew as they came nearer and then from the dark appeared a rickshaw drawn by a healthy Cantonese. Seated in it was a polished young gent with his lassie by his side. Their frolicking laughter became louder as they approached the street lamp by Barney and then drifted away, as easily as it had come, when they disappeared into the darkness beyond.

Lucky cove, thought Barney. Barney compared himself with the Chinese footman who was pulling the rickshaw for a few pence. *Are there two kinds of people*, he thought, *those born to enjoy and those who slave? No. It's not true. It's not true that my destiny could be prearranged.* He drew courage, there by the light, and spoke aloud to himself. 'One day you'll see, Barney Simpson. You'll find joy equal to that lucky cove.' The possibility brought freshness to his mind and he felt at ease. 'This street,' he proclaimed. 'This new street doesn't know me. I can begin here, not again, but for the first time.' The laughter of only moments before tossed from Barney's mind the old and ushered in a new perception of himself. The transition from being the footman to that of the polished gent had not been difficult. There had not been conscious deliberation about the matter. Even the very moment before he heard the laughter there had been no thoughts of any such thing. *How*, he thought, *could such a thing be? At one moment feeling like a pauper and the very next feeling as confident as one of the gentry? How is it that before I thought I was only fit for love with barrow women but now I know I'm fit for all including those who ride in carriages?* The certainty of the shift in his awareness was inexplicable.

But he cared not about its genesis or final derivation. The only thing he knew and cared about was that the change was irrevocable. Barney was now on a high and he whistled a carefree tune as he headed home.

CHAPTER 5

While Barney searched for his father during the next few weeks he learnt much about Cooktown which was hailed the Gold Port. On the streets society ladies, wearing corsets and bustles, and gentleman, dressed in vests and collars, contrasted with the raucous shouts and whip cracks from the bullockies and teamsters. He found a diversity of moral codes. The Victorian code forbidding women from mopping, cleaning and dusting in public places during specified hours was enforced. Yet, off the same streets, in dingy rooms, whore houses flourished. He and the son of a shipwright took to the flow of the tide and oared a few miles upstream on the Endeavour River. They explored the mangrove forest lining the river and further beyond the open forest before returning on its ebb. On another day he went fishing and was shocked when he realized that the ripples approaching him were caused by a crocodile. He left the hotel early one morning to widen his search and trekked many miles out along the Palmer Road. The stark, foreboding landscape and the advice of a shanty keeper turned him back. The alleyways of Chinatown intrigued him. He studied the idols and rituals of the Josh House but could not understand their meaning. Scantily clad Chinaman frequently passed through the doors of gambling dens. A Chinese man beckoned him into an opium den to draw on a bubble pipe but he declined. He regularly read the town's billboard for any mention of his father, exercising caution by reading only when no others were about. There were reward signs but never anything of Tom Simpson. He saw a notice in an office window in the business centre that drew his attention.

A few weeks later he revisited Hicksbury's office and again read the professional notice hanging behind the glass window. The private nature of the service lured him. He read the invitation once more, brushed his fingers through his hair, stepped to the door then snapped the door knocker three times. Nobody appeared so he rapped again impatiently, but still no answer. He became annoyed and muttered to himself, 'Christ ...' There was someone inside because when the office was unattended a small sign read: 'Closed'. Barney soon became discouraged and stepped backwards, bumping into someone and raking his heel down their shin.

'Careful there!' a male voice said from behind.

Barney turned hastily to confront the person but stood in disbelief when he saw a uniformed man looking down on him. He was dumbfounded; his words were stuck. Before him, within a pace, stood a police officer and the braiding on his epaulets identified him as most senior. His blood raced.

'Now there,' said the officer, trying to ease the situation.

Barney stayed silent.

'I'm Inspector Britfield—Peter Britfield,' said the policeman. 'Here, what's your name?' he asked quietly.

Barney still could not answer.

The inspector shifted his attention to the office door then towards the far reaches of the street while he waited. His presentation was impeccable: tall, clean and commanding; clothed in a crisp white uniform, polished boots and spurs; bearing braided epaulettes and a spiked helmet.

While not being aloof he remained in control till Barney settled.

He asked again, 'What's your name?'

'Barney Simpson,' replied Barney.

Surprise crossed the inspector's face but he swiftly covered himself. 'Are you staying locally?' The pointedness of the question betrayed his interest.

'At a pub,' answered Barney with a gravelly voice.

'Which pub?'

'The Cavalier,' replied Barney.

The inspector began to question further, 'What—' But he was suddenly interrupted by the office door opening.

Barney recognised the man at once. He had seen him staggering from the Roarin' Meg Hotel on his first night ashore.

Mr Hicksbury was less dignified than Barney had expected. He erred on the side of slovenliness with a corpulent front, bloated face and a dingy suit. No warmth issued from his blunt, bullish face and searching eyes. Barney quickly framed him as a man of dubious integrity. He was thankful that the door had not been opened sooner.

'Hello, Archie,' said the inspector, looking his way.

Hicksbury cross-examined them both with taxing eyes then, as he spoke his first words, a dribble of sweat trickled down his jowl. His voice sounded deep and thick.

'Who knocked?' he asked in a flat tone. The inspector looked Barney's way. Barney felt insecure with an investigative barrister at law and a quizzical police inspector in his company.

'I—I—did,' he admitted, stumbling over his words as though confessing to some wrong.

Hicksbury showed no favour and interrogated them jointly. 'Do you people wish to speak with me?'

Barney stayed quiet. The inspector replied, 'Mr Simpson may.'

'Then?' asked Hicksbury, curiosity shaping his brow.

'No. It doesn't matter. It was nothing important,' stammered Barney.

Hicksbury imposed by extending a hand of friendship. Barney felt obliged and took hold. They introduced themselves by name. Seconds became moments before Hicksbury let him free.

The inspector then eased the situation. He referred to a recent court hearing and engaged Hicksbury in heated discussion. Barney listened to their differing opinions, with Hicksbury arguing points of law and the inspector the practicality of the judgement that had been made. It became apparent to Barney that, apart from this decision, an ongoing animosity existed between the two.

'You can't argue against precedent,' finished Hicksbury.

The inspector let the disagreement rest.

Hicksbury then mopped the sweat from his jowl and concerned himself with Barney.

'Now, lad,' he began with obvious disregard for the inspector's presence, 'come inside where we can have some privacy.'

Barney sought a way out and said, 'It's all right, Mr Hicksbury. I'm not sure what I'll do. I might call another day.' He then faced the inspector. 'Nice to have met you, Sir. I might see you another day. I'll be off now.' He nodded to each then left.

The meeting left Barney feeling upset and insecure. He concluded that, in future, he would have to be more cautious.

CHAPTER 6

Here, Barney. Snuggle into this,' laughed Laura, pushing a clean bed sheet into his face.

''Ere you dashed wench. You'll smother me.'

'I might do that too,' she taunted, 'but in a different way—all with kisses and cuddles,' she yodelled.

'Hey, quiet there,' whispered Barney, pointing over his shoulder to remind her that a guest was seated further down the front verandah.

'Well! Here! Help me or ...' and she pushed the sheet further against him.

Barney took his end of the sheet and together they began to fold the pile of fresh bed linen. Each sheet was folded with them standing at length then, when it was to be doubled, Laura would step quickly forward bringing her lips close to his. This time she didn't restrain herself. She kissed him loudly.

'Hey—' and he blushed as he looked the guest's way. The knowing smile of the guest made him feel awkward. He turned to leave.

'Here! You're not going away. Come back. I promise to behave if you help me with the last few,' Laura conceded.

When they finished the folding Barney loitered. He stood with his hands on the verandah rail and a boot against the lattice.

Laura stowed the linen then came to his side where she placed a hand close to his. The buildings across the way cast late-afternoon shadows on the street.

'Who's that with Eli and Nick?' asked Barney when four people rounded the corner. Laura placed her hand on Barney's while she gazed, pretending they were too far away to recognise. Neither moved till the group walked closer to the hotel. Laura then patted Barney's hand.

'It's Mr Mulligan, Eli's partner, and Meg Challistine who owns the Roarin' Meg Hotel. Mr Mulligan is the explorer who found the Palmer River goldfield.' The new couple was clothed as though on an outing while Eli and Nicholas—for Nicholas was now employed at Mulligan's Trading—wore day clothes. Meg Challistine's face was partly hidden by a colourful, broad-brimmed hat that caught the wind gusts. She held the hat with one hand and her long skirt with the other. James Mulligan carried his suit coat across his forearm. He walked close chaperoning Meg. When they neared the hotel their voices could be heard and on seeing Barney and Laura they shouted greetings. The jovial crew then stepped to the footpath and entered the hotel.

Barney turned to Laura. His eyes were soft and gleamed with delight. Laura was partly overcome and her passion for him drew tears to the corners of her eyes. She wished to hug him there on the verandah in view of the guest but fearing his embarrassment she restricted herself to taking both his hands, giving them a tight squeeze then adding, 'Let's go. There's work to be done.' Barney followed her along the central corridor and down the staircase.

They met Prue and the other four in the dining room. Barney joined them while Laura continued on to the kitchen.

'... and why shouldn't a man, once in a while, start drinking early,' protested Eli in jest as Prue tidied his upturned collar and referred to his intoxication. 'Nicholas here,' and he beckoned him with a sweep of a hand as though introducing an old friend, 'has just received his first pay and that, we judge, is sufficient reason to celebrate. And what about James and Meg, whiling away the afternoon, lunching and talking business.'

Cherie took James' coat at that moment.

'Thanks, Cherie,' said James with his strong Irish brogue.

Meg stood close to Nicholas displaying her elegance and flair, all a man might seek: beauty, sensuality and wealth. Many tales she could tell; many a bedroom floor she had crossed.

Following a lively conversation Prue stretched out her hands and announced, 'Now. Everybody is invited to dinner. The guests will be down in a few minutes and I'll have to go and help prepare. Meg and James, take a seat while the others have a bath. Cherie,' she called aside, 'a bottle of Chablis that James likes and two glasses please.'

Dinner was served on time and soon after everybody had eaten James called to Cherie, 'Dearie, would you please see if there are any cabs handy. I don't want to be late for a meeting.'

She was back within moments. 'There's one ready, Sir.'

'Gracious me, that was quick.' Thanks were passed around. He then rose, took his coat from Cherie and hurried off.

'Business is brisk at the bar,' commented Nicholas when he returned with a fresh bottle of wine. He offered the drink around but only he and Meg partook.

Later he bought another bottle and when he poured Meg a glass she spoke confidentially. 'You'll have to visit The Meg some time.'

At an appropriate moment Cherie addressed the table. 'Barney, I've got a puzzle for you. Do you want to try it?'

'What sort of puzzle?'

'I'll get it for you,' she prompted teasingly. She soon returned from the kitchen carrying two egg trays with several eggs. She placed them before him. 'There we go. Just turn the eggs upside down and solve the riddle.' Barney turned the eggs over and found that each had been marked with a letter.

'What's all this about?' ferreted Eli enthusiastically. 'Let's all try to decipher what message this dove has brought to us.'

Barney and Meg began switching the eggs about forming syllables. Eli raced ahead with his mind, skating through numerous possibilities. Nicholas sat contentedly admiring Meg.

Eli suddenly exclaimed with excitement, 'Of course! Laura, and then there's Barney.' He stood up, leaned forward and then quickly arranged the eggs: Laura loves Barney.

Laura was called and rounded the kitchen screen rearranging her hair as she came. She was momentarily mystified then became gleeful when she realised what had been done. Barney returned her gleeful look with a silly grin.

The evening continued in a most jolly strain and Nicholas, with the flair of a strolling minstrel, touted for Meg's affection. He let the best of his personality spill forth, leading her along. Meg answered his call, leaning in close and laying herself open. When it came time to go they left together, hand in hand. They whisked along joyfully, snatching embraces along the way within the shadows, hardly able to wait till they reached Meg's bedroom at the Roarin' Meg Hotel.

CHAPTER 7

The Goldfields Shanty on Charlotte Street was a known haunt for drunks and derelicts. The rowdy establishment was operated by Pug Carver and his bawdy wife.

Barney, searching for evidence of his father's trade-mark horse shoeing, approached a horse hitched at the rail in front of the shanty. The grey horse, bearing a saddle and blanket roll, looked as though it had been travelling.

Barney lifted one foot then another and as he moved to the other side of the horse a menacing shout came from the shanty.

'You there! What do you think you're doin' liftin' the feet of my 'orse!'

Barney flinched and stood erect as a drunken stockman approached.

The stockman, hefty and brash, the sort well capable of pulling a wild bull to the ground, blustered forward with his beard flowing.

'What do you think you're doin'?' he repeated when within hand's reach.

Some drinkers stepped to the footpath; others watched from the doorway and windows.

'Go on! Tell me!' he shouted.

An inebriate began beating the tin wall of the shanty to a rhythmic chant of, 'Fight! Fight! ...' Soon, another of the rabble chorused with him.

A teamster with time to spare reined in. A group of school boys hurried across the street. Others, from further along the street, came close.

'Are you goin' to tell me or have I to beat it from you!' threatened the stockman, placing a hand on the whip strung across his chest.

'I was just looking,' explained Barney.

'Just lookin'! I'll give you just lookin',' howled the stockman.

'He's a lunatic!' shouted one nervous onlooker.

The spectators jostled for position. They spoke excitedly, turning from one to another. Suggestive comments became possibilities and, in turn, were passed about as certainties. Soon the consensus was that Barney had accused the drunk of stealing the horse.

A lady of about thirty years and undoubtedly of gentle birth stood alone watching attentively, and when Barney happened to look her way she twirled her open parasol. The swirl of colour and her grace held his attention momentarily.

Pug Carver, with a dirty towel over his shoulder and a mean wolfhound by his side, spoke to the derelict rapping the wall. Pug's wife, barefoot and untidy, squeezed room for her broad hips between those in the doorway and stood holding a broom and a bucket of steaming water.

The supposition of horse thieving firmed, and some tried to decipher the brand.

'It's not from this area,' concluded one.

'It must be a southern horse,' added another.

Barney argued his defence vehemently. 'I was only interested in the shoeing job. Why would ...'

'Lyin' bastard!' raged the drunk while unravelling the whip. 'What you need is a floggin'!'

The ugliness drew the crowd closer. Pug Carver's dog barked wildly, pulling at its leash. Mrs Carver, with a broom and hot water at the ready, hailed insults. The lady with the parasol repositioned herself close to Mrs Carver. Mrs Carver, a commoner who resented the gentry, cast her a dirty look.

Barney, now riled, stood his ground and issued an ultimatum to the stockman. 'If that whip so much as brushes me I'll stuff you between the hind legs of this here horse!' he declared.

The challenge stirred the stockman's ire. He raised his clenched hand and cuffed Barney's near cheek with the whip handle.

Barney's temper, like his father's, soared out of control. The Simpson weakness or maybe the Simpson strength, depending on the point of view, ignited Barney's anger. He instinctively dealt a sharp uppercut to the stockman's jaw.

A ferocious expression contorted the stockman's face.

A second blow by Barney, a sharp left hook, sent another shudder through the stockman's head. Barney followed through with a third, fourth and fifth punch, battering the stockman further. In return the stockman swung blindly, striking Barney at random. Each scored telling hits, knocking the other off balance and nearly putting the other down. A sharp left jab by Barney whacked his opponent on the nose, causing a nose bleed that streaked his beard. Barney then threw more punches that left the stockman quavering above the rigidity of his knee-high boots. A further strike by Barney, a blunt biff to the chin, landed the stockman against his horse.

The stockman clung to his frightened horse for support. He choked on the blood, coughing and staining the horse's withers bright red. Barney stood firm, ready to down his opponent should he try again. The stockman took hold of the saddle with a movement that some thought to be an attempt to mount but not so; he freed a stirrup leather and iron from the saddle then turned to confront Barney.

Onlookers, realising his intent, cried foul. One bushman drew his revolver while another came in close.

Barney moved quickly, stepping in before the stockman could swing the stirrup to its full extent. He intercepted the swipe, receiving a short but cutting blow to the back of his shoulder.

With his temper now wholly adrift Barney laid himself open, abandoning his defensive stance. He launched a barrage of punches, sickening the stockman more with every hit. He beat the stricken stockman relentlessly till he fell unconscious to the ground.

It was then that a shout from the front of the crowd raised a fresh alarm. Pug Carver had released his wolfhound.

Screams and cries of horror lit the street as the dog, frenzied by the smell of blood, dashed towards Barney.

In panic Barney knelt, took up the stirrup and braced himself for the attack.

With jaws wide open the dog leapt at Barney from a distance, springing with mighty strength.

Barney's reflex was instant. He swung the stirrup to its full length then brought it down on the dog in mid flight. A dull thud sounded when the stirrup iron smashed its skull. The dog, convulsing its last, fell at Barney's feet with its brains spilling on the ground.

This stunned the crowd. The shouting lulled and this, together with the sight of the dead dog, sapped Barney's strength. He stood, almost limp, while his sense returned.

Pug Carver shouted vengeance and threatened to kill Barney. His wife rushed forward, screaming and waving her broom but was intercepted by the lady with her parasol. The bawdy hotelier struck out with her broom. 'You rich bitch!' she shrieked while taking a swing.

'Police! Get the police!' shouted a bystander. Others now stood between Pug Carver and Simpson.

Carver's wife attacked the lady, first with the broom then her nails. The lady retaliated, defending herself with courage. Pug Carver spat threats at Barney across the cordon containing him. The dog's brains were trampled into the dust. Shoppers not wanting to be implicated were already departing. Some storekeepers re-entered their shops to attend business. Children compared notes. Friends of the pub woman dragged her into the shanty while condemning her for her stupidity in attacking the police inspector's sister. Pug eventually gave way to the restraint of those about him. Though agitated he listened to his supporters and together they carried the unconscious stockman and dead dog into the shanty.

Most of the remaining onlookers dispersed upon Pug's re-entry to the shanty and soon the street returned to normal. The lady with the parasol approached Barney. 'You handled yourself well. He would have killed you if you hadn't stood up to him. I showed my parasol to warn you of the situation but you did it your way. Bravo to you!'

Barney was taken by her presence. Even before he had fully recovered his breath her blue eyes drew his attention. He accepted her offer to wipe the blood from his forehead and as she did he was captivated by her beauty: tall and elegant with a comely body easily imagined beneath her tailored dress with its full bodice tightly laced at the front and a chiffon skirt that followed the movement of her body.

She introduced herself as Abbey O'Reilly and asked his name. Barney answered as he brushed his hands through his hair.

Abbey asked further, 'What were you doing inspecting that horse?'

'Oh,' said Barney. 'Just interested. I come from a line of farriers and was looking at the shoeing.'

'Really,' replied Abbey. 'I have an interest in horses too. They are magnificent animals and deserve more recognition. We have a couple of mounts at the house that are shod regularly. Tell me, are you a farrier by trade?'

Barney answered with a half-truth. 'Yes, I do a lot of shoeing. Been at it since I was thirteen. I love the smell of horses and the smithy shop—part of my life.'

'Well, in that case you may be able to help with ours. At the moment our farrier has back trouble and the shoeing is falling behind. He does all the police horses and at present they're getting priority over our hacks. Although my brother, Peter, is the police inspector we seem to be last on the list.'

Barney took the opportunity. 'I'm full time employed as leading hand at the Cavalier Hotel but can spare time to fit a few shoes for you.'

Abbey quipped, 'You can shoe my horses anytime!' She went on to give directions. 'It's the big white house on the ridge,' and while explaining she engaged Barney with an irresistible smile.

They spoke on for twenty minutes till, eventually, Abbey had to excuse herself to attend to household duties. When they parted Barney followed her with his gaze, fantasising about what could be.

CHAPTER 8

Later that evening at the police inspector's home, the family sat for dinner in the spacious dining room. Inspector Peter Britfield, a bachelor, sat at the head of the table while his sister, Abbey O'Reilly, and her husband Michael sat opposite each other. Their daughter, Juliette, who was learning to walk, held her mother's knee. Madeline, the live-in maid, stood to one side refilling a cruet. Peter's white safari jacket, starched and pressed, bettered the everyday shirt worn by his brother-in-law. Abbey's burgundy evening dress with its off-the-shoulder design revealed the scratches she had received earlier in the day.

'Ah! That's what I call a good meal,' said Peter, dabbing his lips with a napkin. He then sat with his elbows on the table waiting for the others to finish their pudding. He dwelt on the scratches marking Abbey's shoulders and recalled her account of the incident at the Goldfields Shanty. He considered what he should do, not only about this incident but about the many complaints he had received about the owners of the shanty. His consideration was brief. He then spoke unexpectedly.

'Done!' he exclaimed with authority.

'What's done?' queried Abbey, leaving off eating.

'The Goldfields Shanty will be done as of tomorrow. He's had a free rein for too long. They may even think they've had a win.'

'Peter,' said Abbey with surprise, 'isn't that a little hasty and, I also add, out of character for you. You must keep it in perspective. I can understand your concern and share the same view to a degree but an immediate move would be seen to result from today's scuffle and may not appear even handed. There's not a week goes by without some kind of trouble there so there will be other opportunities.'

'Hmm, maybe you're right. What do you think, Michael?'

Michael had finished his pudding and pushed his plate clear.

'It depends,' he said, stroking his ginger beard. He sounded indifferent as he explained, 'Those types are trouble wherever they are. At least while they're drinking at that establishment other businesses are being left alone.' He chuckled to himself. 'Best idea might be to light the place up when they're all inside.'

'Michael! What a thought,' censured Abbey.

'Well,' reflected Michael, 'you told me yourself that the fellow who caused the trouble had stolen a horse. Now, horse thieves are the worst kind and deserve all they get!'

Abbey became equivocal. 'I'm not even sure if the horse was stolen. The young man that fought him, the roustabout at the Cavalier Hotel, this was his view as well as that of others.'

'Is he reliable?' interrupted Michael.

'Very much that way I would say,' and she unconsciously toyed with her rings. 'He also told me—'

Peter interrupted Abbey's explanation by suddenly shoving his chair back, rising abruptly and pacing to the drinks cabinet. He poured a large whisky. He stayed there with his back to the conversation, listening intently to what was being said.

'However, I still think it premature for Peter to foreclose on them.'

On her closing word Peter turned around quickly and snapped loudly, 'Nonsense!'

The others were taken aback by his sharpness. Madeline winced, spilling some salt. During her two years of service she had never seen Mr Britfield so upset. He was tense and close to rage.

'It's utter contempt!' he declared while trying to restrain his anger. 'A notice shall be served on them tomorrow!'

'Peter, Peter, hush. Let's leave the matter lie,' implored Abbey.

Peter was riled and to contain himself he turned away and poured another drink. Madeline went to the kitchen. Abbey sat still. Michael watched Peter and wondered. Juliette sensed the stress and tugged her mother's dress, asking to be taken into her arms.

During the silence the chandelier lights flickered, casting moving shadows on the high ceiling.

Soon Juliette became restless and began to squirm on Abbey's lap.

'Look at the little stars,' encouraged Abbey, pointing Juliette's hand towards the chandelier. 'Tiny baby ones like you. See? See them shining.' Juliette reached, trying to grasp the wavering flames. Abbey lifted her to the dining table where she stood reaching high. Michael joined with her, playing make believe.

Michael, a man in his mid forties, knew little about law or administration and, in comparison to the Britfields, he had limited social skills. He could not be considered a member of the gentry. He was a humble man content with his occupation as police farrier. His working days were full: leaving at daybreak and riding six miles to the police camp on the Endeavour River and, after a full day, returning home at nightfall. On free days he busied himself in the garden and spent much time with Juliette.

Peter took another drink and now stood by a sizeable portrait of Queen Victoria, an original that had been painted during her younger days. He seemed more at ease, diverting most of his attention towards Juliette and her antics.

'Look, your pretty mummy wants you,' said Michael, waving to Abbey.

'Bedtime, my little darling,' crooned Abbey after having called Madeline.

'Yes, Ma'am?' asked Madeline, entering the doorway.

'It's bedtime for our little girl,' and she kissed Juliette's forehead as Madeline stretched out her arms.

Juliette refused to be parted. She began to whimper and clutched Abbey's dress. Madeline, as she had done many times before, pulled a chair close and took Juliette into her arms. Juliette soon snuggled against the familiar apron and drifted to sleep. Madeline then took Juliette to her bedroom.

Michael leaned back against the cushioned velvet of his chair, placed his hands behind his head and spoke casually. 'It's dry out at the camp. If we don't get rain soon then the boys will have to tail the horses further up along the river. There's still pockets of good grass up there.'

The dryness of the season had been a focal point of conversation during recent weeks.

'The dry's driving the Blacks in close,' added Peter. 'Marty Doolan's seen several within a few miles of town. Apparently Mt Cook and the seaside from there to the mouth of the Annan used to be their favourite stamping grounds in times of drought. One prospector came across a camp of them the other side of Black Mountain. "As thick as flying foxes," he said. Eight or ten were seen at Quarantine Bay. They were caught out on the rocks collecting oysters; two were shot and the rest escaped out to sea.'

Abbey listened without comment but the heartless remarks pained her.

'Incidentally, another packer says he saw Christie Palmerston leading a tribe across the Ah-Chee Tableland. I don't know what they do for water out there this time of the year. You know those Myalls can smell water for miles. Palmerston would perish without them. It's amazing how he deals with them; he's picked up their lingo and all.'

Michael took his hands from behind his head. 'Have you seen him about the Chinese robbery?'

'No, not yet but he'll have to come to town sometime. When the tucker gets really light they'll starve and he'll probably come in.'

'I don't know about that,' said Michael. 'The boys at the camp say he's as good as one of them.'

Peter brushed the comment aside. 'No white man can stand that isolation forever.' He then added, 'One way or another Palmerston will learn who's boss around here.'

'Watch him,' Michael cautioned. 'He's the best shot there is.'

Quiet prevailed while Peter dwelt on the warrant for Palmerston's arrest. He then changed the subject. 'Maybe it will rain soon. The storms are well overdue. Four inches would be a blessing. There'd be no shortage of food then and the Blacks would disperse further west.'

Abbey, who had stayed quiet, now drew the men's attention. 'There's lightning out there.' She pointed. 'It's way off but at least it's a sign. This heat can't continue for much longer.'

'Dearest, I hope you're right. Tempers are beginning to thin out at the camp. Bill Frazer,' and Michael turned more towards Peter, 'he gave one of the Blacks a hiding yesterday and threatened to tie him up at the river for crocodile bait.'

'Which one?' asked Peter.

'Tracker. He's not a bad lad; hardly deserved what he got. Bill's a bit hard on them.'

Peter drained his glass, stepped to the cabinet and tilted the decanter. Since Juliette's departure he had become sullen. He poured half a drink, gulped that and refilled. 'Once the wet breaks they'll feel better. The heat and dry is getting to us all. As for Bill he's just about due to go on a bender. I'll post him back to the town barracks and give him leave.'

Abbey interjected sharply, 'That's rum bottle discipline!'

Peter was incensed by her stinging comment. He thumped the glass on the cabinet. 'My dear sister!' he almost shouted. 'I run this town and the rest of Cape York! It's my prerogative to ...'

Abbey was stunned by his outburst. She struggled for words of apology. 'Sorry, Peter, I didn't mean—'

'It's all right,' he said with a wave of his hand. 'Leave it to me. I'll mete out the justice around here.'

Abbey turned away from him, left the table and moved to an open window. Here she sought diversion by watching the lightning flashing to the north-west.

Peter then foisted himself on Michael. 'Bill's liable to get up one morning, see which way the wind's blowing, roll his swag and go. I don't want that to happen. You can't keep a man stabled forever.'

Abbey pondered the situation; sifting for clues, searching for some cryptic message that would explain what had triggered Peter. Her thoughts returned to the Goldfields Shanty. Mention of the trouble at the shanty had disturbed him. She remained silent at the window, silhouetted by the lightning flashes. She came to the view that the conflict should be left alone and decided to say no more.

Madeline, who had stayed clear, re-entered. She wheeled in a servery and offered tea. Abbey was thankful for the thoughtful interruption and left the window to assist. Michael accepted a cup but Peter declined. Instead, he refilled from the decanter then excused himself, saying that he must water his horse.

CHAPTER 9

Just before daybreak—when the tune of the willie-wagtail filled the air—Barney had a dream.

He dreamt that he was in one of the boarding rooms of the Cavalier Hotel. He was sitting at the far end of a table facing the doorway to the hall.

Suddenly his father, Tom Simpson, appeared in full view at the entrance. Barney was astonished, unable to move or say anything. He was overcome and sat, statue still, staring into those familiar eyes. His father's eyes were wide, gleeful, and his face beaming. Barney had never before seen him so happy. He was clean shaven and his hair neatly brushed. He wore his usual clothes but they were not unkempt as they used to be; they were clean and neat.

Barney's shock passed as quickly as the moment of recognition. He now needed to touch his father. He sprang from his chair and as he did so his father moved forward. Two years of pain were lifted from Barney's heart. Two years of uncertainty vanished. It was true; it was real. They had finally been reunited.

They met halfway around the table. They went to shake hands, to greet each other as men do, but that was bypassed and they fell into an embrace. They stood, unashamedly hugging each other for many moments. It had all been worthwhile; the decision to leave Sydney, the sea journey and the search. Barney's greatest wish was fulfilled.

After more hugs they separated and each took a step backwards to see the other. They gazed at one another before Barney began to speak.

He said, 'This is the best thing that's ever happened to me.' But then, unfortunately, just as the fullness of his message took form, Barney was stirred from his dream. The dream was finished and the vision gone. He clung to the fading image of his father. 'No! No!' he cried aloud when it dissolved.

Barney made no attempt to stop his tears. He sobbed openly till the emotion subsided.

As he lay there the first glow of dawn began to light the feed-shed room, and other birds, heralding their own day with their own tunes, replaced the calls of the pre-dawn songsters.

Barney lay in a confused state trying to accept that it had only been a dream. He lay on the sheets thinking till he heard an outside noise. It was Laura shutting the small side gate as she arrived for work. He did not look but knew it was her because she always arrived before Cherie. He lay for a while longer then rose.

Nicholas' bunk was empty; he must have been at Meg's.

Barney washed in the basin on the rack and finished by brushing his fingers back through his hair. While he was lighting the boiler fire Cherie passed by and said good morning in a sleepy voice. He then fed the horses in the stalls before going for breakfast.

The kitchen stove was hot. Cherie was cooking breakfast and Laura was making bread. Laura offered to wash his clothes.

'And what about the sheets?' she asked. 'It must be time they went into the copper!'

Barney's answer was short. 'If you want.'

Laura wiped the flour dust from her hands, went to Barney, placed a hand on his bare shoulder and gave a squeeze. 'Be a good boy and light the copper for me.'

Barney bent his head closer to his porridge bowl but Laura held her touch. Her thoughts were constantly with him; a desire to be near him, to feel him, to be part of whatever he did.

Barney lit the copper fire. He then drew water from the well, preferring to heave the full buckets hand-over-hand rather than wind the slow windlass. He then went to and fro, carrying a large watering can, dampening the ant-bed footpath fronting the hotel. While he watered he thought about the dream of his father, the warmth and nearness. There was also another matter cramming his thoughts—Abbey O'Reilly. Since their meeting her pretty face, sweet manner and her apparent interest in him had filled his thoughts daily. As he reflected he became more unsettled. He needed to act and, without giving notice, he left and walked towards nearby Grassy Hill.

At the foot of Grassy Hill he left the roadway and stepped into the waist-high grass that covered the hillside. The long shafts gave way as he pushed up the steep incline towards the summit.

The mid-morning sun beat upon him, droplets of sweat dotted his forehead and the muscles of his legs strained. This new ground and his ascendancy from the pit of the town fulfilled his need for space and solitude.

A cool sea breeze welcomed him at the top. For several minutes he stood, almost motionless, with his eyes closed, feeling what was about him. Relief gradually spread throughout his body. The stress that had weighed so heavily on him earlier was easing. He realized that his dream had been but a dream, that it was unreal, that he had not spoken to or held his father. He was then distracted by the sight of a fleet of luggers under full sail far out to sea. He watched them bobbing like white butterflies. He continued watching as other ships plying the channel came and went.

Barney then moved to a shady ridge nearby. From there he studied the patchwork of the town. He saw the big, red roof of the Cavalier and watched the specks of activity there. His attention then slid to Abbey O'Reilly. Her house, in ornate splendour, stood alone and conspicuous on a ridge below. Nobody was in sight. The huge, silver roof of the house was surrounded by a garden and a white-picket fence. As he cooled in the shade he dwelt upon Abbey and their meeting at the Goldfields Shanty and recalled how she had wiped the blood from his face. He imagined her smiling that same sweet smile and speaking in the same playful way. He remembered her interest and, in particular, her invitation for him to visit. Barney's fancy took hold and, before long, he found himself toying with romantic notions.

He observed an eagle flying high above the house and became wholly absorbed with its mastery of the sky. He was held in awe and before long imagined himself endowed with the marvel of flight. He visualised himself as a mystical eagle. In his fantasy he swooped down and plucked Abbey from her silver slippers without bringing her harm. He then whisked her high into the sky and flew northwards. He hid her in an enchanted place where there was fine food, trickling water, books and a golden harp. When they were not otherwise occupied they sat listening to the sea crashing below the cliffs. Their life together ...

Barney kept the illusion alive for as long as possible and when it finally ended he descended the hill to rejoin the reality of the town.

CHAPTER 10

Ezra Cowan, manager of the Gold Bank, Cooktown, sat in the leather chair of his upstairs office. The antique furnishings together with Ezra's sentimental pieces—a set of gold scales, a silver letter knife and an old waxing pad—created an interesting atmosphere. All was quiet except for the beat of the street activity outside. As was his custom he read the *Cooktown Herald* before beginning the day's business. He folded the newspaper and placed it on the mahogany desk.

Though a Londoner by birth his genealogy had its roots in Judaism and hence the thirty years of his adult life had been devoted to the banking profession. During these years, both in England and Europe, he had witnessed financial strategies of mammoth proportions. As an executive of the Rothschild's banking empire he had seen the balance between nations tilted by financial dealings. Whilst in Rothschild's employ he had narrowly side-stepped a scandal involving the diamond trade; a debacle that eventually led to his sailing to Australia.

People who dealt with him observed that he was neither imposing nor retiring, making it difficult to gauge his attitude. Most considered him to be a financial enigma who diverged widely from traditional banking thought. Since arriving in this uncharted, high-risk, high-yield market of Cooktown he had capably managed his bank's finances. 'A most practical and worthy man,' James Mulligan had said of him.

Ezra, now engrossed in thought, rose and moved to the sideboard. He took the weights from beside the gold scales and began to place them on the pans; a few pennyweights in one, a half ounce in the other, then more on the first pan. As he contemplated he continued playing the unconscious game. When he was close to a resolution he evened the weights and, as a plan formulated, he watched the to and fro of the pans till they became steady. A satisfied smile together with a clicking of his fingers confirmed that he had made a decision. He was now well pleased and optimistic that he could recover the two-hundred-pound loan.

He left the weights as they were, walked past his desk and through the doorway to the bank's private balcony. He stood there in his suit and trimmed beard and surveyed the street.

Below him, there on Charlotte Street, a road gang was repairing a stone-pitched gutter. He mused about the street and all it had witnessed since its construction: the thirty thousand miners who had walked its path heading for the gold head of the Palmer strike. Its Chinese component arriving, hundreds at a time, bewildered and ignorant of the recklessness of the country they had just entered; and the European contingent, a mix of seasoned miners and new chums, all eager to be on their way. Men of the land, of commerce, the skilled and unskilled, the affluent and the castaways all melded into a human flux brimming at this frontier. Alluvial gold, everyman's dream, where little capital is required, had been the irresistible promise that had drawn them pulling their carts and humping their swags. Now these men, thirsty for more gold, were turning to reef mining. The cart and swag brigades were being replaced by bullock teams, double-banked at times to twenty head, pulling drays laden with massive boilers and crushing plants destined for the Palmer field. Much of this Ezra financed and often it was backed with uncertain collateral. What value a gold claim on the Palmer more than one hundred miles away?

Ezra's attention was distracted by the sight of Hornet and Barney together with Billy and the cart, moving towards him along the street. He knew Hornet Finnigan well and the circumstance of his father's death and he remembered meeting Barney at the Cavalier Hotel. He watched as they halted at a butcher shop, hitched Billy to a rail then entered the shop.

His thoughts then returned to his earlier preoccupation. His concern was the advance of two hundred pounds that his bank had made to Archibald Hicksbury. He was worried because there was now reason to doubt that its repayment would ever be honoured. Ezra had also learnt that Hicksbury had been first refused the loan by a local Chinese banker even after he had offered to pay them a loading over and above the normally harsh terms they demanded. He was critical of himself as he considered the worthlessness of accepting professional status as collateral. At least opium, which the Chinese sometimes staked, was tangible and marketable. This and Hicksbury's lack of honour had spiked Ezra's determination to retrieve the amount.

His plan was thus: Meg Challistine, owner of the Roarin' Meg Hotel, was a valued and long-time client of his bank. Ezra's advice and finance together with his preparedness to accept her assurances had underscored her success in building the most grand entertainment centre in Cooktown. She was appreciative of this and often expressed her gratitude when they met. Hicksbury, an incorrigible gambler, frequently darkened the doorway of Meg's gaming saloon and had lost heavily. Meg had told Ezra of this and of Hicksbury's pending financial ruin. However, though financially distressed he still had some income and it was this that Ezra intended to seize. Ezra also knew well Meg's ability to fiddle the margins. He intended approaching her with a view to using this avenue to settle the debt— even though it be by unconventional means.

The ganger of the road gang on the street below had called a halt and now he and his men sat on the kerb drinking hot tea by the embers of a fire. Hornet and Barney had loaded the meat into the cart and as they made ready to move off Eli came by. Ezra watched as Eli passed them and waved.

Ezra's association with Eli had begun two decades ago and during the years since they had maintained close contact; first through the

Institute of Academic Perception—a non-profit union of academics that sought to explain scientific phenomena—and in recent years as close friends in Cooktown. Ezra dwelt upon his bachelor friend, bringing to the fore nostalgic memories of their times together and of Eli's past.

Eli had graduated from Oxford University and taken the Hippocratic Oath at an early age. Later, he became a reader in philosophy and was acclaimed as a modern prodigy for his interpretation of philosophic tenets. By this time he was also a persuasive orator renowned for choosing his words carefully. He had a remarkable capacity to distil and crystallise ideas into forms that could be understood; he assigned simple benchmarks to complex philosophic reasoning so that his listeners could understand. His personal belief was that people ought not be coerced but that they should be free to gauge against their own conscience and decide for themselves.

He also worked relentlessly, pressing himself hard, carrying heavy professional and intellectual loads; leading the way for those of his own ilk and others; always at the forefront trying to do good and excel. He coped with this telling situation for many years till, one blustery night, he quit.

Ezra recalled that night vividly. Eli had walked through the pounding rain to arrive at Ezra's, sodden and cold. They had sat beside the fireplace for many hours exchanging views and sharing thoughts and before dawn it became evident to Ezra that the burden was stifling Eli's spirit. Ezra counselled him to make a clean break, to go abroad, to allow his spirit to roam.

This Eli did; he was outside British waters within a month and to this day had not returned.

Ezra reminisced further. He drifted ...

CHAPTER 11

Nicholas rose before daybreak and went fishing in the cool of the morning. Dressed in no more than a pair of trousers and with a jute bag slung over his shoulder he ambled to Chinatown. Here, by piccaninny daylight, that first glow of breaking dawn, he hired a sampan from a dubious Chinese. When he launched, his twelve-stone weight sank the small craft, leaving only a few inches of freeboard. Tiny ripples, flecked with gold by the ripening dawn, gave way as he sculled upstream. He ignored the mangrove's defences of stinking mud and biting insects and cast his line into the most likely place.

Snap! The first bait was taken before it reached the bottom. Nicholas rebaited and soon the still water was striped with dashing silver. The barbed fish shafted swiftly, cutting and pulling, trying to escape to the shelter of the mangrove roots. Nicholas, as joyful as a child, drew the line smartly and when the fish broke the surface it struck with all its might, splashing with blazing brilliance. Three more were soon slid into his sack. He then moved to a fresh patch to bag more.

Before the glare from the water had taken much hold Nicholas had caught a feast of red bream and grunter. He scaled and gutted them by the river and paid the Oriental man with fish. He was now slicing the last one into fillets in the kitchen of the Cavalier Hotel.

'Enough to feed the whole crew,' he said proudly to Prue and Cherie while pointing his knife at the piled plate.

'Must be worth a bottle of brandy,' tempted Prue.

'No. Not at all,' insisted Nicholas, wetting his lips and standing to his full height. 'Barney and I are indebted to you beyond repayment. What, with free rent and little board.' He added as a quip, 'You'll never get rid of us. Not this here Nicholas Hart anyhow. He knows when he's well off!'

Cherie admired Nicholas' Afro stature and syrupy skin and now, seeing him standing half naked and more than six feet tall, she had a fancy for him. She captured one of his glances and briefly held it at call with mocking submissiveness.

The morning's activity and the catch had done Nicholas good and, for the first time since his arrival, he spoke out. He told of his childhood in Jamaica: the bondage, the atrocities, emancipation and the planter's refusal to let go—his struggle to become a free man in a society dominated by colonial rule.

Barney listened while sitting at a table on the landing beneath the rear verandah. He was longways with one foot on the stool and picked his toe nails with a pocket knife.

Unknown to Barney, Laura was upstairs, on her knees, spying on him through the cracks between the verandah floorboards. She longed for everything she could see: his sandy hair, thick shoulders, barrelled chest and his long legs stretched before her. It pulsed within her; a tireless yearning to care and share, to be one. This urge, which of late had become obsessive, could not be dispelled. To attract Barney's attention she took a water pitcher from a room and poured water through the cracks. Everyone heard Barney's outburst when the water splashed on his head.

'What! What's goin' on?' he blurted, looking upwards.

Laura poured the rest through the cracks.

'Plurry hell!' he shouted, tripping over the stool and cracking a shin. He then hobbled to the courtyard.

Laura was nowhere to be seen so Barney, knowing it was her, shouted, 'You wench! Show yourself!'

Laura suddenly appeared at the railing. She had removed her apron and bonnet, dropped her hair and flicked off her shoes. 'Catch me if you can,' she shouted.

A chase began. Barney raced towards the rear stairs as Laura ran along the verandah. He leapt up the stairs then ran around the verandah without sighting her. He was breathless and waited, listening for a sound. For Laura the chase was still hot and before descending the internal staircase she shouted, 'Barney. I'm here!' Barney rushed from the verandah, reaching the top step soon after Laura entered the empty bar room below. She had left the door ajar just sufficient to be noticed. Barney descended the stairs and halted by the staircase post. He heaved a deep breath before approaching her hideout. A floor board creaked as he entered the darkened room. He sensed Laura's presence but was in no rush to make the discovery; the hide-and-seek was all part of the play. The store room door lay wide open but the darkness inside hid almost everything. He paused at the doorway then entered.

Laura stood by the rear wall craving the silhouette before her, but as it slowly came closer she became unsure. Her cheeks began to burn. Barney somehow knew when he was within reach. He stretched out his hand and felt about. His first contact was with her bosom. Laura placed a nervous hand on his to draw it away but he resisted by moving in close, wrapping his other arm about her and clutching tightly.

Laura had no previous experience with this kind of encounter. As the daughter of fish merchants, she had been raised in the fish markets of Brisbane where her mother, as a registered vendor, sold fish that the father netted from Moreton Bay. During this time, she had, six days each week, been woken at four o'clock and accompanied her mother to the markets where, till early afternoon, she sorted and sold fish and scampered about in play with other children. She had been very disappointed when, within days of her thirteenth birthday and still with no formal schooling, her parents announced that the family was going to sail north to harvest the bêche-de-mer fisheries of the Great Barrier Reef.

The first year of this far-away life was idyllic; roving the coastline and docking at Cooktown where the Chinese paid in gold for the sea-slug delicacy. But then the Asians in their small, leaky junks flooded the reef, decimating the fishery. To cope with the threat Laura, together with her parents, established a permanent camp on the Bloomfield River. From here her father, together with a deck hand, sailed their schooner to distant reefs and on return they all prepared and smoked the catch. The family was close knit, being bound by their lifestyle and their belief in the Roman Catholic faith, and within this fabric Laura had developed a sound sense of morality and loyalty.

However, all this changed when, on a mid-November afternoon the unpredictable occurred. Her parents and the deck hand, promising to return before the afternoon storms broke, sailed off and left Laura alone to stoke the smoking fires. By midday storms were beginning to encase the seaward horizon and, soon after, these dark, deepening omens banded together to form a single front. The thunder storm burst earlier than anyone expected, careering landward, raking the coast and whipping the mountains.

Laura had raced through the fury of the storm to reach a hilltop with a view to seaward. But to no avail: visibility extended little beyond the great foaming torrents that battered the foreshore. For days after, every ship contacted between Princess Charlotte Bay in the north and Rockingham Bay in the south scoured the sea for signs. A lady friend, camped further upstream, took Laura into care and when, three weeks later, wreckage of their schooner was found washed ashore at Cape Kimberley, arrangements were made to settle Laura at Cooktown. But Laura's love of her parents, the bonding which had occurred within the family during the period of isolation, made it difficult for her to adjust to new family life. She had, in the main, remained as an orphan. Although, since being employed at the Cavalier, she had felt a parental nearness to Prudence.

While Barney's thoughts and rising intentions left no room for doubt, Laura's were otherwise. She became desperate. *What am I doing?* her mind stammered in silent confusion. Everything was now uncertain, under question. *Why is he slipping his hand under my dress? What is he doing fumbling my breasts?* This was not her wish, her will, or her belief. This should not be allowed. She wished to go, to leave the dark, to separate. But every thought of escape was quickly trapped by another that called for her to be obedient. Like a pup on a lead she allowed him to undo her dress and pull it free. It was unbecoming, embarrassing and wrong; there was no call for mischief of this kind. Laura tried to retreat, pressing her back against the wall. She was unable to utter a word, to tell him to stop, to quit, to leave her alone. She cringed inside when his hand groped its way to her crotch. There was no pleasure, only a sensation of invasion, of abuse. She tripped and stumbled in her mind, trying to express the concern, begging for him to stop, to go away. The insistence of his movements staved off her attempts to stall his advance. With the removal of one then another of her undergarments he stripped her modesty till she was wholly naked. Laura's terror stiffened her posture, expressing revulsion, crying out that this not be so, that some respect be shown. But her silent pleas went unheeded. Laura began to sob, pleading in a childlike way to be spared, for him to please understand before it was too late.

It was strange that at no time did Laura try to move aside, to push free. Neither did she ask nor demand that he stop the intrusion; not one word of objection crossed her lips. Maybe she was possessed by fear but more likely she, in her youthful naivety, knew of no other way to cope. She had been taught to be giving, to be selfless. She had never been taught to say 'No!'

Barney pulled his pants off and exposed himself. Never could she have imagined any of this. This was not love, not Laura's idea of love. There was no understanding, no intimacy, no caring, no gentleness; nothing at all of love.

Barney took hold of Laura and proceeded to rape her with callous disregard, and when finished he dressed and left without a word of consolation.

Laura was left on the floor a crumpled mess. She lay for a time, bewildered and lost, till she was able to clothe herself and leave by the front door.

She was unable to return to the Cavalier that afternoon. Nor was she able to confide in her elderly landlady; there was nobody, she thought, who would understand. She remained in the isolation of her tiny room, trussed by shame.

Soon after dark a thunder storm struck, pelting on the tin roof above the calico-cloth ceiling. The heavy drops clattered like pebbles creating a dense roar in Laura's ears. It made her feel more numb and less aware. She became unaware of the candle burning on the upturned tea chest, of the rapping of the rain on the window panes and of the red quilt beneath her. She lay with her arms cradled against her chest, swaying unconsciously, trying to console herself. Her life to date, all she believed and hoped for, had now been shattered by this one act. Her intermittent sobbing went unheard above the hammering of the storm. The old landlady did not know and neither did Prudence. The candle burnt out without bringing help, and when that tiny glimmer of comfort died Laura lay face down on the quilt and in frightened dismay she bore the agony the whole night through.

Christmas Day was only a few days hence but for Laura the spirit of Christmas was now gone. The secret baking she had done and the small, thoughtful, handmade presents she had hidden away—including one for Barney—no longer held meaning.

CHAPTER 12

The Cavalier Hotel advertised a gala evening to celebrate New Year's Eve: 'To drink out the old and pipe in the new,' the invitation read. It was now mid morning on this special day and everyone was busy. Prue and the two girls baked. Eli and Nicholas slid the concertina doors open and decorated the lounge and dining rooms as a combined entertainment area. Barney mowed the yard, pushing the mower with zeal. Hornet delivered a load of wood.

Cherie's parents, the owners of Vanity Place, an embroidery and fancy glassware shop, visited and Cherie, together with Prue, Eli and Nicholas, joined with them for tea and scones. Eli was explaining the mechanics of a new sluicing technique when all were surprised by the appearance of Inspector Peter Britfield and his aid, Constable Cecil Bean.

'Come through,' welcomed Prue, standing and tucking her blouse more tightly into her skirt.

'No, nothing official,' replied Peter to Eli's question. 'Purely informal.'

'Here, I'll take that,' offered Prue stepping forward to take Peter's helmet.

Nicholas tried to avoid involving himself with the police. His face took on a sullen uneasiness and he remained motionless and downcast. He prayed for his exclusion from the conversation but his coyness was as conspicuous as his colour. Prue soon took the opportunity to make his introduction.

'Nicholas,' she beckoned cheerfully, 'I'd like you to meet our inspector.' She then referred back to Peter. 'Peter, this is Nicholas Hart, one of our boarders.'

Peter was in fine spirit; his remarks so far had been colourful and boisterous, nabbing every chance to cause a spill of laughter.

'Hello there,' he hailed merrily, trying to lower himself to Nicholas' rank. Nicholas, fearful that his misdeed in Sydney might be known, rose clumsily and swallowed hard before meeting the inspector halfway and taking a manly grip of his hand. However, the perceived conflict was one sided. While the purpose of Peter's visit remained unclear, he certainly was not about to arrest Nicholas for the murder of a policeman in Sydney.

Before long Peter and Eli diverted the conversation towards political considerations. They canvassed matters pertaining to their disenchantment with the Legislative Council of Queensland then digressed to the question of Sovereign Rule versus Political Democracy, and later they agreed with Henry Parkes' vision of a confederation of the Australian colonies. This conversation was of no interest to Nicholas and he soon excused himself from their company.

Prior to supper that evening Barney shaved at the wash rack. He stropped the razor on the strap, tested it with a touch to his cheek, soaped himself then shaved with long, firm strokes. He bathed quickly, donned shirt and trousers which Laura had pressed, then stood before the cracked mirror at the rack. He admired himself in the yellowing pane as he tidied his hair with his fingers.

Barney felt good: the freshly cut lawn, the large pile of chopped wood, the busy movements of people and the smell of roasting food all contributed to his high spirits. He ate heartily amidst the good cheer that could be heard from the bar and those closer at hand. Laura had set aside her painful memories and was tackling the demands of a full house. Nicholas had spent the afternoon at the bar of the Cooktown Hotel and was now in Prue's bar waving a loaded rifle about as though it were a plaything.

James Mulligan arrived just as Barney finished arranging the tables and chairs to allow space for dancing.

'Fine, fine,' said James, doing a twirl about the polished floor on his own. Miss Milstred, an elderly spinster and long-time teacher of pianoforte, together with a saxophonist and an amorous drummer, soon filled the wooden building with loud, rattling music.

In coaches, carriages, and buggies, on horseback mounted side-saddle and astride, the cheerful thronged to the Cavalier. Chivalrous men with callused hands and clothes smelling of camphor helped their graceful ladies down and escorted them across the ant-bed footpath and through the doorway.

Jugs and jugs of beer and silver trays full of ladies' drinks were shared. Those present danced, swinging to the tune of the 'Pride of Erin' or dancing in close to a soft waltz. On and on as though wearing enchanted shoes they swirled and stepped remembering all they had been taught in earlier years. White frilly dresses, heavily ornamented and with pumped-up bodices, graced the ladies while dark suits set against white shirts fitted the gentlemen who sported trimmed beards and moustaches.

The Scottish pipers—the Caledonians—arrived full of beer and spirit and upset Miss Milstred for a wee while when, unannounced, they piped through the hotel, upstairs and downstairs. Archibald Hicksbury their Drum Major spun and pumped his mace with a practiced hand.

Those in the bar room and bushmen yarning by the boiler fire in the courtyard listened and imagined, and at times sang along. The rifle at the bar was eventually let loose, blasting a hole through the ceiling. Nicholas, now shirtless, happened to have it in his clutches when Eli appeared but denied being responsible as he surrendered it amidst hoots from his mates. Gold nuggets, won from the reaches of the Palmer, lay on the bar with their ownership marked by whose drink stood nearest.

Barney had been wary of Archie Hicksbury since he first piped in and now, seeing him leaning on the piano and swigging beer, he felt a creeping distrust of the man. Hicksbury's brows wriggled in proportion to his attempts to focus on those across the room. He had looked Barney's way often during the evening and was now peering his way intently. Fortunately Ezra Cowan together with Mrs Cowan and their daughter Philya had just arrived. Barney, who had met the family at the hotel on a previous visit, crossed the floor to extend a welcome. Philya, just sixteen, was striking in appearance. Her pointed chin, pouted lips and high cheek bones created a provocative but regal air. Her dark, attentive eyes, framed by straight hair cut with a fringe, conspired with intrigue. She was as slim as a wading bird and wore a blue evening dress that comfortably clad her modest suggestion of an emerging bust. Barney was enthralled with her cultured accent. He wanted to request a dance but the man from Country Down, James Mulligan, with his dapper style and with only a few words quickly stole the princess and whisked her off about the slippery floor. When it came nearly midnight, blasts from steamers resounded across the harbour and filled the town. Horses' ears pricked and coachmen consulted their watches. Then, at exactly midnight by Eli's watch, Hicksbury's band piped through the main doorway, squeezing out a pitched rendition of 'Auld Lang Syne'. Amid shouts, cheers and laughter people linked arms, formed traditional circles and frolicked while singing to Robbie Burns' best, calling back the good times of old. They sang verse, chorus and then another verse all the way with sentimental fervour. Then they sang again, one more time, right the way through, bringing forth the most cherished memories. Miss Milstred then danced her nimble fingers across the piano keyboard as the season's greetings were exchanged with handshakes, hugs and kisses.

Philya sought Barney in the crowd, took his hands, reached upon her toes then kissed him hard on his lips. He placed his hands on her shoulders ready to engage in talk and maybe even, if courage permitted, ask her to dance, but something suddenly niggled his intention. He drew his hands aside and looked towards the kitchen. Laura stood there alone in her bonnet and apron. She had worked the whole day through and was still dressed as she had been that morning. She was watching him, forlorn and lonely, waiting, hoping that he would notice. Barney became perplexed. He felt guilty and to satisfy his conscience he excused himself from Philya's company. But he could not bring himself to approach Laura for, apart from Philya, there was his nagging desire to embrace Abbey O'Reilly.

He again busied himself with his duty of gathering glasses and wiping tables. Table to table and back and forth to the bar he went, enjoying the rowdy atmosphere. He was handing the drummer a free whisky when his name was called unexpectedly.

'Young Simpson!' he heard from his left side. He turned to attend but was confronted by Hicksbury's outstretched hand. Hicksbury laughed at him, louder and louder, drawing undue attention from those nearby, making it impossible for Barney to ignore his request.

'Here! How about a free pint for the Drum Major whilst you're about it!'

Barney hesitated.

Hicksbury pushed the glass further forward insistently and when Barney took hold their hands touched. All of Hicksbury's laughter was now gone. His expression narrowed as he spoke.

'Just one drink to appease the keeper of the hounds,' he said sarcastically.

'What hounds?' asked Barney innocently and unsuspectingly.

'The hounds that—' Hicksbury left off to breathe deeply then gushed his stinking breath across Barney's face. Barney's nostrils twitched as he pulled the glass free. He then condescended with a nod before turning for the bar.

What hounds? puzzled Barney. *What has hounds got to do with New Year's Eve or a Drum Major?* He bumped against Alexander Trott and Mr and Mrs Agnew, while crossing the floor engrossed in thought. Barney tried to attach significance to the remark. *Was it flippancy arising from a drunken stupor? Was it meant to be polite inconsequential patter?*

He returned with the drink without having formed any firm notion and when he handed the drink to Hicksbury he was compelled to ask, 'You were about to say?'

'Hounds, lad! Hounds!' sounded Hicksbury loudly.

Barney stepped back a pace. He was now more confused.

'I,' said Hicksbury, tapping hard on his own chest, 'I will turn the hounds loose.'

Barney's forehead creased with genuine puzzlement. He had no clue as to the mischief the other was about.

Hicksbury grunted disdainfully at Barney's naivety then swilled his glass, spilling some beer. He commented almost offhandedly, 'You'll hear the barking soon.'

Suddenly, a monstrous realisation flooded Barney's thoughts.

'No, no,' he spluttered involuntarily in disbelief, his eyes shifting from Hicksbury.

'Yes! Oh yes!' he heard when he turned his head further aside, seeing the crowd as only a blur.

Barney did not want to hear more. It could not be true. He refused to accept what he had heard.

Hicksbury set to rattle him further, to gauge his reaction, to reinforce his own suspicion. 'They will soon be on the scent, following the trail that you have laid to your father!'

Barney became oblivious to everything except Hicksbury's persecuting voice. 'You, lad, have laid the trail to Cooktown yourself!'

This sting exasperated Barney. He shoved off abruptly, ignoring the piercing voice behind. He bumped heavily against couples while making for the rear doorway.

He stormed across the courtyard, through the carriageway, then headed north along the street, making for Grassy Hill. His ascent up the hill was rapid. He tripped and stumbled in the dark, exposing himself to injury.

At the top he milled about with his thoughts clouded and confused. It seemed inconceivable that Hicksbury could have linked him and his father, yet Hicksbury's comments clearly indicated otherwise. This admission by Hicksbury confirmed to Barney that his father was somewhere in the region. He recalled the searches he had made for his father, peeping into blacksmith shops and livery stables in and about the town. Also inspecting the style of shoeing on horses that came to town to see if it was his father's work. His dislike of Hicksbury had turned to hate. Furthermore, there was now a dire necessity to protect his father. These considerations gradually turned to a sinister thought. *If Hicksbury were to be killed, maybe in an accident, Tom would go undetected. The police know well of Hicksbury's recklessness when driving his sulky while drunk. I can easily tamper with the sulky harness so that the stitching on the leather breastplate gives way when strained by a sudden jolt.* Barney had the motive, means and daring to implement such a plot. By the time he descended Grassy Hill he had a clear idea what to do.

CHAPTER 13

Nicholas became a regular at the Roarin' Meg Hotel. This Saturday night he was clean shaven and well dressed. He had returned to full health and his handsomeness showed as he stood with a cue in hand awaiting his turn to shoot at the snooker table. Meg was by his side.

Meg's creativity was responsible for the layout of this upper floor. Its design and décor equalled anything to be found in the colonies. The evening was busy with a throng of patrons and others filling the snooker room, gambling saloon and saloon bar. A few were seated on the balcony enjoying the cool breeze. Meg's private quarters lay at the rear with the door locked and windows barred. When it came to Nicholas' turn to cue Meg let him be. She stepped to the central hallway and within a few paces came to the stairwell, the only access to the upper level. She heard the merriment from the bar room downstairs and paused with her hands on the rail. The call of the pit master umpiring the two-up game in the public bar room below could be heard. Down there vixens laid trails with perfume and traps with words. Many were cheap, one-night girls with cracked heels and stained teeth, taking all they could get as quickly as they were able from the diggers. Others, the professionals, engaged in lengthy pretensions to create an image and thus enhance their worth to the high rollers. Fortunately for Meg the Roarin' Meg was a place the police inspector chose to ignore. She then moved to the saloon bar where sounds of a midnight singalong by the piano filled the air. The saloon's main feature was a flag that had been flown at the Eureka Rebellion in 1854. It took pride of place on the wall at the far end of the bar. The flag, blue in colour and emblazoned with a white Southern Cross, symbolised Meg Challistine whose father had fought beneath that flag during the goldfields uprising at Ballarat all those years before. With a will inspired by that flag Meg had built a personal empire that was evidenced by the success of the Roarin' Meg Hotel. 'Rip Roarin' Meg' she had been dubbed, the woman who could smell gold in pack saddles miles out from town.

Meg drifted the length of the bar then crossed the hallway to the gambling saloon where Archie Hicksbury and others were playing Black Jack. Gunther, the gambling saloon manager and former card cheat from Hamburg, was monitoring the play. Meg joined him and in silence they watched several hands played, and each time the dealer cleverly dealt the second card instead of the top card Gunther touched Meg's hand. Eventually Meg drew her hand aside and Gunther, feeling her rejection, withdrew without comment. Meg relied on Gunther—his understanding of the trade and his handling of men—but lately, since her involvement with Nicholas, Gunther had become a concern. His possessiveness of her, for which she had given him no cause, and his overt jealousy of Nicholas were intolerable and she had decided that he must be dismissed. However, she had come to know that he was an introvert with convoluted ideas, potentially dangerous, and this had dissuaded her thus far from acting. Hicksbury was losing heavily and Meg, not wanting to be implicated, withdrew and returned to the top of the stairwell. Archie lost another hand and accused the dealer of cheating. He flung his cards on the table, abused the dealer then left in a disturbed state.

He thundered down the hallway and sighted Meg alone by the stairwell. He ignored her appeasing smile and came close. Meg was forced to step backwards till her buttocks pressed hard against the rail. He came even closer, shaking with fury. He abused Meg, naming her a 'whore', a 'curse'. Meg became terrified and grasped the railing tightly. She dared not scream for he would surely toss her over the railing to her doom. He leaned further forward forcing her to bend back till she pivoted on the brink of overbalancing.

Conflict about riches was nothing new to Hicksbury. His whole life, from when he was the child who had to have more than the boy next door, had been defaced by greed. His days at the University of Edinburgh saw no improvement and his partnership in legal practice faltered and failed as a result of his malpractice.

His most notorious excursion was his involvement some thirty years past in what became known as the Estrangement Trade. It was during the Irish potato famine of the latter 1840s. Rather than watch their children die of starvation in sod huts and straw shelters, Catholic peasant farmers of Ireland had, through an agency which was secretly commanded by Hicksbury, allowed their children to be placed anonymously as servants on what these humble families understood were the wealthy and caring estates of the British Isles.

For their part these blameless but naive land-locked souls agreed that, when their penance was done and divine providence once again greened the fields, they would recompense both the agency and the children's custodians for their humanitarian services. Every aspect of the agency's initial presentation was so dignified and confidence inspiring that these uninformed agrarians were easily fooled into mortgaging their small plots as security. They believed that, in return, their bonny ones—mainly boys aged from seven to ten years—would be treated tenderly and read the scriptures.

So eager were they that scores agreed to mortgages which were third or fourth call on over-encumbered properties, the discharge dates of which were so early as to make them nigh on impossible to satisfy. Even then the realised sale price of the property, in many cases, was insufficient to repay the other mortgagees and then the agency. In such instances there was no legal obligation for the agency to return the child or to disclose the child's whereabouts. Instead the agency sold these dozens of children to unscrupulous labour merchants to do as they chose with them. The coal and iron ore industries, the mines providing the raw materials needed to fuel the Industrial Revolution, sopped up this child fodder. Misfortune was piled upon misfortune, with the most incomprehensible being that only a few of the children assigned to the mines were ever reunited with their families.

The furore which eventually erupted reverberated throughout the British Isles. Even the Protestant English were astounded and incensed at the perpetration of such a shameful and indecent fraud. During those years the agency, under the precepts of British Law, bled the believing people of their children, their land and their livelihood. It was not till the Ribbonmen, an Irish-Catholic secret society, attempted Hicksbury's murder that the foreclosures ceased and, after destroying the files showing the children's whereabouts, Hicksbury fled to Australia. However, word of his damnation had not remained confined to Europe. Eli had been present in Europe at the time of Hicksbury's scandalous exposure; so too had the inspector and Ezra Cowan. Meg and Prudence had also come to know of his infamous deed.

Hicksbury's self-control was now precarious. Saliva dribbled from his chin, his face blistered into purple patches, the hair on his temples rose and his heavy jowl swelled. Meg's fragile position was unsustainable. She would soon follow the dangling locks of her hair and crash to her doom. It was certain, like a woman at the guillotine ready to be beheaded and, like such a woman, bound but not gagged, she hit out, blurting her innermost thought with no concern for its consequence.

'Murderer!' she hissed at his face; and then more specifically, 'Child murderer!'

Hicksbury heard and was shocked. His stare shifted from Meg's face. The stain of murder—memories of the children who had been killed or had collapsed and died of fatigue in the pits—splashed across his conscience. His evil doing had pursued him even to Cooktown. There was no place on earth to which he could escape. Always his reputation would follow, persecuting him with every reminder. Meg's words struck at the core of his being. Without further intimidation he withdrew and blundered heavily down the staircase. When outside he took to his sulky, whipped the mare hard and dashed off at a reckless pace by a ghostly moon.

CHAPTER 14

Hornet was most excited. Today was the annual fete and sports day organised by the Catholic Ladies Guild. He had entered Billy in the goat cart race. Prue, with Laura's help, cut Hornet's hair and clothed him to perfection. His silken shirt of green and white, his chosen race colours, gave him a mature appearance. His jodhpurs, tailored with a slim cut, dressed him with manliness beyond his age. Hornet had prepared well during the past weeks, feeding Billy corn, greasing the axles and practising in secret down by the Finch Bay road. Through Prue's encouragement Helen, Hornet's sick mother, agreed to attend the outing.

After breakfast Hornet, Prue, Laura and Cherie assembled in the dining room. A small difference of opinion arose.

'Hornet!' insisted Prue cheerfully.

'But Ma'am!' protested Hornet vigorously.

'No buts, Hornet. You're to keep these shoes on all day.'

'But they're too tight.'

'Rubbish!' interrupted Laura. 'They look good.'

'But I'll slip. When I drive hard I stand up on the seat and I'll slip.'

'No you won't.'

'Bet ya thr'pence I will.'

'Everything's money with you.'

'Better 'n you. Everything's about love with you. You want to marry Barney. I know.'

'You wouldn't know anything. You—'

'Here. Here,' said Prue. 'Let's not start the day like this.'

Hornet sat quietly whilst Laura knelt and buckled the new shoes. 'There,' said Laura after she fitted the shoes with a mother's care; then when Laura rose to her feet Prue saw that she was pale. Laura held a hand to her stomach to relieve the morning sickness.

Hornet was about to leave when Nicholas, happy but weary from a night at the Roarin' Meg, entered by the small side gate. He mustered interest and, together with the girls, inspected Billy's polished horns and the spruced cart. Barney kept away. He quietly attended a guest's horse at the stable. His concern lay elsewhere. His thoughts were full of Abbey O'Reilly and the approach he intended making at the fete.

Barney shaved and bathed then took his best clothes from a tin trunk and went to the kitchen to iron. Laura, alone and lonesome, offered to press them but Barney declined the offer and ironed them himself.

The new clothes, his indifference to her and all the girls who would be at the fete added to Laura's anxiety as she watched. Then when he gathered his clothes Laura with moistened eyes asked, 'Can I come, please?'

Barney replied by shaking his head and turning away from her.

Laura felt sick and held her stomach to fight the nausea. All that had passed between them in the store room six weeks before and its consequence was being felt. For her there was now nothing, only the prospect of a bastard in arms.

She was bewildered by the rejection. She felt spurned, cheated, deserted. All had turned to darkness. She could see no way out except to turn to the teaching of her upbringing. She left the hotel and trudged tearfully along the windy street towards St Mary's Church.

Father O'Gorman, the parish priest and a man of nearly three-score years, met Laura by the side door of the church and guessed her plight without having to ask. He took her into his arms and held her tightly, reassuring her of the only thing she needed to know—that somebody truly cared. They later drank tea in his reception room. He listened patiently and spoke compassionately, encouraging Laura to confess all. He prayed, asking forgiveness for her, giving her hope. He spoke of the miracle of birth, of the future, the blessing that the child would be and he asked her to be brave for the babe's sake. He suggested to Laura that she confide in Miss Swanson whom he said was 'a most understanding lady'.

Hornet remained anxious. Although the goat cart race was scheduled for that afternoon, he had arrived by mid morning and tethered Billy in the shade. The venue was the town park, on the river side of Charlotte Street, midway between the wharf and the Sovereign Hotel; the place where Captain James Cook, more than a century before, had beached his barque, *Endeavour*, to repair its damaged hull. There, upon the soft grass of the esplanade, the ladies of the Guild had erected sail sheets and beneath them laid out all sorts of niceties. Hornet dodged between the people, inspecting the stalls, fingering his treasured sixpence. Many families were still arriving and, at this rate, the park would soon be full. When children arrived they made direct for the sweet stalls, pulling their parents forward, and the parents followed knowing that there would be no peace till this wish was satisfied. All the choices to be made—coconut ice, marshmallow, toffee, popcorn and assorted lollies—helped make the children's day.

Barney made a manly appearance at noon. He was dressed casually, wearing a white shirt, fawn trousers and tan shoes. He had thirteen shillings in his pocket and, if necessary, would spend the lot.

He scanned the crowd, sorting through the bowler hats and umbrellas. More than five hundred people mingled about the stalls and half that number again were gathered by the roadside watching the children's foot races. Barney expected Abbey to be wearing the same dress, twirling the same parasol and to greet him with the same smile. He walked by the stalls then checked those by the river side sitting on rugs, nursing babies and lunching. Abbey was nowhere to be seen. However, the day was yet young and horse-drawn vehicles were still being reined in.

He strolled to the roadside where an excited crowd were encouraging their young to win. Peter Britfield was the chief steward and with his personality, free from the restraints of marriage, he was a favourite of both the children and adults. The children, being honoured that Mr Britfield would start their races with a live revolver, gave each race their best. Barney loitered there and was studying Peter Britfield closely, guessing what traits bore a resemblance to Abbey, when Hornet came to his side. Hornet's cheeks and silk shirt were stained with red toffee and his shoes were missing. He offered Barney a try of his half-sucked toffee apple. Barney replied coarsely; he wished Hornet would scat. After all, courting is a man's business not to be hampered by kids. Hornet took no notice and stayed with Barney till the rooster chase for the children began. Barney was relieved when he saw the rooster then Hornet disappear over the river bank.

Barney watched the races till two o'clock by which time almost everybody had arrived. He then began a fresh search. Up and down the lanes then criss-crossing between stalls he went checking then rechecking. He began to see people for the third and fourth time and while many of those ladies had pretty faces there was none he wanted. He went further, pacing the street side, searching for the family carriage. He was now hot and frustrated.

The foot races had finished and the mounted police were delivering a display of tent pegging, an exciting sport of horsemanship that was a popular pastime of the British Cavalry in India. Four troopers had already galloped, individually, with a lance at hand, spiking one of the small wooden pegs from the ground with each pass by. It was now Sergeant Bill Frazer's try and Barney watched as his horse side-stepped to the middle of the street. To everyone's surprise Bill drove his lance, point first, into the road then rode clear. A hush settled upon the crowd when he steadied his horse. At the crack of the starting shot the horse leapt into full gallop with Bill leaning over till his head was level with the horse's underline. With a loose rein the charger held a straight course towards the pegs. At the first peg Bill, with a snap of the wrist, plucked the short peg free and tossed it aside, then the next and the next catching all seven pegs at a full gallop. The spectators shouted applause, and when Bill cantered back Peter fired two more shots to the crowd's cheers.

Barney, however, offered no accolades. He was cantankerous. Time was beginning to slow with events appearing to crawl. None would move fast enough to present the moment when Abbey would appear. Yet, ironically, at the same time he wished to forestall the afternoon till she arrived. He moved off to continue his hunt. He scanned the moving sights and sounds till late afternoon when the lads assembled for the goat cart race.

Father O'Gorman arrived just in time to officiate. He held a loud hailer with both hands and began his commentary as the carts were circled.

'Ladies and Gentlemen,' he announced with his Killarney brogue. 'Attention please so I can introduce the contestants.' Father presented the crowd with an eloquent preamble outlining the short history of the annual race. He then proceeded:

'I'll take them as they are numbered. Number one in the orange silk is Sam Fox driving Harriett. Sam is eleven years old and this is his first try at the race. Number two is Stinker, trained and driven by Jim Glade in the blue and white silk. I see the odds are short on Stinker, so there, Ladies and Gentlemen, make your own assessment of this upstanding buck. Third, and a late nomination, is Charger, bred, trained and driven by Ces Buxton. Ces, I'm told, is responsible for those wild drives along Charlotte Street.

'Ah! Next we have my man Hornet Finnigan, number four, with his famous Billy Boy. Watch for his white silk with the green shamrock on the back. A true Irish lad is our Hornet.'

Father O'Gorman paused for longer than necessary for breath in order to give Hornet extra exposure. Hornet took the opportunity and trotted Billy quickly, making a wide circle outside the others. Prue and Helen exchanged devilish comments at the sight of his bare feet. 'Yes!' returned Father. 'A combination like that is an Irishman's sure bet.'

'Number five in the purple and gold silk is Manfred Fudge driving Sir Sudan. Sir Sudan is from the south and a fine specimen in fine fettle. Good luck Manfred. And finally, number six, we have Jamie Axford driving Tempest.'

The course had been set: from the park the boys were to race their carts along Charlotte Street, steer around a barrel abreast the Sovereign Hotel then return. When all was set Peter Britfield pulled the trigger, startling the goats and plunging them forward. The backlash from Charger's quick start nearly tipped Ces Buxton from his cart. The drivers jostled, wheel to wheel, fighting for the lead. Sam Fox's goat careered sideways and his axle rattled in the spokes of Stinker's cart. In return Stinker tried to butt Harriett. Jamie Axford's cap blew off when he slipped. Hornet and Fudge were jammed in centre field. Fudge's big white Angora goat took bold strides, whisking his custom made gig along the wide street. Billy pulled gamely, whirling the wheels of his makeshift cart. At the quarter way mark Fudge laid his whip hard across his goat's back. Sir Sudan flinched noticeably. The saddle horses hitched nearby fidgeted nervously. Billy and Sir Sudan drew level; Charger was a length behind followed by Stinker then Tempest. Harriett had bailed-up somewhere behind. Hornet, with the red drape of his cart fairly flying, edged sideways aiming for the barrel.

Fudge glared at him from beneath his riding cap which featured his family crest. He then beat his goat furiously and in the flurry his cart tripped Billy, sprawling him to the ground.

'You mongrel bastard!' shouted Hornet as Fudge sped off. 'Get up, Billy, get up mate!' urged Hornet frantically.

Billy staggered to his feet then lurched forward.

'Go get him, Pint Size!' shouted the umpire at the barrel.

Billy wavered till he regained his balance then lengthened his stride.

Fudge looked back and, with a dirty grin on his thin lips, estimated that he had a winning lead.

Hornet, now ablaze, stood upright, flung the slack of his reins forward and shouted. Billy responded and scorched after Sir Sudan.

The crowd's sympathy was apparent. 'Come on, Hornet! Come on, Hornet!' was their cry.

The prize was now only yards away but Sir Sudan was nearly spent. He was beginning to falter.

Hornet shrieked, 'Go for it Billy! Get him boy! That goat ain't got the steam!'

Billy held his pace, gobbling the distance between them till, only strides from the finish, he again drew level with Sir Sudan. Sir Sudan strained valiantly but Billy took the lead, crossing the line triumphantly.

The people gathered around offering their congratulations but Hornet was overcome and soon he pushed through the crowd towards Helen and Prue. Prue put her arms out first and hugged him proudly then Helen, a gentle wisp of a lady, lovingly embraced her son David.

During the presentation Hornet became embarrassed and repeatedly spat on the ground.

'Oh, dear,' whispered Helen.

'Never mind. You should be proud,' said Prue, touching Helen's forearm.

Peter spoke following Father and during his address he placed a hand lightly on Hornet's head and expressed the opinion, 'I hope that one day Master Finnigan will join our force.'

Father O'Gorman then concluded the outing with a prayer which, surprising to some, sought forgiveness for sinners.

Barney had lost interest in the people. He now cared not a jot about them. He had not foreseen that Abbey may not attend. No such possibility had occurred to him.

He was upset and walked to the wharf seeking solitude. There the ships with tall masts and furled sails lay like becalmed galleons on a grey sea. At the pier end he gazed into the grey water not knowing what to do, where he should go.

Sunset arrived with still no resolution at hand and as the silhouette of Mt Saunders faded Barney became depressed. He remained at this post till the turn of the tide then laboured homewards through the uselessness of the cloudy night. Then he crept to bed.

CHAPTER 15

Moonlight flooded Charlotte Street, spilling through windows and doorways, softening everything it touched. It flicked between wheel spokes and glinted from horses' shoes as Saturday night merry-makers converged on the town. With pockets full of gold and riotous intent these men and ladies filled the music halls, saloons, theatres, public houses and the footways courting, joking and sparring. The gaiety of the street activity had drawn Meg and Nicholas to the balcony rail of the Roarin' Meg. Meg was speaking, telling of the coolness of the river breeze when, suddenly, a disturbance erupted in lower Charlotte Street. Others also heard and moved to the railing, and on the street below there were visible signs that they had also heard. Horses pricked their ears and a dog barked. Meg took Nicholas' hand as patrons crowded the railing. Others, further down the street by the Sovereign Hotel, were closer and crowded the street from both sides.

'Where is it?' shouted a short stocky man unable to find space at the railing.

'Down the street somewhere!'

'Where?'

'Down the street! See!' called a banker as he made room for the squat man.

The music and laughter were now gone. The entertainment rooms, all along the street, were being emptied. People spilled forth cramming the roadside, with ladies caring not that their long dresses dragged in the dirt. Coaches halted and passengers alighted, with coachmen forfeiting fares in the confusion.

Nicholas released Meg's hold to lean further over the railing.

'What is it?' she asked urgently.

'Seems like somebody's being dragged. There's a runaway horse coming along the straight.'

'Where?'

'Just below the Sovereign.'

People below shouted to those up top for confirmation while further down the street, in the pale of the moonlight, men moved to block the horse. Another reached for his rifle. Some ladies screamed, others put their hands to their faces in horror. The dog's barking became swamped by the uproar.

The bolting horse rushed through a cordon of men at the intersection of Green Street and as it careered by the Sovereign Hotel the bright lights revealed more.

'They're mounted!' shouted a little twerp standing on the balcony railing, grasping a post for support. 'Three of them! See them! See their black hats!'

A duty policeman who had tried to intercept them earlier had now reached the police compound. The onlookers on the successive balconies cried out to those further along to stop the ugly stampede. A rifle shot from near the Sovereign Hotel cracked overhead as the front rider passed the Gold Bank.

'Wedge them!' roared a burly bushman to his mates as they made ready to intercept and manhandle the galloping horses. Some horsemen had mounted in the wake of the threesome and were pushing through from the back of the crowd.

Those on the balcony gasped as the hideous reality reached the Roarin' Meg. The horsemen, hunched over their horses' withers and with their heads low, spurred wildly. The horses, crazed from fright, bolted blindly, ripping up the damp roadway and flinging clods into the crowd. Those watching were sickened by the gruesome spectacle of a Chinaman being dragged by the ankles behind the lead horse. The

Chinese man, midst screams and cries, bounced and rolled, being flogged against the ground at full gallop.

'Murderers!' shrieked the proprietor of the Bull's Head Inn.

Somebody on the balcony tripped over a cane table, smashing glasses to the floor. The twerp on the railing shouted a commentary to those behind. Angelique, one of Meg's barmaids, became distraught. Nicholas, spiked by his memories of persecution, gripped the metal railing to contain himself. A corn merchant who had arrived from Brisbane just that day was aghast.

The inspector heard the fracas from the verandah of his hillside mansion and frantically saddled his stallion. Chinatown by Adelaide Street became calamitous as masses of Chinese with sticks and shovels marshalled.

The murderers could not be halted. With bloodied spurs they drove forward clipping and trampling all who dared. They tore past the Goldfields Shanty with the thunder of feet echoing from the tin walls. A teamster, who challenged them with his whip, lashed a burn mark around the lead man's neck but was then himself shot in the leg by another of the cohort. A young couple at the corner of the Palmer Road hid in the grass. A lady in the cooking annex of her cottage near Chinaman Creek heard the screams. Further out horse bells rattled when spelling horses leapt in fright. Angus Goodlad, the father of Madeline, the girl servant for the Britfields, was returning to Cooktown with his pack team of mules and was the last to witness the madness.

By the time of Goodlad's sighting the breadth and depth of lower Walker Street was strung with hundreds of riotous Chinese. They turned into Charlotte Street and began to march downtown, waving their sticks, forks, shovels and lighted flares while shouting for retribution.

A police contingent led by Sergeant Frazer rounded the corner from the police compound and spurred past the Sovereign Hotel. Sergeant Frazer, dressed in trousers and boots and with a cartridge belt strung across his bare chest, roared for the way to be cleared. A new pathway opened through the crowd as twelve troopers galloped towards the barricade of Orientals. When it seemed they could get no closer the half-dressed troopers spread across the street, pulled their mounts to a halt on their haunches and drew arms. Frazer's intention was announced by a blast from his carbine. The Chinese, dressed in loin cloths, baulked three carriage lengths from the troopers.

Frontier men with weapons drawn shouted instructions and made hasty plans. The twerp on the balcony rail repeatedly howled, 'Rotten Chows!'

A pall of terror clouded Charlotte Street as more shots scattered overhead. The inspector's stallion was head high and hard on the bit when he swung into the street. He frisked through the crowd and drew to a halt at Frazer's side.

'Hold up!' he commanded his troopers as his stallion plunged further forward. 'Hold your fire!'

The Orientals roared vengeance while moving forward by pace then pause. An alien clad in rags and wielding a heavy staff struck for the inspector but the stallion, rearing and striking, drove him off. The inspector, pulsing visibly at the throat in the night light, held his revolver hand high as he bellowed at the rioters, demanding that they disperse.

'Cut the yellow scourges to pieces!' roared Frazer. 'Sir, give the order to shoot!' Some civilians also called, urging the inspector to be decisive and shoot. Five more troopers joined the police cordon and several civilian horsemen stood by. Nicholas grabbed Meg's revolver from beneath her pillow.

There would be no retreat. The Orientals' march was to be black and final. The challenge to Peter Britfield's authority was also final. He turned and waved, bringing his troopers forward. Frazer fired a shot into the mass. A man reeled with blood spilling from his shoulder. More shots sounded off. The advancing horses and cruel weapons, the tags of European dominance, struck fear into the Chinese. They halted only paces from the troopers and began thumping their sticks on the ground.

They beat faster and faster and continued shouting until a lithe, partly clad Cantonese who carried a lighted flare broke from the ranks and raced towards the Roarin' Meg. The inspector stayed Frazer with a shout then spurred in pursuit. The flame of the torch, fanned by the movement, became even brighter, flaring skyward. Some on the footpath braced themselves, others ran clear and a few, bewildered by the lunacy, just stood. The inspector spurred further forward and was nearly within grasp when the Cantonese suddenly propped and tossed the torch into the foyer of the Roarin' Meg. He then turned to flee but the inspector wrenched his flying pigtail and hauled him aloft. The heathen, stiff with fright, struggled little when carried by the hair back to the fore of the confrontation.

Peter dropped his reins across his horse's withers, lifted the slight coolie higher and, without hesitation, put his revolver to the doomed man's head. Frazer knew he would shoot. So did others, for the inspector's word was law. The pawn, feeling the muzzle against his temple, trembled violently in expectation of death.

'Shoot the bastard or I will!' raged Frazer.

Peter was about to pull the trigger but was suddenly interrupted.

'No! Wait!' came a shrill cry from a woman somewhere nearby in the crowd. This appeal from a feminine voice drew attention and Peter was distracted when a woman, plain and uncultured, a washerwoman, pushed her way through. Out of breath and near to tears she bustled across the open space to the inspector. Then, before acknowledging the inspector, she put her arms around the young Chinaman's bare torso and held him tightly. Almost everyone was drawn by her courage and the shouting was checked on both sides, giving enough calm for her to be heard.

'Please, Inspector,' she begged, still clutching the young man and now addressing Peter's dark eyes. 'Please let him go.' The woman's sensitivity, the expressive compassion of her plea, won her an audience.

'Why should I?' demanded Peter loudly, addressing everybody with authority.

'Because, Sir, he's a person. He's no different to you or your sergeant. Please spare him. Please, Sir. I myself have lost two sons. I know the pain.' She spoke bravely, pouring forth a genuine love of mankind and though few of the Chinese understood her words her tone conveyed a spirit of accord. This lady of at least three score years and greying then spoke more slowly. 'Please put him down.' Her calm request like the mellow of the moonlight touched almost every soul present. The sticks, forks and carbines took easier, oblique angles as the truth of her message spread.

During this brief time she and Peter made silent exchanges. Her tired face, worn from a life of work as a mother, implored him to be merciful, to understand the right of sparing a life. Peter glanced at the Chinese headman who, now quiet, acquiesced by looking at the ground. He then slowly lowered the Cantonese to the roadway and set him free.

'Thank you. May the Lord take you into his divine care,' whispered the washer woman before quietly turning away. By the flickering torchlight Peter dwelt silently till the anonymous lady became lost in the crowd.

This humble lady had averted a calamity. She, with a mother's instinct, proved to be more powerful than these men of war for, within moments of her disappearance, the Chinese leader turned his men back and Peter turned his aside.

The following morning the Inspector compiled a report for immediate dispatch to Brisbane Town:

Cooktown Police Station,
27th February 1877

The Colonial Secretary

Dear Sir,

For some time racial unrest has been a concern within the Cooktown Division and a particularly nasty incident which occurred yesterday evening has prompted me to again report direct to your office.

At 8.40 pm civil disorder erupted in the main street of Cooktown. Three horsemen riding at full pace dragged a Chinese man along Charlotte Street by the ankles and out into the hinterland. Being a Saturday night the townspeople remained relatively calm. However, the local Chinese community took umbrage to the strife. Soon after the incident several hundred of them, being very irate and assertive, confronted me, my officers and the townsfolk on the street. They became riotous, threatening violence and destruction of the town. They continued with their intimidation and threats for one half hour then upon the issue of an ultimatum they dispersed.

This morning I have been informed that the battered body of a Chinese male known as Wo San was located at Mosquito Creek. Chinese sources indicate that the incident occurred over a dispute concerning non payment of a gold tribute. At this time I have no knowledge of who the assailants are. If you require a more detailed report then a full report of the incident is available from the Office of the Commissioner of Police.

My main concern, however, is not specifically the incident itself but with the circumstances which precipitated the riot and it is in this context that I write as follows:

Ever since the Chinese first arrived there has been civil disorder on the Palmer goldfield. On the field they outnumber the whites ten to one. They live like dogs, preferring to remain emaciated rather than part with gold. Further, while Sovereign Patriots are out searching for new prospects these imports pilfer the claims left behind, leaving our men nothing to fall back upon in times of dearth.

In and about Cooktown Chinese merchants are accruing enormous estates of which the proceeds will eventually be returned to China. They operate with villainous greed and extortive measures. There is no limit to how far a local Chinese Tong leader will go to bribe and extort. It is invasion by stealth. They are deleterious to the Colony and unless their numbers are checked the Free Settlers will soon be bearing yellow yokes of servitude.

Smuggling is rife. No accurate estimates are available but the practice of smuggling gold to China is common knowledge and oft done with blatant disregard of the Crown. I have received several reports of Chinese junks in the Annan River and others anchored off-shore. Indeed, there are even rumours emanating from Hong Kong that a Chinese invasion of our continent may soon be a reality. I add further that a credible, first hand report from Macaw informs that the Portuguese, for their own covetous reasons, are party to this subversion.

Ever since the first reported case of leprosy amongst the Chinese the townspeople have lived in fear. They are also potential carriers of cholera and yellow fever, the sinister consequences of which I need not elaborate.

Their numbers (15,000 to 20,000) and degree of civil disorder cause us inordinate administrative problems and the colony a huge cost. Currently, at Maytown, groups of them are brought in daily in chains for not paying their Miner's Permit. They are incorrigible in this vein yet bemoan every moment of their internment. Our horses are worn and bare from policing them and only recently one hundred and ten remounts have been ordered from Lyndhurst cattle station.

The port facilities are oft jammed with eastern ships offloading hordes of Chinese whilst legitimate European traders carrying needed supplies have to stand off. As the colonial press is currently stating: These Pagans are foreign to our beliefs and we would be best served if they were returned to their treadmills!

Whilst acknowledging that there are Anglo/Chinese treaties to be considered I assert that the Chinese have no sovereign rights in Australia and therefore should be banned from immigrating to our country.

The Crown has an Imperial duty to this colony. The subjects of the Empire should be considered first and foremost.

I wish to put to the Governor and the Home Government as I have in previous correspondence that if political remedies to these problems are not instituted soon then Cooktown might be torched and the Palmer might run red with blood.

I therefore recommend the following:

> *(1) The immediate cessation of all further non-white immigration to the southern colonies.*
>
> *(2) That there be a tightening of the Goldfields Act and the Masters and Servants Act to ensure white supremacy.*

I request, with respect, that you convey my recommendations to His Excellency the Governor in Council and request that he make representation to the Home Office in respect of these urgent matters.

Yours faithfully

Peter M Britfield
(Inspector of Police)

CHAPTER 16

Ever since the day of the fete Barney's mood had remained glum. His obsession with Abbey O'Reilly had him nearly visit her on several occasions and often he walked the streets hoping to sight her. He saw her on two of these outings but neither was rewarded. On the first, at Alt's drapery, she was accompanied by Juliette and Madeline and on the second the trio passed along Hope Street in an open carriage driven by Constable Bean. On each occasion Barney had wanted to approach her, to call out or, at the least, wave to them as a group but a fickle restraint over which he had no control held him back.

Barney had, this morning, whitewashed the tin fence surrounding the hotel courtyard and already the lime coating was cracking in the stifling heat. The task had strained his mood, making him more uneasy. Soon after lunch he felt an urgent need to escape from the confines of the white fence. He laced his boots, then, dressed in nothing more than boots and shorts, he left via the carriage gateway.

He strode through the sweltering heat to Grassy Hill then ascended, clambering over rocks and pushing through shrubbery. He sought solace at the top but there was no reprieve; the salt air from seaward made his skin clammy and the sun, as intense as a flaming tallow candle against his skin, turned his cheeks and shoulders bright pink.

Barney moved to a vantage point on a nearby ridge. From there he surveyed the vista of the town. The hot roofs glinted like sparks spraying from a blast furnace, showering the townscape with a fiery intensity, and Abbey's estate, hedged by stark granite outcrops, shimmered as a blazing fortress.

Barney held his post determined not to leave till his depressed mood eased, but to no avail. The melancholy deepened as the blistering heat intensified. He became giddy then nauseous and held a hand to his head. He fought the dizziness but the condition would not pass. He suddenly felt weak. An eerie fainting spell forced him to the shade of a nearby tree. He leaned against the tree to stay standing but sunstroke had taken hold. He fell to the ground and began to hallucinate. Spasms twitched and jerked his body. These hallucinations opened a rift between reality and macabre imagery. Sparks of fire began lighting his mind, creating vivid scenes.

There below him, with clarity and detail, Cooktown was suddenly torched on every side by unknown torch bearers. The fire spread with gruesome determination and soon the whole town was ablaze, with pandemonium on the streets.

The bells of the churches tolled, with the friendly Catholic priest, his hands raw from rope burn, frantically tugging the tail of his bell rope.

Cholera had struck, a severe outbreak in Chinatown. All and everybody had to be sacrificed.

Awesome, fiery cones turreted high in the sky and the people's screams matched its roar.

The town was bewitched.

Chinatown burned like tinder, trapping a writhing morass of life.

The streets were chaotic with people both dead and alive choking the pathways.

Horses crazed the streets, dragging capsized carts and carriages through the mobs.

These images of damnation continued, scattered and sporadic, while Barney drifted between semi-conscious and unconscious states of mind; on and on, relentlessly persecuting him and for what reason?

What bizarre concoction of his mind could wish for the destruction of those about him?

Nobody knew anything in this kaleidoscope of imagined horror where people ran, scrambled and were trodden underfoot and where distorted faces held mindless expressions.

A footman carrying his master's baby caught fire and was incinerated.

Men and women carrying lighted bodies battled to wells then fought for rights to the water.

Eli stood between corpses and warring parties at the town well, shouting for reason to prevail.

When the Cavalier Hotel ascended in a spiral of fire and smoke Barney saw, most vividly, the white-washed fence turn black then buckle, destroying the confine.

He witnessed Hicksbury's death: his sulky overturned, then, ablaze on Charlotte Street, conscious and gasping, blinded and hairless and burnt almost beyond recognition, he struggled then died.

The gunpowder magazine near the wharf exploded, showering the harbour with fiery rain. Ships pushing free from the blazing wharf were set alight. Men in the rigging shrieked as they fell from flaming sails. Ships were ignited in succession by the swirling flames and falling masts. The sand dunes on the north head of the river glowed an iridescent red.

Billows of smoke, piling high in the sky, cast a black shroud of death over the devastation.

The run-away fire swept the countryside with jagged flames, racing upwards on the hillsides, licking life from all it encountered. All that man had made was being destroyed and finally Abbey's house, the last bastion, flared and dissipated into a monstrous fireball.

The carnage in all its horror plagued Barney's oppressed state till the imagined stench caused him to vomit. He began to choke, coughing and spluttering, rallying to full consciousness.

The fireball, the sun, the catalyst for his aberrations, had just set, leaving a fleshy radiance on the horizon. Barney, badly sunburnt and parched, sat decrepit, disorientated and totally distraught. The images of his hallucinations haunted his every attempt at thought. His head throbbed as he tried to focus his foggy eyes on the giddy town below. Barney had no desire to return to the peeping lights which by the minute were appearing brighter in the pit of the town. He abhorred any such thought so, when enough of the dizziness had passed, he rose to his feet and staggered down the seaward side of the hill.

In his clouded state of despair he stumbled across the windswept, heath-like slopes in the semi dark. The descent became steeper and he tripped more often on rocks hidden in the brush underfoot. He reached the cliff top above the crashing sea where the temptation for self-destruction beckoned him to jump. The lure of the bare rocks after each wave receded drew him closer till only a foothold on a tiny ledge held him aloft. He could see no way out, absolutely no possibility that the agony would ever pass.

His thoughts were surreal:
It would all be very simple to end.
The cord of life could simply be severed.
So what if my noble attempt at earthly ways failed.
Few would be stung to the quick.
No death certificate would evidence my disappearance.
No grand event for which a memorable epitaph would be scribed.
Memories of my humble doings would soon be forgotten.
It would be as if it were an anonymous passing ...
These depressing thoughts held his sanity in a precarious state for what seemed an eternity. Eventually, exhaustion took hold, weakened his resolve and a stalemate was reached. He then turned his back on the bane of death and staggered homeward where he would rest and, hopefully, rise tomorrow to once again be master of his own destiny.

CHAPTER 17

Coach horses, wet and glistening by the light of the street lamps, plied Charlotte Street in the drizzling rain. Many were drawn to a halt at the Roarin' Meg Hotel where doormen, wearing galoshes and oil-skin coats and carrying umbrellas, assisted patrons to alight. The rain seemed to hamper them none and now at ten o'clock more were still arriving in cheery spirit. Upstairs, in the gambling saloon, the atmosphere was thick with cigar smoke; spirals drifted upwards passed the hot chandelier lights then out through the lofty windows. In this saloon a card game of Black Jack absorbed everyone's attention.

At centre place sat a new arrival to Cooktown, a dapper young man with an obvious education; an aristocrat and mathematician it was whispered. The ladies in particular admired his engaging face with its resolve and taunting blue eyes. They were also enthralled with his pearl-buttoned vest and full-length, swallow-tail coat. From comments made, it was apparent that the ladies present would grant him favour in return for the solitaire diamond ring on his finger.

To the silent menfolk the Pitt Street gambler was also a hero. Who else in the history of the Roarin' Meg had ever stung the dealer for two hundred pounds? Who had ever come close to breaking the house? They were happy that a payback for what they themselves had lost was about to be made. With smug daring the gambler studiously played his own game; placing bets, keeping count of the cards dealt and, all the while, adding more to his pile.

Meg stood beside Nicholas, gauging the rush with an icy cool. Her white satin dress, lavishly laced about the cuffs and bosom line, together with the dainty crimson tie holding her piled hair, disguised nothing of her dire expression. Gunther, the saloon manager, stood opposite, straining at the seam of his vest pocket with one hand and stroking his moustache with the other. He was as concerned about the newcomer's challenge to his captaincy of the saloon as he was about the loss of the money. The dealer agonised further with each successive loss. He eventually looked Meg's way seeking a directive and was relieved when Meg nodded to Gunther to switch dealers.

Pierre, known as the cheating dealer, then took to the stage dressed in smart black and white. With silken movement he confidently set to business. Several hands were played showing no particular bias but then, gradually, the odds began to weigh against the gambler. Four consecutive games were lost, one won and now another three lost him each bet. The gambler became suspicious and began to lose concentration. Pierre sought to raise the limit but the gambler did not follow the lead. All was now apparent to him and during his last game he intimidated Pierre by ignoring his cards and closely scrutinising Pierre's movements. Then, with a handsome bounty still at hand, he quit as quietly as he had entered.

Gunther claimed full credit for saving the house from ruin and, for the first time, sought sex from Meg as recompense. He openly laid claim. Throughout the evening he harassed her. He repeatedly came in close, talking suggestively and touching her. He bragged of his past, weaving a web of lies and innuendo: a man of military service during the Franco-Prussian war of 1870–71; a man of cultural appreciation visiting the Louvre; his involvement in his family's holdings in the docks of the River Elbe. He told of gambling sprees and bloodletting duels. All sorts of nonsense; reminiscing about unbelievable escapades. Meg resented his presence and, to avoid a scene, she retreated to the balcony where others were seated. But Gunther soon followed, became unbridled and openly propositioned her. He showered her with remarks about his sexual prowess and made erotic insinuations about how he could satisfy her. He declared himself as the only man fit to be her lover.

Meg hit back contemptuously. She inferred that he had been born into poverty and had led the life of a pimp and petty criminal.

The criticism stung Gunther; he became offensive and pressed for a fight. He accused Meg of encouraging his advances and as a final insult referred to her association with Nicholas and his colour. He then said that she was nothing more than 'a lady of the night!'

Meg turned on his foul tongue with a stinging rebuke. She slapped him sharply across the face and shouted, 'You're finished!'

The altercation upset Meg terribly. She turned away with tears clouding her eyes, found Nicholas in the snooker room, took his hand and led him to her room. Here she became awash. She wept openly and held Nicholas tightly. Gradually, the warmth of his body, his feel, the nearness of his spirit, the ... All those feelings which embody caring found their way into her awareness. They waxed together, joining lips, fondling and fornicating, just *being* as the rain intensified.

Nicholas had, in his past, been a worldly suitor: there had been the promiscuous, dark eyed girls of the Caribbean; a lady in Tierra del Fuego, the wife of a high official, whom he met as a result of shipwreck; the blissful Tahitians; a memorable summer in Mauritius comfortably sharing the wife of a plantation owner; all these and more, together with the fickle ladies of Europe from which he excluded the Irish lassies whom he regarded as the most sensual of all women.

However, of all these women there were only two or perhaps one that he truly loved. All the others had been little more than rambling romantic interludes. Louise, the daughter of white planters in Jamaica, was his first true love. Nicholas had then been in his seventeenth year, when emancipation from slavery was only recent and colonial dominance still prevailed. Their roadside meeting and subsequent courtship blossomed and progressed until they met regularly in secret in a water-wheel hut. Here Louise, an innocent and giving child of sixteen, conceived, and upon her parents' realisation of her condition she was forbidden to ever visit her secret lover again. She later bore a healthy bronze baby, a boy she adamantly named Nicholas. Soon after the babe's birth, after the implications were apparent, Nicholas fled without ever having held his child. His young mind agonised, first in sugarcane fields elsewhere on the island then at sea. This hurt was so profound that, to this day, he had never returned to the Jamaican valley of his boyhood. And now there was Meg whom he envisaged as Louise and who he adopted as a surrogate for his first love. The interchange had become so profound that he now wished to marry Meg.

For Meg, in her late thirties, Nicholas' attention was timely. She had made her run, starting early in life, dashing ahead through her twenties, turning her hand to business and becoming wealthy. By the age of thirty Meg had consolidated her position with the ownership of a popular music hall in central Melbourne. Her style invited the moneyed barons to patronise her theatre where feminine performers whetted the men's appetites whilst on stage, then extended their business from the corridors out back.

Meg tired of the dancing, the feathers, the fans and the favours. She became weary of city life and sought adventure elsewhere. This spirit led her to book passage on a steamer and sail to Cooktown where real gold was for the taking. As in Melbourne her Cooktown venture was hugely successful, so much so that the challenge had waned, leaving Meg seeking a new direction.

Odd as it may seem to some Meg now wished to settle, to do those things that others do early in life, to marry and, nature permitting, bear children. Though Nicholas might seem an unlikely choice to many, Meg found him endearing. He was an uncomplicated man who had experienced life, understood its ways and could accommodate Meg. Although neither Nicholas nor Meg had yet declared their wish for marriage, the tie each felt there in Meg's bedroom bound them so tightly that escape was unlikely.

The rain continued beating on the bedroom windows, causing a clatter that muffled the whispered exchanges passing between them.

The locked door and barred windows prevented any intrusion. Privacy was theirs to be enjoyed on the soft covers.

CHAPTER 18

'Miss Swanson, there's a man downstairs who wants to see you,' said Laura, bridging the doorway between the back verandah and the sewing room of the hotel. Prue interrupted the pedalling of the sewing machine.

'He's a fat man,' said Laura. 'His name is Mr Hicksbury and, and ...'—she was puffing from climbing the stairs—'he wants to talk to you.'

'What does he want?' Prue sighed as though an unwanted message was at hand.

'I dunno, Ma'am,' replied Laura apologetically for not having asked.

'Very well, Laura, tell him I'll be down soon. And Laura ...'

'Yes, Ma'am?'

'It's not "I dunno". It's "I don't know". You understand?'

'Yes, Ma'am. Sorry, Ma'am. I'll remember better next time, Ma'am,' apologised Laura, bowing slightly before leaving.

Before following, Prue finished the stitch and quickly tidied her hair. She fingered the top button of her blouse into place as she descended the carpeted staircase. Hicksbury's reputation made her tense and uneasy as she approached him across the dining room.

'Good morning, Miss Swanson,' he greeted, appearing amicable behind a pretentious smile that did little to conceal his state of alcoholic remorse.

Prue guardedly offered him a chair.

97

'Well, thank you, thank you.' He shuffled across, pulling the flaps of his vest together to hide his frayed braces. Prue took the chair opposite.

For Laura it was one of those easy, nothing-much-to-do mornings in the kitchen. A good day for biscuit making, and she stirred a mix whilst listening to their conversation.

'Miss Swanson,' she heard Hicksbury say, 'let me say at the outset that most of my work is interpersonal, but in addition much work is offered by the Crown. All manner of lawful matters for which they engage my services: assistance with Crown prosecutions, administrative requirements and, of course, investigative services which are something of a speciality of mine. My success with the latter has been exceptional with ...' His introduction continued, tedious and rambling, revealing nothing of substance. So much so that before he had broached the purpose of his visit Prue set to clip the meeting.

'Mr Hicksbury,' she interrupted. 'I'm quite busy so ...' She broke off, allowing Hicksbury to infer the rest for himself.

'Yes, I understand. Sorry. I was about to explain ...' and he began to fold the cuff of one sleeve.

Curiosity lured Laura. She came to the kitchen doorway and stood shielded by the privacy screen, unaware that her feet were visible beneath its lower edge.

'For some months now I've been searching for the whereabouts of a fugitive believed to be in or around Cooktown. He's a farrier by trade, approximately forty-five years of age, nearly six feet tall and with a ruddy complexion ...' Prue listened in silence. 'Miss Swanson, the terrible trouble with this kind of case is picking up a lead. Why, on some cases I've made folly after folly; spent days, weeks chasing the wrong scent. What seems like a certainty often ends as a file piled high with useless information. The amount of detail I've accumulated on some cases would boggle the layman. Then there is the pitfall of having accumulated an excess of material and being confronted with a confusing mass of comment from which no real conclusion can be drawn. Many times I've outlaid enormous amounts of money in a search; hired all sorts from politicians to pimps, passing rolls of cash and gaining nothing in return. It's a thankless occupation. After all, apart from the client, who else regards you as a friend?

'All these experiences have equipped me well for such tasks. It's a specialised business, requiring acute perception, not letting go of a single clue. The tiniest snippet is oft the piece that threads together the whole. It's remarkable the insight one gains into human action and interaction. There's no limit to the quirks of human nature. I've had cases where the motive is far removed from what appears to be the situation.

'Almost invariably it's only a matter of time. Time is a great revealer. Give the suspect time, I say, and he will come from hiding, visit old haunts, reacquaint with old friends, return to old habits and invariably expose himself. The human mind, though fickle and evasive, is also predictable to a large degree. In a given situation it's possible to predict from among a few courses of action what the fugitive will do. Some are so clumsy as to permit themselves to be apprehended almost immediately. Others, the more devious, relocate, change their name and occupation and try to create a new lifestyle. They go to extraordinary measures to cover all trace.

'A locality like Cooktown is an attractive destination for criminals. They think that distance and frontier disruption will dissuade the law from pursuit. However, that's not the case. The law has a duty to fulfil irrespective of any difficulty it may encounter. In fact it's oft been the case that fugitives in these situations become complacent with a resultant arrest.'

Hicksbury's as yet undisclosed purpose together with his arrogant disrespect of Prue's time quickly exhausted her hospitality.

'Mr Hicksbury,' Prue interjected, 'I'm quite familiar with most of what you have said. There's a dozen ways of catching a criminal I am sure. And it's probably true to say that some of the people who pass through my hotel have criminal records. But, as to their status I never enquire. It's, as you say, a matter for the law enforcers to investigate. Really I prefer not to know. From whence they come I care not. It's caring for people at the present and in some instances helping them into the future that interests me; not some past doing from which they are trying to escape.'

'Miss Swanson, I appreciate the charity of your viewpoint. It's very magnanimous. However, we all have a function to perform and mine is devoted to wrestling with criminals, criminals who will probably re-offend. Most of them do, it's been proven.'

Prue's distaste of Hicksbury, his intrusion and his still unspecified interrogation—the total vileness of the shabby man—pressed her patience.

'Mr Hicksbury, since you haven't been courteous enough to state your purpose I ask you in what capacity do you seek my assistance?'

'Therein lies the reason for my call, Miss Swanson. It's with difficulty that I persuaded myself to impose and now I am hesitant to broach the delicate matter that necessitates my call. Each of us is duty bound to assist with the application of the law. Every person has a duty to contribute for the benefit of the whole. Even in the smallest way, by offering information we can all help. We must, at all times, remain loyal to the Crown. For the sake of all that is British we all must, where possible, assist with the maintenance of law and order. In this regard—'

'Mr Hicksbury! Who is it? Who is it you suspect I'm withholding information about? State your purpose for I am fast losing patience!'

Prue abhorred his attempt at innuendo and his attempt to conjure guilt on her part. Laura remained statue-still with her ears cocked, straining to hear everything, wholly absorbed in the intrigue created by Hicksbury.

'Very well, Miss Swanson, since you are reluctant to co-operate I will state my request. It concerns murder! Murder of the first degree! Some two years ago a police farrier, for no apparent reason, apart from his own ill temper, thrust an officer of Her Majesty's Service into a fired forge, burning him to a ghastly death. It's alleged he then fled Sydney, bound for Cooktown aboard a sail ship. The sequel to his departure from Sydney began almost five months ago when his son arrived here in Cooktown, presumably in search of his father. It may come as a surprise to you but since his arrival you have been harbouring this lad. Miss Swanson, Barney Simpson is the person of whom I enquire in relation to the whereabouts of his father, Tom Simpson.'

'Harbouring! You accuse me of harbouring!' blurted Prue.

Laura, turning tight lipped and pale as chalk, shuddered from the impact.

'Mr Hicksbury, I suggest you keep your blind assertions to yourself. There is nothing to implicate myself. I have no knowledge of your allegation. As to your presumed reason for Barney's presence I suggest that it's nothing more than wild speculation, probably unfounded hearsay. What! Two years later you say! It's absurd to presume that after an absence of two years Barney has suddenly decided to visit his father at Cooktown!'

'Why else!' demanded Hicksbury.

'For the sheer adventure of it! That is why! Barney himself,' and Prue began to fabricate a defence for Barney, 'has intimated as much. His stay is indefinite. He could move on any day. There's never been any suggestion that his inclination is anything but a desire to experience the frontier. It's commonplace that the likes of Barney seek adventure and fortune.'

Hicksbury cut back, pressing his point, and as he argued his face assumed a grave colour and his jowls became a deep purple. 'Perpetrators of crime must be dismembered from society!' he shouted while clutching his chest and wincing in pain. He then rose to his feet to assert his authority further. His acid tongue became unmanageable.

'Law and order is a tenet of our organised society and there can be no tolerance of any challenge to this premise. The Law has been master-minded by the masterly for the benefit of all. Clearly, capital punishment is the only remedy for premeditated atrocities such as murder. Murder is inexcusable!'

Prue now also stood, stockaded for confrontation across the table. The colour of her eyes had hardened and an acute alertness chiselled her features. She was ready to pounce with her Irish blood pulsing Catholic vengeance.

'Mr Hicksbury! Followers of your creed are hypocrites!' she asserted. 'The carriage of justice is oft as not maliciously manipulated by those with the power of the law at their disposal. Justice, Mr Hicksbury, is what I refer to, justice as it is meant to be interpreted. Not the debased misconstructions presented by the likes of you for self-interest.

'Law and justice, the high ideals for organising society, have never been properly practised. Never has English law been consistently or fairly applied. What price at English law for stealing a loaf of bread! Tell me! Torn from one's family, transported to Australia as a convict, never to return. Is this justice? Why, in the first instance, was the loaf stolen? Is the man indolent, a malingerer, by nature a petty thief? No, Mr Hicksbury, he is not. He is a man who, by the very acts of law you esteem, has been denied an opportunity of earning sustenance.

'You can brag about the English notion of equality before the law. But I tell you, Mr Hicksbury, that it is all a sham. Yes, one gigantic sham to protect those with power. Political power and that of capital are bed partners, always found together. English tyranny, for the common man, is nothing less than serfdom!'

'But Miss Swanson—'

'No, Mr Hicksbury, you listen to me. A system specifically designed by the peerage for the peerage. Not by the people for the people. It's always been that way. The judiciary, Mr Hicksbury, is the instrument by which it manipulates its subjects.'

'But—'

'No buts. You listen to me. I'll tell you very clearly. I know nothing of this Tom Simpson of whom you speak. I have no knowledge at all. But, and I warn you, if you implicate Barney Simpson then you'll have me to deal with. I have means and I have ways, you Protestant curse!'

Laura immediately thought of Eli; she was familiar with Eli's just ways, his principles, his capacity and his determination. She had been present on many occasions when Eli, as was his way, had spoken freely and informatively about all manner of lawful considerations. She was certain it was he to whom Prue was referring.

In the general flurry of cross assertions that followed much was said that was regrettable. Each denigrated the other, flinging, almost in abusive terms, accusations pertaining to professional and personal conduct.

Much of Prue's thrust decried the English hierarchy from Queen Victoria downwards. The persecution of the powerless poor remained her constant concern. She treated Hicksbury as an effigy of this shameful regime, portraying him as an ogre with an insatiable appetite for plunder; plundering people's labour and holdings and the riches of nature for the sole aims of exercising power and flaunting conspicuous indulgence.

Hicksbury, palpitating at the heart, became reckless with his words. He declared Prue as unworthy of being British. That she was nothing more than a commoner with common views. That, in spite of her views, the Empire, in its benevolence, had provided every opportunity of which she had availed herself. As to her defence of Barney Simpson he was totally appalled. How did she, a mere hotel proprietor, think she could interrupt the course of justice? He cautioned her to mind her place otherwise she may be considered an accessory.

There could be no meaningful discussion between them. They were bound to be antagonists. The common ground of opinion was too narrow to accommodate both safely. The situation was impossible from the outset.

Hicksbury's greed was behind his every ploy, and he cared not who or what he destroyed. He targeted every source from which manna might be extracted. The affliction of his mind—his greed and sinister addiction to gambling—commanded and consumed him wholly, channelling his every effort towards hatching grand schemes of deceit. He had gained not one merit mark during his lifetime. All he had to show for his journey was an agonising pile of human misery.

Prue was otherwise. She was angelic, giving of herself and sharing her lot; protecting, as far as possible, everybody within the fold of mankind; sheltering them from marauding predators like Hicksbury and providing warmth and comfort from the cold chills of life. With zeal uncommonly found she took in the lost lambs of society: the runaway Barney, the fugitive Nicholas, the orphaned Laura, the truant Hornet, the injured miner and the destitute traveller. She excelled during every waking hour, giving, at every turn of the clock, help to the needy who chanced her way. With patient and attentive concern she attended to their needs through the avenue of the Cavalier Hotel. Her selflessness was effusive; everyday, somebody somewhere gave thanks to her.

It was no wonder that, there in the dining room of the Cavalier, confrontation with Hicksbury was inevitable. It was as impossible as the Devil from Hell trying to bargain with the Mistress of Heaven. Hicksbury was both foolhardy and a fool. What offer of bad, what amount of ill will could ever induce a disciple of good?

Hicksbury's contemptuous assault, his vicious outpouring, began to slow. The sharp pains bracing his chest told of his sick and labouring heart. His face turned ashen. His clenched fists unfolded to grasp the table edge for support. His vision blurred, spinning Prue and the surrounds into a dizzy vertigo. Hicksbury was approaching the end, the end of this initiative, if not of life itself. All thoughts of anything Simpson had gone. He left the table, staggered across the dining room and disappeared down the hallway.

After Hicksbury had left Prue settled herself while Laura made tea. They then sat at the kitchen table and discussed the allegation at length. It was decided that the matter should, at least for the present, be kept secret—even from Barney.

The frank exchange led to the disclosure of another worry. Laura, flushing about the cheeks, confided that she was pregnant. She also gave details of how it happened and told of her love for Barney. Prue, her eyes again soft and colourful, accepted the overdue admission. She then began making suggestions that set Laura at ease. Their talk focused on the pregnancy and all that had to be done before the baby was born.

Later that evening, after closure of the hotel, Prue and Eli retired to Prue's bedroom.

While Prue undressed, Eli, a modest man when engaged in bedroom romance, occupied himself by looking through the window and gazing at the stars.

'Darling,' she called when nude, 'what about some music?'

Eli roused himself from his dream of the galaxy and when he turned the lamp light presented him a revealing view of her. At the sight of her soft body, he modestly turned away again, asking as he did, 'Beethoven or Shubert?'

'Beethoven's "Moonlight Sonata" please, darling.'

Eli crossed the room, sat at the piano and began to play whilst Prue slipped into a negligee. She then joined him and said, 'You are a Maestro.'

'Do you really believe that?'

'Sure do, darling. Nobody else in the colony can play as well as you.'

The opening of the melody, soft and wistful, drew her close to Eli's side. She knew the piece well and turned the pages of the manuscript precisely at the right moment. The notes filled the room and spilt outside for Laura and others to hear. The rendition took her back to her childhood in Sydney, to the family home overlooking the harbour, to memories of her father sad and forlorn, playing this sonata, alone, consoling himself after the death of his wife and her mother. Tears came to her eyes as she recalled how the unresolved grief gradually reshaped a man of means to one barely able to care for himself by the time of his death. Eli sensed her upset and played with a passion, taking her through the first and second movements. He then played the third movement, heightening its tempo as he went, bringing it to a crescendo and belting out the final tumultuous bars. The lull that followed left them pensive till Prue put a hand on his shoulder, leant down and kissed him on the cheek.

She said, 'Darling, you're too clever for Cooktown but I'll never let you go. You're the world to me.'

Eli laid his head against her and replied, 'My love, I'm sure we will grow old together.'

Prue then suggested, 'Darling, you ought to stay with me tonight. I need your company and also wish to talk more about Barney, about how best to implement Laura's and my plan.'

Barney was near Vanity Place when, by chance, he saw Abbey O'Reilly. Madeline, Ces Bean the constable and baby Juliette accompanied her. They alighted from a carriage and came his way.

Abbey, with her hair in ringlets and tidy bows, a velvet ribbon tied high around her neck and long flowing dress appeared more dashing than any other woman on the street.

Barney quickly groomed himself. He spat on his hands, rubbed them together then brushed them through his hair exposing his cowlick. He did this twice. He then polished the toes of his boots by rubbing each foot against the back of his trouser leg. Luckily he had shaved and bathed the previous night and donned a clean shirt that morning.

The foursome paused by the turnstile at the laneway between the offices of the Golden Lode Mining Company and the Pacific Trading Co. It was from here, only one shop away, that Abbey sighted Barney.

'Good afternoon, Mr Simpson!' she hailed with a wave.

Barney replied with a silly grin.

Madeline and Ces, arm in arm and only a pram's length from Abbey, exchanged a questioning glance before Abbey turned to introduce them and baby Juliette.

'It's a nice carriage and four you drive,' said Barney addressing Ces, the meek young police officer in the blue uniform.

'Yes, all Percheron crosses.'

'Thought so. Can't mistake a line of greys like that.'

'He's got gentle hands as well as a gentle nature. That's why they perform so well for him,' added Madeline affectionately. 'There's no other officer allowed to touch them, only Mr O'Reilly, Ma'am's husband, who's the farrier. Although, he had to have a hand to shoe the team last time. He's laid up with a sore back. Poor fellow. Ma'am has me rubbing liniment into his back each day but it seems only a little better. Even had trouble tying his boots the other day. Didn't he, Ma'am?'

'My father's a farrier too,' Barney admitted spontaneously. 'There's no doubt it's hard work and bad backs are common. Part of the trade I reckon.'

Ces nodded agreement.

'I've seen my father shoe a wing of horses, fifteen mounts or more, in one day with only a lad as help.' He hesitated. 'But that was a while ago. He wouldn't be able to do it now.' Barney was momentarily wistful. 'I was buyin' horses from auctions at the City Pound in Sydney when I was twelve. Got them for a price little more than they'd fetch for boiling down as pig food. I then on-sold them for double the money. I reckon I could start the same trade here.'

Madeline bounced Juliette in her arms causing the baby's forelock to flutter. 'Here,' said Abbey, addressing Barney and leaning forward to fully expose Juliette's forehead with her palm, 'you both have the same cowlick. You could be kin. The Star of Ireland I call it. Everyone with it is blessed.' Madeline then passed Juliette to Ces who jovially tossed her high and brought her to rest on his shoulders.

'That reminds me of our jaunt last week,' Abbey recalled. 'Never again will I do that,' and she related the story of their recent excursion to the summit of Mt Cook.

'And Ces, poor Ces, he carried Juliette all the way on his shoulders, just like this.'

'Ma'am, tell him about Sir!' prompted Madeline.

'Well,' and Abbey put a hand to her chest, 'Peter was horrified and furious that we should attempt such a feat. You see, we thought of the idea soon after breakfast one morning and, knowing that Peter would be at court most of the day and could do without Ces, we took it into our heads to do something for ourselves. It was a wonderful outing. You ought to do it sometime; the rainforest at the top is magnificent and the view out across Quarantine Bay from the granite outcrop is magnificent.'

Juliette now wanted to get down.

'Ma'am, bubs is getting hot and would like a cordial.'

Abbey dug into her purse and took out a shilling. 'I'll be ready in about an hour,' she said to Madeline.

'They're suited,' commented Abbey after the trio had left. 'They're going to announce their betrothal soon. It's still a secret. It's to be announced when they've saved a little more. They're really such a sweet couple. I do believe that Ces is too soft to be in the force though. As for Madeline, she's the strength there. There have been times when I would have been desperate if I hadn't had Madeline. She knows most of what goes on but, quite rightly, maintains confidentiality.'

Barney made mention of having met Peter.

'Oh, I wasn't aware that you'd met,' replied Abbey with surprise.

'Yes. It was before last Christmas. A chance meeting down the street.'

'How did you find him?'

'Good. We didn't talk for long but I liked the way he carried himself.'

'Peter used to be an officer in the British Cavalry before we emigrated six years ago. It's vastly different here though. The force here has nowhere the amount of regimentation there was back home. Peter seems to have taken it on himself to rule the northern division. He feels constantly obliged and does most of the administrative thinking and planning for the district; particularly the gold escort with the huge amounts of gold they're now carrying. It's not good. He's become very authoritarian.

'He seems to have got himself into a bind about the Chinese and the Aborigines during the past months. It's a point of contention between us and he's so adamant that I daren't mention it when he's about. In his zeal he overlooks the fact that the Aborigines have been here the longest and are dependent on the rivers for their survival and that the Chinese are free settlers. It's reached the point that every time a patrol sees the Aborigines they disperse them with firepower. It seems they're steaming up for all-out war on both sides. It's fearful to contemplate. The problem I have is that, in my position, I'm expected to maintain a certain respectability which includes supporting his ideas.

'Sometimes I wish we hadn't left England—the autumn leaves of the elm trees, the clipped hedges and the peddlers passing by. It's all so peaceful compared to here.

'The thing is, Peter's ten years my senior and has always cared for me; right from the time our parents were lost with the sinking of the *Rotterdam* in the North Atlantic.

'While I appreciate this, he forgets that I can't always live by his standards. Things are not always as they appear. In reality, things are seldom that way. I'm even finding it increasingly difficult to confide in Peter and, for that matter, Michael as well.'

Abbey's pensive mood continued, outlining her marital situation, telling Barney that she had been married barely eighteen months and now, even so soon after, she held regrets; that she should have taken a much younger man.

'It was circumstantial,' she explained. 'Michael was employed by Claude Henge who took up the contract as farrier for the garrison. We always have a couple of horses stalled at the house and of course they had to be shod. Michael was a troubled soul and it also filled a need for me. He would choose his days and we had the house to ourselves for hours at a time.

'Peter has only himself to blame. If he hadn't been so possessive I might have been married years ago; children too, who knows. I used to send Madeline shopping and nobody would have suspected except—you can't hide a pregnancy. Peter was furious for weeks. I think the difficulty arose partly due to Michael being just a farrier. It's difficult to accept.

'If Madeline hadn't been there I'm unsure what the outcome would have been. She spoke to Father O'Gorman who told Peter and eventually calmed him. After the wedding—small, but the most talked about affair to ever occur in Cooktown—Peter terminated Henge's contract and employed Michael as the garrison's farrier.'

Primrose Thumpkin, a pinched-faced lady wearing a cheap stole, had come into view. She observed Abbey and Barney's attention from a distance and then, as she came close by, she peered from beneath the brim of her black hat. Her jealousy of Abbey's social position upset her mood and once passed she walked on quickly. She was the middle-aged wife of Basil Thumpkin, a clerk who pencilled in the magistrate's office; a man who, although he had sacrificed almost everything of himself, had been unable to provide the status his wife demanded.

Later, Leopoldine Bonapart, better known as Poldine, joined Abbey and Barney for conversation. She was the ambitious and attractive daughter of Andre Bonapart the manager of Empire Stevedoring. Nothing less than a lifestyle of eminence and conspicuous comfort would be acceptable to her. Her obsession was commonly known and for the past year Peter Britfield had been dodging her. He even tried to quietly pass her to the visiting French Consul. She was agreeable but the Consul, after having soiled her during his stay, sailed from the port without notice. 'Not even a goodbye' she had complained indignantly to Peter when she again started on his trail.

'Best she stays out of Peter's way. He's in no mood for courting at present,' said Abbey when Poldine had gone. 'Tell me,' she asked suddenly as though she had wearied of the street observations, 'tell me something about yourself. It's much more interesting than talking about others.'

'Like what?' replied Barney.

'Well,' and Abbey stalled briefly as a tease. 'Anything, anything that will give me further insight into you.'

Barney stroked his fingers through his hair before commencing. 'What about a crazy story, the craziest thing I've ever done. Like looking down the barrel of a gun?'

'Truly! Did you! I can't wait! Quickly, tell me!' she insisted with girlish glee.

'Well, Ophelia was a lightweight filly with fiery red hair and a wolfish face. Her father was a drunken photographer. I never met him until—well, that'll come later.

'She used to dress in garb from a shop for the poor—all loose rags hanging off her shoulders—and always wore pyjama pants and slippers. Sometimes she wore a wide waist band that pulled the ruffles in close and showed that she really was nice underneath.

'I met her the first day she ever came to the dock and she came back the next day and the next. We became friends, spending nearly all our time together.

'We were only sixteen at the time. She wouldn't do anything more than horsin' around, like youngsters nibblin' and kickin' up—you know the sort of thing.

'She mightn't sound much from the way I've told you but she was just so special.

'We kept seeing each other for weeks, every day, except for Sundays. We used to go everywhere together and everybody got to know us and thought it was lovely.

'Then one day we were on the pier holding hands when a strange man came upon us from behind. He was drunk. I remember he was dressed in black with a bowler hat and cloak. He had a craggy old face, full of rage. It was her father.

'He ordered her to go home, raising his voice as he spoke. She bailed-up and told him "No!" She told him half-a-dozen times. It was then that I stepped in to help, but he pulled a gun out from under his cloak.

'He pointed it at me and, within a second, the end of the barrel looked as big as a biscuit tin. I grabbed the gun and tossed it in the river. Then I caught hold of him and rolled him in too.

'I thought I had done good, but straight away Ophelia lays into me, belting me with her fists. I tried to explain that maybe I'd saved her life but she wouldn't listen so, before the old man spluttered to shore, I upended her and tossed her in as well.

'And that, I think, is the craziest thing I ever did. She never talked to me again and I fretted for months.'

The morning sun continued warming as they swapped more tales and asked more questions.

'You're one who won't be persuaded against your will,' said Abbey. 'I like that. You maintain a reserve that preserves your individuality. I see it clearly in you.' Her lips pursed during the pause. 'You have a strong character. I once met another man like that. He was the same age as me. It was during my eighteenth year; that's eleven years ago now. It was spring and I visited my uncle and aunt in the pastoral district of Suffolk. The man I tell of was a herdsman on their estate; a most unlikely occupation to be seen as a threat to the household.

'I recall the event vividly. I was drawn as if by force. Without ever having set eyes upon him I was lured by talk of him at the breakfast table. Seems my uncle was displeased with the apparent disrespect he returned when spoken to. Nothing particularly offensive, just a self-assuredness that my uncle couldn't manage. It aggravated him no end and he declared, there at the table, that he would terminate his service for this reason only. He declared that a disrespectful herdsman was an unworthy herdsman. He riled himself, ruining his breakfast. But the herdsman wasn't disrespectful, just independent of mind. One of the man servants told me this later and I still believe his word till this day.

'Soon after breakfast—it was eight thirty by then—I dressed and tidied and ... Oh, I can remember it so vividly. The feeling! I ran to the dairy, scrambled over the gate and followed the fresh prints of the herd. I followed the winding pathway over a creek, through a small forest, then into a large field. There was a small graveyard to the left with wrought-iron railings and daffodils galore. I then saw him in the distance, trailing behind the patchily coloured cows. I caught him up to see for myself. We wandered along together in perfect harmony as though we had always been friends, and when the cows were settled we held hands and before long went to a nearby glen. It was the first time in my life but I will never forget his spirit.

'Uncle dismissed him the following day without notice. The manservant told me how my friend had received the dismissal calmly, without question or recrimination.

'Uncle was never told of our frolic but I have always derived some ironic satisfaction from having done it. A sort of compensation for what Uncle did to him.'

Barney had not shifted his eyes from her and now, with his gaze holding hers for much longer than was seemly, Abbey flushed about the cheeks. She quickly digressed by saying, 'Let's get a cool drink, shall we?'

They entered the Outpost Cafe and sat at the most secluded table. They sipped fresh fruit juice from tall glasses and talked.

'You're a man of extremes, aren't you,' said Abbey.

'In what way?'

'You're a man capable of everything from the most violent to the most passionate. Take, for instance, that fight you had at the Goldfields Shanty; you knew no restraint, no limits. The odds couldn't have been more against you but it made no difference. I've often thought about your courage. As for the passion, you can't hide that. Even Madeline showed interest in you at first sight.'

'Did she?'

'Yes, a woman can sense these things. Nearly made me jealous.' Abbey laughed lightly then leant forward. 'Even when you're silent its presence is there. Like now. I can feel the warmth from you as though you have a lot to give. But you'll never give everything of yourself. You'll always hide that inner core and that's what frightens me. If I give of myself ...' Abbey left the sentence unfinished. She escaped to another thought, something simple about the dainty flower arrangement in the bowl on the table.

They continued talking, passing compliments and furthering their interest till the others returned.

CHAPTER 20

The horses plodded and the ten-man detachment under the command of Sergeant Frazer rode in silence as they approached Dray Creek.

Condamine, one of the native troopers, was sick with fever. He had been that way since leaving Maytown and now hung over the pommel of his saddle, shivering and clutching the horse's mane. Match-Tin and Governor, the other two native troopers, were faring better than Condamine and the white troopers.

The Gold Escort had departed Cooktown on April 16 and overlanded 160 miles along the Macmillan track to arrive at Maytown on the Palmer River goldfield. They arrived on the twenty-third without incident and reported to the mining warden. Light duties occupied the following day at the Maytown police barracks. At daybreak on the twenty-fifth they loaded the wagon with twelve boxes containing 15,000 ounces of gold and rode off, leaving behind the rhythmic beat of the ore crushers.

Ces Bean, like all the other troopers, was obliged to take his turn at escort duty. He was wholly unsuited for the duty—everyone knew that—and so far on this escort patrol he had agonised incessantly, and the loneliness of night guard had almost driven him to distraction. To ease his fears he diarised the daily events so that, in the event of being speared, somebody could give Madeline his account of his last days. He wrote with a lead pencil:

25th March: Poor Condamine. He should have been left at Maytown. He hasn't even the strength to click his horse up. The other black boys seem unconcerned about his condition. Only the first day out and I have begun to stare at the ammunition box again. I must not ride behind the wagon tomorrow. Night duty is the worst. I find the tinkling of the horse bells a comfort but when they stir I fear—my love—that I may never see you again. Please be brave if the worst happens. Abbey will always be there—go to her.

26th March: This must be the most forsaken place on earth—nothing but hills and rocks. All a-rubble. Too horrible to note. I will always love you, my love.

27th March: Camping at the Little Laura River tonight. Am writing by moonlight. The boys saw plenty of tracks downstream. The Boss doused the fire at dark so the men had half cooked 'roo meat. Jack Hamley had words to him. I couldn't stomach it so ate this morning's Johnny cakes with treacle.

28th March: I have a feeling for the worst today so am writing in the dawn light. No tent flys pitched last night. My blanket is wet from the heavy dew so my swag will probably stew in the hot sun—that is if the pack horse doesn't roll at the first crossing and wet the lot.

29th March: Boss detoured 'cause Blacks about. No waterhole at the camp tonight and only half a hogshead of water on board. Horses not watered. He could have at least given them a gallon each. I was tempted but dared not. There's nearly no grass about. Expect the horses will be hide-bound in the morning.

30th March: Left before daybreak. One horse had the staggers and had to be left behind. Ted Shack's got a carbuncle. He's been using blue stone but I don't think it's doing much good. He's been driving the wagon most days. Tiger, the little gelding I like best, he's doing more than his fair share and I wish Ted or the Boss would give him a spell from the wagon traces. The pull over the range today had him on his knees.

No diary entry was made on the evening of the thirty-first.
Condamine had been shaking uncontrollably in his swag and Ces had
sat by his side till late.

There remained one day's ride to Cooktown, with a dinner camp
at the well-watered and shady site of Dray Creek.

The sight of the winding tree line of Dray Creek raised the
expectations of both men and horses. Some of the loose saddle horses
trotted past the wagon to bury their muzzles in the cool current. The
two lame horses hitched to the wagon moved more freely. Bill
Drummond, Ces and Match-Tin blocked the pack horses on a clearing.

Governor, who had transcended into an oblivious state to pass the
time, was stirred by the movement and when he awakened his instinct
caught a slight smell. There it came again, stronger this time, on
another drift of breeze from the river. He raised his nose and sniffed
the air, whiffing more. It was odd, a smell not quite strong enough to
be identified but suspicious. The hitherto emptiness of his thoughts
was now occupied. He dragged the shaggy locks from his rugged face
and peered from the shade of his heavy brow but saw nothing unusual.

The escort closed on the creek with Hamley and Robb scouting
out front. The wagon, shadowed by Vincent and Governor, rolled a

safe distance behind. Condamine lagged. Frazer stayed behind, helping the other three catch the pack horses. The team horses sank to their fetlocks while the wagon wheels furrowed into the sand with each turn. When Hamley reached midstream he called to Ted Shack the wagon driver, 'All clear, Ted! Roll her in 'ere. We'll have dinner camp on the other side.' Tiger, leg weary and drawn at the flanks, was the first to take water and the last to raise his head.

Governor peeled shy of Vincent when halfway across the sandbar. He reined downstream and disappeared into a grove of trees. Tim Vincent scooped up a quart-pot of water from the belly deep stream, drank then passed it to Condamine. Hamley and Robb gathered about the wagon and lazed in their saddles.

None of the white troopers sensed the unusual stillness; the only bird life to be heard was the cawing of two crows that flapped about in the tops of the tall paperbark trees.

Much jostling occurred when Frazer, Match-Tin, Bill Drummond and Ces lead the thirsty pack horses to the water. After the horses were watered Ces and Drummond joined those at the wagon. Match-Tin halted by Condamine. Frazer turned his mount about and rode back to the sandbar where he stood watch. His years of service made him wary and he scanned the bushy crossing nearby and the far bank some eighty yards distant.

Governor suddenly reappeared from the trees. He forced his horse along at a quick walk to report to Frazer. He was frightened.

'Boss, bin mark here. Myall mark longa side water. Dat way,' and he pointed nervously downstream.

'Bin sure?' asked Frazer.

'Proper one, Boss. I bin see em ant,' and using his lithe fingers he made like an ant crawling across the pommel of his saddle.

Frazer nodded, wanting to hear more.

'Bin ... bin,' stammered Governor trying to find the words. 'Bin walkabout,' and he cupped the fingertips of his left hand while trying to grasp white man's language. 'Ant he makum new gunya. Old one bin broke.'

'How long ago him bin broke?' asked Frazer tensing his legs in his stirrups.

'By 'n by small one.' Governor lifted a hand and held his thumb and forefinger a match width apart to explain. 'Ant bin run em fast. Make em new gunya on black fella track.'

'How many dat fella?' quizzed Frazer.

'Yeah, Boss. Plenty track. Big mob.' He then spread ten fingers to show.

'Where dem Myall bin now?'

'In dare,' said Governor in his soft native voice and pointing to the left. 'Plurry wild, Boss. Big fella one. Plenty.'

'You bin sure?'

'Plurry oath, Boss. Him bin catchum trooper by 'n by.'

'Did you bin see em this fella?'

'No, Boss. Bin smell em.'

'No tracks here,' followed Frazer nodding at the ground.

'No, Boss. Dem fella go longa creek.' Governor explained by crawling his fingers across a knee pad.

Frazer muttered to himself again and fingered the cartridge belt strung across his chest. Governor wore khaki shorts, a forage cap and a cartridge belt. The remainder of his uniform hung from a stick beneath his bark shelter at the Cooktown camp.

'Gov'ner you bin tell em Match-Tin and them fella there. I tellum Ted to move em team. You go like steady one. If plurry Myall catchum us in dis one we dead.'

Frazer spoke in a low tone to the lean men at the wagon, 'They prob'ly think we'll unsaddle on the other side.'

Ted Shack then called to the wagon team.

'Hup there. Hup there, boys.'

The team hardly took the strain so Ted flicked his whip and then cracked it above their heads. Its echo resounded like a revolver shot and then, in an instant, a quivering spear creased the air overhead. More spears followed falling mostly about the wagon.

'Fire! Fire!' shouted Frazer as carbines were drawn. 'Shoot the Myalls!'

The roar of the first blast reverberated amongst the trees. The horses panicked, rearing, lunging and trying to bolt. Hamley got in a tangle trying to reload while his horse spun and floundered. Governor, a wily native trooper from the New England District, took to the forefront, blasting the mob.

The wagon moved but one turn of the wheels then stalled. Shack was in trouble with the team. Both lead horses, Tiger and Gold Dust, were down, kicking at the fouled trace chains.

'Get up, you bastards! Get up! For Christ's sake get up!' he ranted.

The second pair of horses, jammed between those down and the wagon, struck out against Shack's whip lashes.

Eddy Robb's Snider jammed with a shell wedged in the chamber.

The natives—fifteen, probably nearer twenty—all exposed their nakedness and yellow ochre stripes each time they stepped from behind the paperbark trees to fling their spears. Their attack came from downstream and extended right the way across.

The spare saddle horses had fled and the last of the pack horses followed, careering up the far bank heading towards Cooktown.

The war whoops from the natives were more frightening than the carbine blasts going their way.

Bill Drummond scored a kill: a native took a hit to the lower jaw, tearing it away. In a crazed stupor the warrior rushed to the open sandbar then wheeled and cut sideways in front of the troop to collapse into the stream. His struggle soon ceased, leaving only a swirl of red.

Frazer still shouted between shots, 'Fire! Fire!'

The wagon became hopelessly stuck. Gold Dust was still grounded, sitting upright with flaxen mane and tail floating on the current. Tiger, with a hind leg hooked over a trace chain, thrashed wildly, trying to keep his head above water. Ted Shack, with whip in hand, leant forward and flogged Tiger.

Ces Bean was startled, confused and utterly dismayed. Though he had drawn his carbine, not a shot had clouded its muzzle. He watched Shack flogging Tiger.

Condamine, with his strength sapped from fever, had fallen from his saddle. He knelt in the water shielded by Match-Tin's horse.

Tim Vincent, stressed and driven beyond caring, rode towards the native cordon, exposing himself fully at close range. He felled one then another of the attackers without a flicker of remorse.

Tiger was failing; his nostrils were filling with water. Shack continued beating him. In the chaos, Ces urged his horse through the churned water, passed the wagon, then leapt to Tiger's rescue. He shouted for Shack to stop. Shack, in the uselessness of his temper, threw the whip aside then took up his carbine.

Tim Vincent aimed for the stretched tribal marks of a poised warrior. His shot went astray but the warrior's spear struck his saddle flap, penetrated and punctured his horse's ribs. Tim slid from the saddle as his mount collapsed into the stream. He then half lay, half knelt by its side, firing from the foaming water.

More than two hundred rounds had been fired and Frazer still bellowed for more, 'Give it to 'em! Lay it into 'em!'

Suddenly Eddie Robb shouted, 'Jack! Watch your flank!' Jack Hamley spurred his horse into a turn just in time.

Match-Tin, a small native from a coastal rainforest tribe, blew a piece out of his horse's ear. In its frenzy the horse reared against the bite of the bit, fell over backwards and immersed Match-Tin in the stream. The horse writhed then found its feet and rose with Match-Tin still grasping his carbine and holding his seat in the saddle.

Ces cared not for himself or the others; his whole focus centred on saving Tiger. With Tiger's strength almost done and his will fading Ces struggled to keep his head above water.

Another native fell, this time to Ted Shack's bullet. The head man, positioned behind a bunch of small trees, shrieked when struck. The horror of his scream outstripped any agonising cries that had gone before. His loss immediately shrank the command of the natives causing uncertainty within their rank.

Frazer ordered a charge. 'Give it to 'em boys! Move in and cut 'em down! Bill, you and Gov'ner take the left bank. Jack and Eddy the right!' he bawled midst the smell of gunpowder and the blue smoke haze.

The troopers spurred hard, driving their mounts out of the water, across the sand and then up the banks on either side. Their piercing shots cracked and echoed whilst slaughtering the fleeing natives trapped in the depth of the tangled river course.

Tiger finally submitted, his lungs flooded. The last bubble rose and, when his eyes glazed with death, Ces held him in wasted hope, staying by his side, still and distraught, unable to understand anything of these ways.

Shack opened the ammunition box to replenish supplies while Frazer investigated a movement in a nearby thicket. Frazer suddenly shouted, 'You, Myall!' then aimed from his fidgeting horse.

The elderly native carried only a nulla nulla but Frazer's blast was immediate, striking him in the shoulder. After fleeting recognition of his wound the elder staggered to the openness of the sandbar where he stood with his nulla nulla raised in defiance. Ces and those at the wagon watched as Frazer holstered his carbine, drew his revolver then rode towards the crippled man. He halted only a few paces from the waving nulla nulla and took aim. Ces closed his eyes when the explosion sounded.

Ces knew little about British law or the sanctions of the Union Jack but he knew in his own conscience that the execution by Frazer was wanton murder. What of Christian England!

The loose horses headed towards Cooktown and when the lead ones approached the town they were seen by Freddy Threadgold. He was making bread deliveries and realised that the horses were part of the escort contingent. He left Mrs Appleby by her tin gate, took to his buggy and sooled his horse towards town. He shouted wildly to those he passed, 'The escort's in trouble! There's three horses coming in!'

Madeline saw him from the front verandah of the Britfield home. Ever since Ces' departure two weeks earlier she had gazed out across the distant ranges to the pastel blue horizon. In recent days her spirit had sunk to such an extent that Abbey had hired Frances as extra house help.

'Ma'am!' she called urgently. 'Here, quickly!'

Abbey came in haste. Michael appeared from the central hallway. Frances arrived wiping her hands on her apron.

'Look!' and she pointed away down the hillside to the activity gathering on Charlotte Street. 'Those horses coming into Charlotte Street. Are they—are they the escort's?'

Her anxiety swept to the others. Frances stood on tip toes, Abbey turned for Michael's opinion and Michael, now at the railing, peered to see.

'See them—three of them. Just coming into the corner now. Mr Threadgold just galloped downtown shouting something. It's about the horses, I know. I'm certain of it. Look! Everyone's looking at them!' Madeline's agitation became extreme. She repeated herself, directing her attention to Michael, insisting that he confirm that she was right. 'You must know, Sir!'

Michael was unsure. They were a mile distant.

'What about the one in front breaking into a trot again. Which is that?'

'I'm not sure.'

'But you must. You'd know them in the dark. They are, aren't they?'

The sight of the horses, that one small fragment, turned Madeline's imagination into a nightmare. She turned stark and pale. She began to tremble and cry.

Freddy Threadgold arrived at the police station and explained to Inspector Britfield.

'A tall chestnut, a mousy brown and a good type of bay.'

'Are you sure?'

'Yes, Sir, the chestnut at least has the police brand. They're headin' this way for water.'

Peter was incensed. He left Threadgold to answer those crowding the steps and stormed to the rear entrance. He shouted instructions for McPherson and three others to saddle immediately and to saddle a horse for himself.

Madeline could not be reasoned with. She gripped the railing, watching out along the road, shaking her head in disbelief. Abbey, not knowing what to do, stayed close with an arm about Madeline's waist. Michael refrained from speaking lest his emotions gave way. Frances, a lass of only fifteen, stayed aside. Madeline's crying was all that interrupted the impasse.

Some civilian horsemen had joined the patrol making ready at the police station. They were about to leave when Frances exclaimed.

'Look! On cemetery hill! What's that coming?'

Madeline shrieked when she beheld the sight—mounted troopers and a wagon team cresting the rise at a jog.

'Is he there, Sir!' she screamed while trying to pull free of Abbey who was holding her against the railing. 'Please, someone, tell me!' she begged. 'There's ten of them! Ten went out!'

Madeline crumbled from the shock. She turned and pressed her head against Abbey's chest and whimpered. Abbey cradled Madeline's hot, clammy body and stroked her hair.

Michael could count only seven men including the wagon driver and a glance from Frances told that she counted likewise. Michael shook his head in answer to Abbey's distressed look. Abbey clutched Madeline with precious care.

'How many, Sir?' sobbed Madeline. 'Please. Is he there?'

Michael trusted his voice enough to tell Madeline what he could see. His words struck her a maddening blow. She wrenched herself free from Abbey, looked at her with horror then ran along the verandah and down the stairs to the garden. She flung the picket gate open, tripped on the step outside, righted herself then fled down the gravel roadway.

The others watched in silence, feeling pain and pity as Madeline bolted down the slope. She slipped and fell, skinning her knees, then rose and raced ahead.

When Madeline disappeared behind the buildings on the street below Abbey asked Frances to follow. Abbey and Michael remained at the railing and when Frances neared the bottom Abbey spoke quietly, expressing an anxious thought. 'Thank God we have a daughter. I couldn't bear the anxiety of having a son.' Michael made no comment.

Peter and his troop met the escort on Charlotte Street. Madeline was close behind, arriving at the scene breathless, shoeless and bleeding from her knees. She stumbled into the crowd of babbling onlookers then pressed forward. She saw Tim Vincent and Condamine seated on the wagon with Ted Shack. She then saw Ces at the rear with Match-Tin. She pushed recklessly through the crowd, shoving and wheedling her way. Ces saw her when she broke free. He dropped his reins, swung from his saddle and met her halfway. Without concern for others they embraced, almost squeezing the breath from one another. Hugs and more hugs, a look into each other's eyes, a kiss and another hug. Madeline marvelled at his presence and held him tightly to reassure herself that it was really true. Ces, craving her touch, wallowed in the affection of her arms.

They then walked arm to waist, following the escort to the Gold Bank, and when Ces helped carry the boxes of gold Madeline held his horse before the crowd. They then hurried off to be alone, tired but thankfully secure in each other's care.

To this day the curlews at Dray Creek mourn the dead Aboriginal warriors who fought to defend their land. When the moon is high and the tree tops cast shadows along the creek banks the curlews can be heard. Their plaintive cries, bleak and mournful, call to the dead.

CHAPTER 21

The servant class of Cooktown was particularly prone to trifling chatter about the smallest of happenings, filling the kitchens and maids' parlours with exaggerated stories of everyone's doings. Their masters also filled much of their time dissecting lives and creating rumours but their efforts were more often contrived and conspiring than those told by the more humble.

It had been noted that Laura and Barney had attended a comedy evening at the Endeavour Restaurant. It was also held that Laura was beginning to 'show'. To this observation much speculation had been attached, particularly with Barney Simpson so close at hand.

However, Poldine Bonapart was less certain. She referred to her meeting with Barney Simpson and Abbey O'Reilly and her 'guarded opinion' was that Abbey had behaved 'quite demeaningly' with 'that commoner' and that there was 'no telling' what might eventuate. After all 'everyone' knew of the disquiet Abbey had expressed to Poldine at a recent afternoon tea party. It seems, as far as can be ascertained, that Abbey had referred to Michael as 'ageing', a most disrespectful reference by any measure. Poldine also said, 'She's been speaking to Simpson in the street again. Truly, she must revel in guilt. No, not alone. She usually has her maidservant with her but I suspect there's something of a trade-off there. Cecil Bean is more oft at the Britfield's than down at the station.'

A spiteful maid whispered, 'What of Laura having taken residence in the Cavalier Hotel soon after Easter? What a surprise! She was,

127

supposedly, being accommodated almost as a guest, making a contribution of only one shilling each week towards her keep. And so soon after the Resurrection. Surely it would have been more proper to wait at least another month. Prudence Swanson ought not to condone nor encourage such unholy conduct. It's almost as though she has arranged it to have them wed-locked in time. It's most distasteful really.'

And whilst Poldine was telling about Abbey O'Reilly, others spoke of Poldine: '... thwarted by the quick departure of the French Consul, that's what happened. It's Peter Britfield she's after now.'

Meg Challistine was also scathed by their tongues: there was the matter of Gunther, her gambling saloon manager, whose favour she had most certainly won. 'And did you know that she passed him over for an older man, one much older than herself. Yes, a mulatto and a very dark one at that. She sent Gunther running like a common cur last month but much had happened before. Gunther makes no secret of his want for her. She's driven him to distraction. Why, almost everyone at some time has seen him standing in the street just gaping, yes, gaping at the balcony, hoping she will appear. This I believe to be so. So upset, the poor man, that he hacked the head from a goat and left it in a cane basket at the back door of her hotel. Now, if that's not madness? Only the Lord knows what he will do next. She's most wicked. She even influenced the inspector to her aid—at a price I could not really say—except to say that he apprehended Gunther, took him to the station and told him to stay clear of her place and person. Now, one may ask, why would the inspector chastise him so if it weren't to his own benefit? Further, why does he allow such goings-on to occur in that hotel and to such late hours? They're all signs.'

Neither did Archibald Hicksbury escape their attention. 'He's fallen apart! He's in tatters! Why, Mrs Nightingale told me only yesterday that his office never opens before mid morning—it's the drink you know—and most days he's gone by school-out time. It's that gambling den he goes to upstairs and that Challistine woman—she ought to be put in stocks for the lives she's ruined. Pounds and pounds he loses on the tables. Hardly ever a night's win. Mind you, he deserves it. Did you know! Last week Pastor Nesbet, the cleric of the Methodist Church, was punched in the mouth by Hicksbury. Yes, apparently he approached Hicksbury to represent one of his parishioners and that was the acknowledgement he received. Short and blunt. Also, the lies he tells. Mind you, he must have a predisposition there. Nobody with proper breeding would succumb like that.'

And so it went, day after day, greasing the way with innuendo, making way for further talk ...

CHAPTER 22

t one hundred yards I might miss but at fifty you'd be dead!'
The voice was that of Bill Frazer, Sergeant of Police, Cooktown, speaking in the upstairs saloon bar of the Roarin' Meg Hotel. For Bill most events of life ended in smoke. As a country lad from Tasmania he had learned the harshness of the lash from his ex-convict, bullock-driver father. He had also adopted his father's attitude that women were created for man in order to serve and provide him with pleasure and offspring. Without an ounce of schooling and little more than a threadbare blanket he had fought his way from town to town, shearing, timber getting, cavorting with girls serving the public houses, drinking, brawling, waking to threats and hurriedly moving on. After many years of wandering he reformed himself enough to gain office in the Queensland Police Force. His fifteen years of service had provided the force with the brawn necessary to quell the frontier from the New South Wales border to Cape York. 'If it moves, shoot it!' was his tenet of law enforcement. His hat, swag, rifle and saddle were the only meaningful objects of life. Sensitivity was something buried deep beneath his childhood beatings in the woodshed and later drowned by bouts with the rum bottle. The inspector had again given him leave and his past four days of hectic drinking had left splinters at the Commercial and Great Northern hotels and now Angelique, the head girl serving the saloon bar of the Roarin' Meg, refused to give him another rum. The ructions were immediate. Bellowed threats of

retribution filled the hallways. Meg and Nicholas hurried to the bar when alerted.

Meg was startled on her entry. Frazer had pulled the Eureka flag from the wall. Everyone knew its importance to her. She had related the story of her father's defence of the Eureka Stockade many times. Frazer knew this and the affront this posed to Meg.

Of this Meg was aware but, even so, the threat of damage to the flag ruled her temper. She came within striking distance and demanded that he surrender the flag. Frazer rebuffed her words with a snarled reply then swirled the flag above her head in a belittling manner. Meg made a grab, took hold and drew the furls her way, stretching the flag taut between them. Frazer pulled his hand back, straining the fabric further.

'Tear it and you're dead!' she threatened with a piercing glare from behind her pale face.

Frazer held the strain, giving no leeway, allowing for no compromise. His rum-induced paranoia reeked with contempt. No one was going to issue him orders. No authority but his would be tolerated.

Nicholas knew well the paranoia that besets a rum-filled mind and set to deal with the situation in the age-old fashion. He took three paces to bring himself within close reach of Frazer then followed the movement with a swift punch. The blow hit the side of Frazer's head, concussing him and laying him back against the bar. But, powerful as the hit was, Frazer weathered the assault and retaliated. His right arm, as rigid as a gun barrel, struck out, landing his broad knuckles across the bridge of Nicholas' nose. Nicholas returned a hefty punch to Frazer's skull. There followed a volley of punches, a stand up fight, a test of strength from which neither would retreat.

Bystanders, tasting the blood of the match, shouted support for one or the other. Meg called for Angelique to pass the revolver from beneath the bar.

Nicholas continued dealing with Frazer in the manner he knew best. He flung himself at Frazer relentlessly, pounding everything of Frazer that came within reach. Frazer, with more bone than brain in his head, defied the onslaught, shaking off one then another of the blows. He became manic, unleashing into a brawling melee of wild swings, landing many solid hits, dealing Nicholas a beating. With bleeding knuckles they boxed on till a smart right hook by Nicholas caught Frazer beneath the chin and downed him to the carpet.

While Frazer struggled to regain consciousness, Nicholas stood over him as victor. Indications were that the dispute had been settled but suddenly, from Nicholas' near right, came a shout of warning. Nicholas half turned to confront a mean man standing at close range with a cocked pistol pointed his way. Nicholas, having before felt the searing pain of hot lead, stiffened with fright.

Onlookers shrank aside, pressing their backs to the walls, leaving Nicholas, Frazer and the gunman in the open. The gunman stepped closer, bringing the long-barrelled pistol to within range of a few feet. A morbid expectation gripped the crowd, quietening their mood. It was then, during this lull, that the sound of galloping horses was heard.

'It's the police,' shouted a man on the balcony.

'Five of them,' confirmed another standing close by.

Nicholas' fear mounted. He saw the man behind the pistol as a maniac ready to kill. Also, the police might, in a moment of rashness, decide to shoot him dead. He hovered in uncertainty until he heard Meg shout from near the bar.

'I'll blow you to bits!'

Nicholas looked across. He saw Meg coming his way with the revolver sighted directly at the gunman.

She repeated her simple threat, 'I'll blow you to bits!'

The gunman nervously held his aim, ready to shoot Nicholas.

A thought akin to prophesy flashed through Nicholas' mind. It seemed that his life was about to end in a pool of blood on the bar room floor—a scenario he had sometimes imagined in moments of contemplation. He had predicted his own fate—a messy end to an unfulfilled life.

Without a flicker of hesitation Meg advanced, bringing the revolver nearer. Her thought was singular: to pull the trigger at the slightest move. Her approach terrorised the gunman. He shook with fright and called for her to stay clear. But when she came to point-blank range and held the muzzle to his cheek his resolve crumbled. He signalled defeat then dropped his pistol to the floor.

Without turning her head Meg called to Nicholas, 'Run for your life, darling!'

The crowd stepped aside, allowing Nicholas to dash through the doorway and to the staircase. He defied the two troopers ascending the stairs and their commands to halt. He clashed with them part way down, falling into a brawling scuffle. He took one trooper by the shoulders and tossed him over the edge. The other tried to pin him to the step but Nicholas delivered a sharp punch that laid him unconscious.

Nicholas then stumbled to the bottom and swung about the balustrade post to escape through the back door, but a shot from a trooper covering that entrance turned him back. Bystanders on the street were startled when Nicholas burst onto the footpath. They scattered immediately, narrowly escaping the advance of two mounted troopers. Then, like the hunt, the troopers pursued Nicholas across the street with the first rider crashing him to the ground and the second collecting his skull with a carbine barrel.

Hornet appeared in the crowd, horrified and trembling. He waited till Nicholas showed a sign of life then groped his way through the rabble to flee along Charlotte Street, scorching towards Mulligan's Trading. Meg, now hysterical, fell to her knees beside Nicholas on the roadway. She spat at the offending officer.

'You'll pay for this! I swear!'

She then shouted, bit and kicked while being forcibly set aside. Three more troopers, led by a senior constable, galloped from the lower end of the street, bristling with firepower and marching chains. The senior constable took command.

'Chain the bastardised nigger!' he ordered.

Nicholas shuffled on his knees, trying to escape the policeman cuffing the marching chain about his throat.

Without waiting for Nicholas to collect himself the officer instructed, 'Move off!'

The metal clasp gripped Nicholas' throat, choking his breath. Meg screamed. Others began to involve themselves. One teamster fingered the stock of his long whip. Another man cried, 'Mongrel traps!'

Nicholas, with his eyes agog, grappled with the chain when the horse stepped forward, dragging him through the dust. He was dragged mercilessly for fifty yards before an authoritative voice shouted from behind. It was Eli, red with fury and heaving for breath. Hornet followed behind. Eli ran by Nicholas, passed the man dragging the chain, then confronted the senior constable. He grabbed the steel bit in the horse's mouth and jerked it hard.

'Stop!' he demanded of the constable. 'In the name of natural justice! Stop this abomination!'

Eli's rage confronted the constable's authority.

'Let go!' demanded the constable, pulling the reins. 'I instruct you to let go!'

'You instruct me of nothing till you let this man loose!'

'This man's under arrest!' protested the officer.

'Under arrest he may be but I remind you that you are obliged not to use more force than necessary!'

'Here, here,' concurred some nearby.

'He—'

Eli gave another sharp jerk to the horse's bit.

The senior constable became unsure of his position. He scanned the noncommittal faces of his men. Hornet stood alone, pale, silent and intent. Meg knelt by Nicholas' side, pulling to slacken the chain. The senior constable became uneasy before Eli's adamant glare. He then conceded.

'Thompson! Take the chain from the prisoner!'

Three rich Chinese merchants dressed in sandals, pyjama pants and silken kaftans and with faces as smooth as porcelain stood in silence with their hands clasped while Thompson undid the shackle. Eli and Meg assisted Nicholas while Hornet stood protectively alongside. A stark and incredulous stare was all that Nicholas exchanged with Meg and Eli when they helped him to his feet.

Meg defied her critics by clutching her half-caste man dearly. Eli and Hornet supported Nicholas by flanking his pathway to the police station. The duty officer at the station attended to Nicholas' imprisonment then advised that the inspector was unavailable. He agreed to make an appointment for Eli to speak with him at eight o'clock the following morning. Meg distrusted the police, particularly Sergeant Frazer. She maintained her own guard, sleeping on the step of Nicholas' locked cell till the duty officer arrived soon after daybreak.

CHAPTER 23

Two troopers, grooming horses in the yard behind the police station, had observed Eli's early arrival and speculated on the lengthy discussion he had with the inspector. Now with his departure and the inspector stepping from the rear door and headed for Bill Frazer's barrack room they wagered on the outcome of the proceedings.

The less scruffy of the two tapped his grooming brush against the hitch rail as he spoke.

'That Eli, he'll be doin' some kind of deal. You wait and see. I bet you the nigger walks out of here a free man.'

'He couldn't,' replied the other.

'A florin he does,' challenged the trooper touting the bet.

'All right. A florin he goes before the magistrate.'

Frazer's open door and window allowed for a breezeway through his small room. At the inspector's arrival he rolled in his swag then sat up with his long legs extending from the canvas stretcher.

'A bit battered,' he replied to the inspector's enquiry. 'How's the nigger?'

'I haven't seen him yet; thought I'd get your story first. What's the gist of it?'

'Well, Boss, everything was all right until that sooty bastard pestered me ...' Frazer's morose report of the incident was hampered by the pain in his right leg. He winced often and paused at intervals till the pain again became bearable. He implicated Meg Challistine with her use of a revolver. 'She's a proper one she is, Boss.' He cussed, blaming her for yesterday's intoxication. Peter remained patient allowing Frazer the time he needed to tell the story his way. They then discussed certain aspects in detail with the inspector expressing some of the assertions that Eli had argued.

'Eli was adamant that it was your intimidation that started the trouble. His camp, those at the Cavalier, are prepared to pursue the case if we proceed. Eli quoted some provisions of the Emancipation Act which he says protects ex-slaves from harassment. Word of your having shot that Myall at Dray Creek has upset his part of town.'

'Plurry hell, Boss!' retorted Frazer. 'Without us no gold would get through. Then what would they do? Listen here, Boss. Who's payin' us to do the shootin'?'

'We discussed that also and it's not that simple. He's threatened to write to the commissioner about our patrolling and says that if need be he'll have the matter put before the Privy Council. He's really riled. He also canvassed the current mood of the southern press. He says there's been a lot of coverage about atrocities against Blacks. Apparently they're covering a lot of space with stories about human dignity. Things are changing, Bill, and we may have to go their way.'

'Plurry hell, Boss. Them Myall lovers with plenty of money make me sick. We've got to stick together, Boss. The boys are with me.'

'I know, Bill, and I'm with you too. You know that. But we're dealing with public opinion and politics now. It's not like the old days. We'll have to be a bit careful.'

'Careful! Any more careful and they'll overrun the town,' insisted Frazer.

'You're right but I may have another way.'

'Like what?'

'I'm waiting for Christie Palmerston to show himself in town. I've got a deal to put to him.'

'What sort of a deal?'

'Can't say at the moment. Leave it with me and if that doesn't work then we'll go back to the old way.'

'What about the nigger? What are you goin' to do with him?'

'I'm going to free him.'

'Free!'

'Yes, it's all part of the plan. It's important to keep the peace at present.'

'Well, whatever you say, Boss. You're runnin' the camp.'

'Incidentally,' added Peter, 'you know Dan Hart, the selector on the Mossman River?'

'Yeah. The mulatto who thinks he can tame the Myalls there.'

'That's him. Well, he's a brother of this Nicholas Hart.'

'Sure?'

'Yes. I did a bit of a deal with him some time ago. Helped him with the paperwork for his selection in return for his efforts with the Blacks.'

'I didn't know that.'

'There's lots the boys don't know about, Bill. Best I go and talk to him now. You stay indoors till he's gone.'

Nicholas watched Peter leave the barrack building and cross the square. He stood respectfully when Peter unlocked the cell and entered. He listened attentively while Peter addressed the purpose of his visit.

'Sorry about yesterday, Nicholas. It's one of those unfortunate examples of being overzealous. It's a trait of young officers, not that that's any excuse.' Peter paused momentarily. 'Tell me, what's your side of the story?'

With a voice husky and plaintive, Nicholas put his case openly and directly, proclaiming his innocence and claiming police brutality. Peter concurred with a nod each time a pertinent comment was made.

'So,' said Peter in an ambiguous way when Nicholas had finished, 'so, so.' Nicholas followed Peter's expressions, glimpsing his real thoughts. 'So,' repeated Peter, this time with a trace of affirmation, 'maybe somebody has erred in their duty.' A hopeful smile parted Nicholas' lips, showing his willingness to accept a compromise. Law courts were no place for a man with Nicholas' record. Peter set to strengthen the suggestion of an accord.

'Tell me. Where were you born?' he asked in an affable tone.

'Jamaica,' answered Nicholas.

'British?'

'Yes.'

'Nicholas Hart of Torrens Estate, Parish of St Andrew, I dare say.'

'How—' Nicholas was confounded. Not a soul, apart from Meg, knew of that.

'Well, there can't be many Nicholas Harts from St Andrew's.' Peter then added, 'What about Dan Hart?'

'Dan!' blurted Nicholas, whirling into further confusion, for not even Meg knew of his brother Dan.

'Yes, Dan Hart, explorer and pioneer. He has a selection on the Mossman River.'

Nicholas was amazed. In all his years of absence from Jamaica he had only met Dan once. It had been in Mauritius some fifteen years earlier.

'He's a go-between with the natives on the Mossman. I came to know him through the land commissioner. Dan enlisted me to write a recommendation that his homestead selection be granted. Of course we had to provide detail of his birth place and family. He is your brother, isn't he?'

'Yes, sure, but ... It's been fifteen to twenty years since we last met. He's about fifteen years older than me. Haven't seen him since we met in Mauritius. We both went back there. We're full brothers. Our father's name is Henriques and our mother is a Jamaican born negress. We were both given her name.' Nicholas stumbled with excitement. 'Our father was descended from the French in Mauritius and went to Jamaica as a young man. I've got a string of brothers and sisters and half ones from both his and mother's side; all sorts of mixtures. Dan's religious and has always been more stable than me. How far away is this Mossman River?'

'Only seventy-five miles to the south. He has a schooner and can do a trip to here in one day in good weather.'

Nicholas listened keenly.

'He originally worked his way from the northern rivers of New South Wales to Maryborough then to Cooktown. Interested in cedar timber then. He's credited with leading expedition parties up the Johnstone and Mulgrave Rivers and the Mossman, Daintree and Bloomfield also. He's widely known and makes regular visits to Cooktown with loads of produce. He's also trading with the new settlement of Port Douglas. It is only a canvas town at present but is bound to grow as it's now the main port for the Hodgkinson gold field. You might like to visit him. If you do, go up the river as far as the junction of the north and south branches then walk upstream about a mile along the north branch. He's not hard to find. He's the only one there and lives in a bark and slab hut perched on the high river bank. It's idyllic. The valley is beautiful—towering mountains disappearing into the clouds, dashing streams and fertile river flats so dense with rainforest that much of the cedar can't be logged. Why don't you visit him? I'm sure Eli and Jim Mulligan will be happy to give you leave. There's thousands of acres yet to be selected. Could be a good opportunity for you.'

The two troopers grooming the horses sharpened their attention when, after a half hour's discussion, Peter accompanied Nicholas down the laneway to the street entrance. Then, on seeing them shake hands, one trooper slapped the other on the shoulder and declared the bet. 'He's free. A florin thank you!'

Nicholas did not return to the Cavalier. Instead he made direct to the Roarin' Meg where he and Meg retired to her bedroom.

Although it was not judgement day it was certainly reckoning day for Nicholas and Meg. Their near appointments with both murder and death, together with Nicholas' confinement in the cell, stormed their complacency. The bubbles of last week's concerns drifted afar, fading into obscurity behind yesterday's furore. As yet nothing, apart from Nicholas' innocence, had been determined. It was time for talk, serious talk requiring frank admissions, consideration of the now and resolutions for the future.

They discussed the matter at length and set a plan: Meg was to sell the Roarin' Meg Hotel. They would then marry and settle on a selection as close as possible to Dan Hart's. There was no conflict of thought. The surrender was complete.

CHAPTER 24

The morning was clear, crisp and statue still; the kind of morning that tells the heart to rush out and forgive everybody of everything, to clean the slate so that the joy of life, in all its fullness, can be lived; a day to forget intolerance, prejudice and differences and get on with the business of living.

All this joy bounced within Hornet's heart; that is, until soon after breakfast when he discovered that Billy had escaped. A gap nudged between the sticks of Billy's makeshift yard told the story. Hornet's concern was immediate. He raced off searching, running from one street to the next, peering from beneath the brim of his cabbage-tree hat. The rope halter dangling from his hand left a dusty drag mark telling of his travels. His fear was that Billy might have been captured by those of Chinatown and may already be butchered and hanging for sale from a ridge pole. His friend, his mate, his companion of five years since Billy was a scrawny kid goat, was dear to him, so much so that Hornet was near to tears. Here, there, around and about; even a visit to the wild herd roaming Grassy Hill was in vain. He nipped along Adelaide Street, the centre of Chinatown, and ducked into alleyways in search of signs but found no trace. He asked the barber who knew most things; he quizzed a drunk who slept on the street; he whizzed by the Cavalier just in case, but none of them were of help. Eventually it was Freddy Threadgold, doing his bread run with his horse and cart, who was able to assist.

'I saw him with his head down in Mrs Swift's cabbage patch,' he called in reply.

'How long ago?' panted Hornet.

'About the time it takes to eat a cabbage I suppose.'

'Is she home?'

'No. But you better be quick. She'll soon be home from church.'

'Thanks,' called Hornet, waving goodbye to both Freddy and the horse.

Mrs Swift, a widow, had only two interests in life. She attended church services regularly to ensure salvation and devoted the remainder of her time to her magnificent garden with its petunias, shrubs and stone pathways and a vegetable patch equal to the best Chinese garden.

Billy was up to his knees in cabbage leaves when Hornet charged through the open gate.

'You mongrel bastard!' he raged, swinging and striking Billy with the halter. Billy bucked and bolted, tearing a strip through the cabbages, flattening the tomatoes, ripping down a trellis of beans and leaving further evidence by raking through a flower bed before scuttling through the gateway. Hornet scurried after him, raising nearly as much dust, trying to overtake Billy before he reached the scrubby mulga footing Grassy Hill.

'Block him! Block him!' cried Hornet to a lone horseman up front. Billy knew the town well and swerved into a side street to avoid the horseman. The spirited horseman took rein and spurred to a gallop. Billy was no match for the horse but even so he was overtaken only yards from the next corner.

'Whoo! Whoo!' shouted the rider when he spun his mount to face Billy.

'Watch him! He'll have ya!' shouted Hornet who was still at a distance when the horseman dismounted. Hornet's knobbly knees were weak beneath him and he slowed to a trot on his approach.

'I'll hobble the bastard! I'll fix him!' threatened Hornet trying to cover his disappointment at Billy's behaviour. Hornet sidled close by and was quick to introduce himself.

'I'm Hornet Finnigan. What's your name?'

'Christie.'

'Pleased to meet ya, mista. We'll jam him against the fence.'

Christie dropped his horse's reins and together they went to edge Billy across the footpath. Billy's morning had been ruined and he was now in a fighting mood. He charged them several times, propping just short of impact. His opportunity came when Hornet tangled in the halter lead and tripped. Billy leapt over him, broke free and raced back along the street. Christie took chase, sprinting hard, careering up the outside in his race against the wily buck. He drew level then flung his battered hat into Billy's pathway. Billy baulked and swerved into a neighbouring yard, sideswiping the tiny gate as he went. Hornet followed, leading Christie's horse.

Billy trotted around the fence returning to the front without finding any getaway. He then trotted off again disappearing behind the cottage.

'I'll choke the rotten bastard!' promised Hornet as he slammed the gate shut. The doors and shutters of the house were closed. Evidently nobody was at home.

Though knackered, Billy claimed his independence for another quarter hour by circling the house, rushing to and fro across the lawn and ducking clear of the attempts to hedge him into corners. Finally, after having exhausted Hornet's temper beyond caring, he stood quietly by the rear fence and allowed himself to be haltered. A slight northerly breeze had risen and it cooled Hornet about the collar. Christie watched while Hornet waived his threats of vengeance and, instead, put his arms about Billy's neck and spoke words of disguised approval.

All now seemed well but their return to the street front was met by Inspector Britfield astride his stallion. A certain officiousness moulded his stilted greeting. The inspector then dismounted, and soon into his conversation with Christie it became clear to Hornet that the men were acquainted. Hornet began to ponder the ambiguous character of his new friend.

In appearance he was a bearded bushman in his prime, lean and hardy and studded with two revolvers and a cartridge belt loaded with shot; but Hornet also noticed that when Christie spoke the civil and informed manner of his speech branded him as a man well versed with the ways of those of gentle occupations. The inspector's manner continued to be less than easy. He left his helmet pulled firmly across his forehead as he spoke. There was no mistaking the officialdom of the visit. No accusations had been made but Hornet detected a pending confrontation between the two. He followed the discussion with interest and gradually a realisation began to dawn. *Is it possible? Could it be?* It was not until the inspector pointedly asserted that 'The Blacks will be controlled one way or another,' that the truth suddenly struck Hornet.

Christie Palmerston! his mind blazed. *Holy cow! Christie Palmerston the outlaw, here in town, helping me with Billy and now in trouble with the inspector!* Hornet was excited. This was the biggest event yet in his life. He needed to tell someone; so with grins rather than with words, he thanked the men for accepting him into their company then trotted off with Billy in tow. The men continued their serious exchange.

'Christie, it's clear from the evidence that you were in the area at the time. A Mr Alex Doe, a teamster, reported speaking with you just the other side of the Normanby on December eighteenth. Later that morning five distressed Chinese gibbered to him and made signs of having being held up and robbed. They came straight to Cooktown and lodged a complaint through an interpreter. They allege that a band of wild Blacks led by a European held them at spear and gunpoint and relieved them of forty ounces of gold. They also stated—and here's the incriminating evidence—that the white man had a slightly withered arm, his left arm.'

Christie clenched his bridle reins, drawing the knuckles of his good hand.

'You're probably already aware that a warrant for your arrest has been issued.'

'What for?'

'A charge of Robbery Under Arms. I add that I didn't raise the warrant, the magistrate did. The Chinese are readily available and hot to testify. One of their business leaders initiated the complaint and has tendered substantial affidavits by the plaintiffs.'

'What? Testimony by Chows? Suffer me, what's the north coming too? Little China? I've more to do than worry about them,' said Christie before turning to mount his horse.

'Not so fast, Christie. You want your freedom don't you?'

Christie paused with the back of his faded shirt still to the inspector.

'Freedom, Inspector, is not something you can give.'

'No, but I can take it away!'

'What, on the word of Chows? I'm innocent.'

'Maybe, but the magistrate will decide that on the evidence. The case against you is quite convincing.'

'I bet it is—hearsay from some Chows who can't speak the lingo.'

'You know the system, Christie!'

'You bet I do—guilty if they want you and innocent if they don't!'

'Put it how you like, Christie, it makes no difference in the end. St Helena prison knows no different.'

Christie needed none of this. Twelve weeks of roving in the bush with the natives had tattered his reserves. He was in need of decent food, an obliging dame, rest and resupplies.

The inspector recalled sketchy images of Christie's past while he waited for Christie to consider. The text of Christie Palmerston's history was a volume pitted with inconsistencies. Accounts ranging from those claiming his nobility of birth, to those claiming he was an orphan had been passed about. The illegitimate son of the famous opera singer, Madame Caradini, and fathered by Lord Palmerston, was the most colourful lineage so far propounded.

'Lordliness' was clearly evident, it was said, in the character himself. Often, clear traces of aristocratic flamboyance surfaced. Many a time, in Cooktown and elsewhere, those at the helm of public affairs had enlisted his services and invited him to join their circle where his presence stirred passion among the women folk. He had accompanied the likes of James Mulligan on prospecting expeditions, providing geological and geographic reports to government agencies. He was acclaimed as a pathfinder and one who had successfully initiated himself into many Aboriginal tribes on the northern frontier. Many a newspaper column told of his achievements as 'Lord of the Bush', a man equally at ease with either black or white, a man undaunted by hardship or danger. Fellow explorers and travellers praised his objectivity and evenness of temperament; even when suffering terribly from bouts of the northern fever he remained companionable and stout of resolve. The future was his to choose. Fame and gain were readily at hand. Public recognition and a comfortable colonial lifestyle were there to be had.

However, these possibilities lay latent. He was, as many had said, 'a dark horse'. While he fraternised with dreams and aspirations he left them largely unfulfilled. He consistently returned to the bush, living with and as a native; speaking their tongue, knowing their customs, gaining a mysterious acceptance wherever he went. But there was also his less popular side. Innumerable reports from a variety of sources cited instances of his atrocities against the indigenous tribes' people. For the Chinese he held the common resentment.

Some said that his arrest as a lad for the theft of a horse and saddle near Rockhampton and his subsequent imprisonment in St Helena jail at Moreton Bay for eighteen months was responsible for his ruthless excursions. Others said not. Their contention was that his intentions were always at the behest of his changeable nature; one not constrained by firm conviction and hence largely free from the dictates of conscience. This, they supposed, was the crux of his enigmatic personality, which could inspire and win confidence in spite of his mischievous ways.

Christie's jaded horse awoke from its doze when he turned to face the inspector again. His expression, although concerned, was by no means that of a man bereft of options.

'Inspector, do you believe in the individual, in individuality?' he asked, taking an unexpected tack.

The inspector, wary of Palmerston's ways, licked his bottom lip rather than reply.

Christie's gaze was steady and direct as he continued, 'I'll tell you something, Inspector. The civilised world is a strange place. Indeed a strange place. I find I have more in common with the Blacks.' Christie paused. 'Do you know what freedom is?' He paused again. 'To me it's being able to stand on a cliff top, miles from anyone, to shout out and listen to the echoes ringing about the ranges. It's being able to ride, cross-country, one hundred, five hundred, a thousand miles, living off the land, taking chances. A place where a man's success depends on his own ability.' Christie added a solemn conclusion. 'Inspector, don't try to interfere with that—it could be dangerous!'

Peter took no exception to the threat. Instead, he removed his helmet and relaxed his stance. 'Let's forget about hog-tying for the moment,' he said. 'There's more important considerations than your warrant. The escort was attacked at Dray Creek a while back with 15,000 ounces of gold aboard. What the Chinese were robbed of pales into insignificance compared to that and, quite frankly, this is far more important from my viewpoint. I'm certainly not going to allow any more shipments to be jeopardised. It's not on, not while I'm in command. We're running escorts almost continuously at present and can't afford this sort of nonsense. I've increased the escort to sixteen and instructed them to fire at will. Now that the wet season has gone the Blacks will be on the move and even more troublesome. They— especially the Laura River mob—defend their territory ferociously.

'Ideally, what I would like to do is form some sort of truce with them. There's thousands of square miles they can tucker on without interfering with us. Their concentrations seem to move about. No matter where we go they eventually arrive, bringing trouble. There's fresh activity down on the Daintree River. The timber getters there were attacked and decamped, leaving thousands of super feet of cut cedar behind.'

Christie smiled at the inspector.

'What's the smile for?'

Christie was unable to contain his cryptic sense of humour and his unabashed smile broadened, showing his teeth.

'You wouldn't?' said the inspector indignantly.

'Wouldn't what?' countered Christie.

'You leave it right where it is—all timber forfeited belongs to the Crown.'

'I didn't say I would.'

'No, but you've been accused of worse.'

'The world's full of accusers, Inspector, particularly the civilised world.'

The inspector digressed. 'And while talking of Daintree, how come you and that black boy of yours, Pompo, can overland from there to here in three days? None of us have been able to find a way over those scrubby ranges.'

'It's my trade—path finding!'

'With the natives,' qualified the inspector.

'Most times but not always,' replied Christie.

'Listen,' said the inspector, getting to the nub of his purpose, 'what I want to put to you is this. You're the one who best knows these tribes, their territory and their lingo. If you're prepared to act as a go-between to talk sense into them then I'll see that the warrant is withdrawn. Your work would be that of pacifier. If they don't take notice then ...' The inspector detailed his plan, specifying areas by priority and outlining what he considered to be a meaningful result.

Christie gave no indication of his attitude. He continually toyed with his bridle reins, but this was due to his inherent restlessness and not the inspector's imposition. He listened patiently till the inspector had fully explained his proposal then asked, 'If I go along with this, what's the guarantee?'

'My word is your guarantee, Christie. You know me well enough for that.'

'And what if the Myalls think different?'

'Well, it's left to my judgement. If I'm satisfied you've tried then the same applies—no action will be taken.' He then added as an afterthought, 'Think about it for a day if you wish.'

Christie slapped the reins against his moleskin trousers. 'No,' he replied abruptly, 'we'll straighten it out now. How long have I got?'

'Well, how long will it take to talk sense into them? We can't wait for weeks. The escorts ...'

'I understand,' said Christie, nodding. 'What if I haul them off the main tracks for a start then work from there?'

'How long will that take?'

'Not sure. There's a lot of country to cover. Especially the ... It'll depend on my horses. They're too cursed for much work at the moment. What if—' and again Christie's compulsive smile tossed a line.

'Don't tell me you want horses as well!'

'Put it down to police work, Inspector. Requisitioned by Constable Palmerston if you like.'

The inspector's hesitation was only momentary. 'Very well, two saddle horses and I'll also provide one pack horse compliments of the commissioner. All to be returned in fair order within six weeks. And Christie, let's keep this quiet. Don't be parading about on police horses. It mightn't sit right.'

'Not a problem, Inspector. Best you mention it to the magistrate though. I'm to meet Pompo near the Annan crossing the day after next. We'll come by the police camp early the following day.'

On concluding the deal with a firm handshake Christie mounted his tired horse and rode off towards Charlotte Street.

CHAPTER 25

Laura rustled in the fresh sheets. She was almost awake and snuggled her face into the soft pillow. A little later the crowing of roosters aroused her further. She hovered in the felicity of that in-between time which graces a gentle awakening from a blissful sleep. The faint, golden tint touching the window panes filtered through, capturing the tenderness of her moment. The sound of Barney chopping wood woke her fully. She lay for a few minutes then felt for her baby—just to say hello.

Although Laura had been in residence for several weeks she was still in awe of the kindness that had been expressed by members of the Cavalier 'family'. Prudence bought most of the clothing, accompanying Laura to the shops, accepting only the best and always conscious of the changing needs as Laura's maternity progressed. Cherie and her parents gave a large parcel of embroidered work. James Mulligan together with Eli opened an account at the Gold Bank and deposited thirty pounds in Laura's name. Nicholas delivered rather terse words to Barney, insisting that he accompany Laura on some outings. Hornet stumbled on a clue or two, a word here, a comment there. He was excited at his guess of the situation but, to date, had not mustered enough courage to ask. However, Barney had not, as yet, given any positive indication. It was even wondered by some whether he was aware that Laura was pregnant and, if he was, whether he realised the full significance of parenthood. He had not, since that day in the storeroom, tried to seduce Laura. But it could not be said that he did not care. Apart from his lapse on the morning of the fete, he had been considerate towards her. Maybe he knew no better, but more probably his desire for Abbey O'Reilly overruled his sense of what is right.

Laura left the warmth of her bed, washed in the basin by the window then dressed for a Saturday morning's shopping.

The merriment during breakfast was not without purpose. Eli declared the importance of family. Nicholas took the liberty of rising to his feet and announcing that he and Meg intended to marry. Prue gathered pencil and paper and began drawing the list of supplies to be purchased. She involved all there and insisted that Barney accompany Laura. Cherie cautioned Laura to be careful when shopping in Chinatown. 'Especially,' she said, 'in your condition.' Barney accepted the situation and dressed in his Saturday best. Cherie insisted that she alone attend to the kitchen and that Laura and Barney get themselves to Chinatown before the best was sold.

Laura carried herself with pride as Barney chaperoned her to Adelaide Street, the heart of Chinatown. Her blue, cotton dress, amply endowed with lace, moulded her figure with a quiet elegance and her shoes with their half-heels added a touch of high fashion. The light breeze played through her shoulder-length hair giving lightness to her step. With the joy of one in love she chattered incessantly to her man.

They entered by lower Adelaide Street where Barney took time to observe the manoeuvres of a tug boat. Ships held a special fascination for Barney, ships of all kinds, and this tug with its large paddle wheels, one propelled on each side, was of special interest. The port-side paddle then the starboard, ahead then astern they revolved, churning the harbour water as a large sail ship of Indian registration was berthed. 'Come on, Barney,' said Laura, tugging at his arm, dragging him away from his boyhood amusement.

The Chinese jostled on Adelaide Street. Far from the terraced hillsides, canals and rice-straw huts of their native China these much misunderstood and maligned men with a history of struggle hastened to make what they could of the day. They lived their culture, practising age-old customs, making best use of space and time. Fresh vegetables ferried from upstream on the Endeavour River and unloaded at rickety jetties before first light crammed the front benches of the traders' stalls. Busy, busy, always busy they cluttered the roadway with carts, barrows, sticks and baskets, exchanging the coin of commerce in wondrous ways.

Laura, though a prudent shopper, found so many bargains that, during the hour it took to wend their way abreast of Walker Street, she had purchased a sizable load for Barney to carry. Barney stood near a Chinese vegetable stand while Laura bargained for four live cockerels a few stalls further along. He was surprised when, suddenly, Abbey appeared by his side and whispered, 'Hello, Mr Simpson.' She was unaware of Laura's presence and sought to pick up from their last liaison. She quickly added, 'Fancy finding you at the markets. It must be my lucky day.'

Without a flicker of hesitation Barney responded, 'Hello, Mrs O'Reilly. I've been thinking about you.'

'And I about you.'

As they spoke on, it became clear to those close by that their interest in each other was more than mere courtesy. Madeline and Ces Bean, Abbey's entourage, observed from a distance. Laura had also seen and needed no tuition to understand that this society lady, whoever she might be, presented a challenge. She left the disappointed trader holding the cockerels and quickly weaved her way through the crowd. 'Barney!' she called when within earshot, and when she reached his side she coupled an arm with his. He accepted Laura's company willingly and, not wishing to exclude her, introduced her to Abbey. Laura immediately joined the conversation to stake her claim. Soon, Madeline, with Juliette on her hip, and Ces, carrying groceries, joined the trio and were introduced to Laura.

To Laura, Abbey's freshness, her willingness to engage in the chase for Barney was clear. She flaunted herself. Her supple movements, loose and swish, together with the charm of her voice made play for Barney's attention.

Laura was not about to sacrifice the gains she had made. She engaged Abbey with zest, matching, in her own way, Abbey's attempts at courtship. With hand flicking, lip pouting, boisterous movements and flair common though effective, she showed that she, too, had the ways needed to win a man. Head tossing was something new that Laura introduced into her repertoire, flicking her head upwards and to one side. She tried to mimic Abbey's stylish body gestures but seldom captured the true grace. The winning aspect of Laura's performance was her devotion to Barney. She spoke of him highly at every opportunity while clinging to his arm tightly and snuggling in closely.

Barney was stranded between the two. The roundabout of play left him confused, so much so that, for the moment, he was unsure where his loyalty lay. Abbey had ignited him with her passion, dared him to run off down the street with her. Yet the callings from Laura, with their undercurrents of solidarity and sureness, beckoned him to follow that lead. The sincerity which underscored Laura's thrust kept untying the bows of passion looped by Abbey. Time and again the suggestions of Abbey's remarks were matched by the depth of security offered by Laura.

Eventually, after a half hour of pull and tug, Barney came up with a solution. He would accommodate both of them. *Why not?* he thought. *They both want me. Why hadn't I thought of this before? Laura as my homemaker and Abbey as my lover.* He began to scheme. He devised dual roles, devoting his lustful ambitions towards Abbey and reserving for Laura his necessity for home and security. He contributed more to the rounds of conversation, preparing enclosures within which to pen each of his two admirers. There was no counting the number of times Barney tactfully flattered one to the exclusion of the other. With remarkable adeptness he balanced his complements between them, keeping the expectations of both alive, inducing them to flaunt themselves even more.

Madeline, as an outsider, clearly understood the strategy being employed. *Mercy be upon them*, she thought. *How blind. What gooses they are.* She set to save her infatuated mistress from possible embarrassment or implication. She referred to the lateness of the hour and the need to be home to prepare Sir's lunch.

The trio, however, would not be dissuaded from their individual pursuits. Barney enlivened his chatter, adding fresh impetus, providing ample opportunity for all to participate. Abbey chartered her eloquence, using French words and phrases to set herself apart from Laura. Laura shepherded Barney by positioning herself nearer the forefront.

This strutting, this play-acting, this peaceful means of establishing dominance was conducted with all the trappings of amorous rivalry.

Ces remained as a considerate bystander, but Madeline, with a mistress to rescue and a household needing her attention, limited her patience only till the strike of the hour. At eleven o'clock she again made mention of the lateness of the time and used Juliette's fidgeting as another excuse to draw a close to the meeting. Then, after a final round of courtship, Abbey and her entourage excused themselves.

CHAPTER 26

Dinner at the Templeman's home was always a grand occasion, an invitation to parade with style. Alfred Templeman Jr, the son of Alfred A Templeman and grandson of the famous Alfred M Templeman, invariably entertained with generous enthusiasm. With enormous annual dividends from his holding in the mighty Seaways Shipping Co. he, together with his middle-aged wife Eliza, had chosen early retirement and selected Cooktown to indulge in their elitist lifestyle. Nothing was spared: their property, set in a location known as the Four Mile, sprawled across many acres of land. Its hillside aspect commanded a magnificent view, sloping to the Palmer roadway and extending beyond to the upper reaches of the Cooktown harbour. From the broad verandahs of their huge lodge the view of the immediate surrounds was excellent. The lush garden, which held centre stage, was attributed to Eliza's influence and displayed traditional English design together with a profusion of Australian shrubs and flowering plants. A citrus orchard, hedged in neat rows and bearing an abundance of fruit, extended from the eastern side of the garden to a copse of native bushland. The main carriageway bordered the other side of the garden. This avenue led around a long curve then presented an imposing view of the grand architecture of the residence. At the approach to the curve a lesser driveway veered off to the employees' quarters, allowing them access to the outside community without passing by the master's hall. Here, beyond the range of the master's ear, servants and husbandmen together with their families lived a humble life reminiscent of old England. The estate with its regal grandeur was, this evening, hosting another of its famed banquets.

About thirty guests had arrived and were taking drinks on the verandah. A further sixty were expected within the hour. The rays of the setting sun, filtering through a feathering of cloud, spread a golden hue across the landscape. Nothing escaped its touch; the colour was so dense and rich as to assume form. Everything in its way was cast to bronze. As each carriage, sulky, chaise and hackney pulled to a halt, footmen, with manners befitting their station, assisted the guests to alight then took charge of the horses. Of those attending most were dignitaries, with the others being associates or friends of these principal guests. Some of the more familiar faces were: Eli and Prudence, Peter Britfield, accompanied by Michael and Abbey O'Reilly, Ezra Cowan and Mrs Cowan, and Andre and Poldine Bonapart. One uninvited arrival by the name of Archibald Hicksbury swaggered to the door. He was granted entry when Alfred Templeman, upon being alerted, gave the doorman a nod of approval.

By eleven o'clock all guests had satisfied themselves with fine wine and food. Now, with waiters waiting on them, they spirited themselves into the midnight hour. Mr Templeman, with his bald and oiled head glistening beneath the chandeliers, boasted to a group about the role his family had played in England's Imperial march around the globe. Mrs Oliveford seemed quite in love with herself, sitting alone, twirling the tips of her hair with her fingers and gazing from deep within her dark eyes. Everybody, she thought, was looking her way. The flushes of pink which lit Miss Heatherington's cheeks revealed the suggestion being put to her by Colonel Ames, an elderly gentleman whose reputation was well known. Mrs Bradmere had eyes for the lordly Mr Barrett but her not-so-cautious glances were intercepted by Mr Ernest. Others with personal motives also found their company then proceeded to steal their way. Fits of boisterous laughter, sometimes spontaneous, other times pretentious, added gaiety to the evening. The butler, Henry Pennyman, retained an aloofness from the servants at his direction and returned composed courtesies to the guests who kindly acknowledged his part in the proceedings.

Peter, Eli and Ezra Cowan settled themselves on the verandah of the terraced wing where they discussed problems common to the constituents of the district. Ezra was putting his view on the effects of the hefty freight rates being charged by some carriers when Archie Hicksbury came their way. As he hobbled closer the men's conversation lulled and a leathery reluctance moulded their expressions. Nevertheless Hicksbury, with a wave of his hand and a few grunts that confirmed he was drunk, brought himself within their circle. He took no notice of the men's silent disapproval and proceeded to extract an acknowledgement from each by addressing them individually. His hollow compliments drew little more than simple phrases of reply. He then tried to enlist Eli's support by complaining about his sore knee. 'Eli,' he burbled, 'it's my knee. It's unbearable,' and he rubbed it hard.

'Maybe it's gout,' said Eli with noticeable disinterest.

'Yes, gout it surely is but what of the cure?' Then, without being invited, he took a chair and joined the men's company. The trio grudgingly accepted his intrusion and resumed their talk. Hicksbury included himself in the conversation, making comments that, most times, canvassed the darker side of the issue being considered. It became apparent that Hicksbury was sizing Peter up for some kind of trouble. Once, then twice, he took exception to a viewpoint put by Peter and not only did he disagree, he disputed at length, stooping to spiteful inferences regarding Peter's credibility. Peter stirred to the challenge. Eli deferred, refraining from comment and reclining in his chair. Ezra, a righteous man, stayed middle ground, ready to venture an opinion if needed. Hicksbury pressed harder, referring to police handling of criminal matters, citing one then another instance where he considered that Peter's office had fallen short in its diligence to duty. The sting of these accusations was met by Peter's demand that he elaborate. In his reply Hicksbury added more to his discrediting of the police then referred specifically to a Mr Tom Simpson.

'You!' He addressed Peter directly and with a snarl. 'You're the one who has something to answer. Tell me, Inspector,' and Hicksbury leant forward pointedly, 'have you ever heard of a man by the name of Tom Simpson?'

Peter remained noncommittal. He replied, 'Archie, if you want to talk business then the office is the place to do it.'

Hicksbury was not to be off put. 'Inspector,' he opened afresh, 'I'll discuss what I like, where I like.'

'Not with me you won't.'

'Is that so?'

'Yes. If you've a complaint then lodge it in writing. You know the procedure.'

'Writing, eh, writing,' grunted Hicksbury. 'Commit it to paper you say. Come now, Inspector, you wouldn't want that. An ink copy for all to see? Evidence that's non retractable? No, that's not what you want. It's the very last thing you would want.'

'Archie, that's the best I can do for you,' stated Peter with discernible awkwardness.

'Best you can do,' followed Hicksbury, again mocking what Peter had said. 'The best, eh.'

Peter refused to reply. A tight interval lapsed before Hicksbury spoke again.

'Inspector, you claim to be a dutiful man, don't you?'

Ezra interjected, 'Archie, Peter's already given his view. Let it rest at that.'

'So, you want to be part of it too,' snapped Hicksbury. 'Maybe you're not fully informed. Maybe the inspector can tell us all why this Tom Simpson, murderer and fugitive, is not officially listed in Cooktown as a wanted man!'

Others, further along the verandah, were roused by Hicksbury's raised voice and, as he elaborated, detailing more of Simpson and the allegation against him, more ears were pricked.

'Yes, there's a conspiracy in this town and I intend to expose it! I have a sworn affidavit from the sea captain who landed Simpson in Cooktown!'

'Have you now,' taunted Peter, going on the offensive. 'And who is he? The infamous Captain Hogg, the knacker slave trader? You're a loser, Archie, and you know it. Go home and sober up. You've enough problems without—' Peter's sharp criticism sent Hicksbury into a fit of rage.

'We'll see!' he shouted. 'We'll see who's the real cur in this town! I'll destroy you before I'm finished!'

Peter had regained the initiative. He closed on Hicksbury, saying, 'Try if you will, but remember, I'll be watching you!'

'We'll see, we'll see,' he shouted for all to hear. He then rose to his feet and staggered away.

Without a doubt the argument affected Peter. He became morose and engaged little in the ongoing conversation between Ezra and Eli. He excused himself soon after and sought Abbey and Michael with a view to leaving.

Abbey had not strayed from where Peter had left her. She was still seated on the green velvet sofa against the portrait wall of the drawing room with Poldine Bonapart seated by her side. Ever since Peter had sacrificed Poldine, excluding her from his romantic ideals, she had, invariably, attached herself to Abbey at functions so as to gain his attention and, hopefully, renew his affection. Of this Abbey was fully aware but, as she had explained to Peter, she always had difficulty extracting herself from Poldine's forceful personality. For Peter, tonight was to be the same as other nights. He met Poldine's charm with polite disinterest, speaking directly to Abbey and with no more than a passing word to Poldine. Poldine's attempt failed with her words trailing behind as Peter and Abbey crossed the room to thank their hosts. Michael, as usual, had found refuge outside. He was at the foot of the stairs of the reception porch, engaged in talk with a footman. Within a few minutes their open carriage with its team of four greys was led around and handed to Michael.

The smell of horses and harness, together with the sound of clopping feet, was always welcome on the homeward journey. Everyone was quiet with Michael managing the reins from the driver's seat and Abbey and Peter occupying the rear carriage seat. At about halfway to home Michael noticed an unmanned horse and sulky parked amongst the trees some distance from the road. He steadied the horses to a half trot then called 'whoa', bringing them to a halt. Peter went to investigate but soon returned when, to his disgust, he found it to be Archie Hicksbury lying on the driver's seat, drunk and unconscious.

'It's Hicksbury, drunk as a fool,' he informed the others and when he went to step aboard without having made any offer to assist Abbey asked, 'Should Michael drive him home and we follow?'

Peter ignored her suggestion.

'Peter,' she insisted when he had closed the carriage door, 'he might come to harm out here.'

'Pity he didn't,' said Peter uncaringly.

'But anyone might come along. He could be robbed.'

'Or killed,' added Peter with marked insensitivity.

Abbey displayed her annoyance by drawing her legs well aside. 'I don't see the need for your attitude,' she stated indignantly. 'He may be in trouble. A little help doesn't go astray.'

'Help!' blurted Peter. 'The man's a cur and deserves to be treated as such!'

'He's crossed you, hasn't he,' countered Abbey, knowing well Peter's nature but not the reason for his taking exception in this instance.

Peter chose to ignore the slight. In preference, he seated himself on the front seat, away from Abbey, and called to Michael to set the horses for home. Peter and Abbey stayed shy of one another all the way home and then retired to their bedrooms without having reconciled their difference.

Abbey's evening had not been enjoyable. Apart from the imposition by Poldine and the spat with Peter she had felt constrained by the expectations of others who attended the party. As the sister of the inspector of police she was expected to conform to the restrictive ethics of Victorian ways, to follow the pretentious protocol adopted by society ladies to preserve their status and position. But, if the truth be told, Abbey abhorred these obligations that stifled her wish to be natural and wholesome, to shake free, to explore, to be herself, to melt into the arms of another man's caress. This need had, as on previous occasions, been aroused but not satisfied by the outing. The frustration now gripped her fancy, turning her to Michael. Their bedroom custom was to undress privately, either at the same time or separately but always apart and without notice of each other. In fact neither had ever seen the other fully naked. This night Abbey left the lamp wick turned high and proceeded to undress in the centre of the room for attention. She stood with her back his way, allowing him the opportunity to admire without being embarrassed. She slipped from her shoes and flicked each aside in a playful manner. With tender movements she removed the small ties from her hair and let the locks spill about her shoulders. She fingered the many buttons binding the back of her evening dress, undoing one, then another, exposing the small of her back. Then she slipped out of her dress. Her light corset was easy prey for her practiced hands and its removal revealed the soft lines of her back. Without any hesitation or show of modesty, and aware of Michael's gaze, she then, with her fingers and bending her knees, removed the last of her underwear, leaving herself nude before the revealing light. With ease she stretched her arms, passed her fingers through her hair and then stroked her thighs. She turned, presenting herself to Michael. So perfect was her form: her face with those sensitive blue eyes and asking lips; her breasts, uplifted and crowned with nipples of mushroom pink, beckoning to be touched; and her firm thighs, yearning to cradle another.

Abbey turned her gaze to one side allowing Michael time. That he was aroused was certain but of his ability to perform he was unsure. So many times had he failed, unable to reach a climax or keep an erection long enough for Abbey to be satisfied. Michael began to undress and when he undid his shirt Abbey allowed her eyes to drift his way. Though he was willing, his modesty hampered his effort. He unbuckled his belt then stalled as a virgin might. Abbey gave him space by turning aside and slipping into bed. Michael was now more able to adjust and was soon naked by her side, taking his part, making ready to embrace. They fondled, trying their hand, being adventurous, shaping new moves. They then joined and spliced, wrestling and writhing and at times floundering when Michael's erection softened. Time and again they tried, only to experience a softening of Michael's resolve, something he wished to overcome but found insurmountable. Abbey pleaded. It must be! She could not bear another shortfall. After another unsuccessful try Abbey, sweating and trembling, rolled herself upon Michael and set herself astride. She begged him with every sensation to stay firm, to allow her to burn her desire. Her imagination raced off, running wild, creating situations erotic and bizarre, making the most of what can possibly be imagined. Nothing now stood in her way. She was released, flying high, taking all that she had dreamed of. This one then that, a fantasia of lovers taking her. Men she fancied in real life all took their turn with her and she allowed them to treat her as they chose. Relentlessly she took of Michael's body, making him stiffen for her to charge yet another round of passion. This liberation, with her groans, shrieks and tears, this tearing away from the past, carried Abbey into a second half hour. Familiar figures returned, taking more of what they wanted; and of these takers, images of Barney Simpson were the most frequent. More so than any other, Simpson covered her, causing her to wail her way to fulfilment. She compromised herself wholly on his behalf, allowing him to take charge, to cover her again and again, to reduce her to a worn and sobbing mess. When Abbey was finally spent she rolled aside, cradling Simpson in her mind. She could not let him go and she dared not fall to sleep for fear of losing him. She lay awake till dawn when, with the rising of the sun, reality was once again forced upon her.

CHAPTER 27

By arrangement Abbey and Barney met again at the Outpost Cafe. Although a wicker screen shielded the entrance to the French style cafe it was by no means a hideaway. The cubicles, formed by wicker partitioning, gave privacy of view but not of conversation between one and the next. The owner of the cafe, a corpulent Marcel Dubois, was courteous and discreet. Marcel quietly speculated as Abbey and Barney sat at the most cosy of the settings.

Abbey, with her hair elegantly braided and wearing a silhouette dress that revealed her breasts and slim waist, had dressed especially for the occasion. Though Marcel was not formally acquainted with Abbey he knew she was Peter Britfield's married sister. Of Barney he had no knowledge. He watched as Abbey placed a shopping bag beside her feet. His attention again returned when Abbey removed the locket from her neck and placed it in the bag. He dwelt longer but not imprudently, admiring her femininity. He surmised that her ancestry lay with the ancient Norse and Germanic tribes of Europe, having inherited her blue eyes and fair complexion from the Norsemen of the Icelandic shores and the directness of her manner from Germanic heritage. The likeness pricked Marcel's memory, arousing fond reminiscences of his bygone days as an itinerant artisan wandering the Parisian boulevards.

Barney owned only one set of clothes suitable for these occasions. At each meeting he had worn the same white shirt, fawn trousers and shoes. Central to his appearance were his hazel eyes, burning with passion and daring. Each sat with their forearms extended across the table and their hands nearly touching. A fascination locked their gazes to one another. The essence of their conversation, though not audible to Marcel, was conveyed to him by the expressions being exchanged. He stayed away, allowing them time, till Barney summoned him with a glance.

'Madam, Monsieur,' he announced with a smile.

Abbey requested Marcel to reread the fruit juice selection then held his complete obedience whilst she deliberated. Barney decided to have the same—two lime juices. After serving the drinks Marcel conveniently occupied himself with polishing glasses behind the counter.

Abbey relished Barney's nearness: his sensuality reached out, touching and stroking her senses, heightening her infatuation and soon, when their hands touched fleetingly, the certainty was sealed. Like young lovers they chattered, leaving aside the drinks in favour of their soft talk.

'Guess what?' said Abbey with a hint of intrigue, 'Peter's taken exception to my seeing you.'

'How does he know?' asked Barney, seemingly untroubled.

'Apparently Poldine Bonapart spotted us together and told him. I'm not concerned though. I'm not going to be a dreary subordinate soul for the rest of my days. Life's too short for that.'

'I agree,' Barney chipped in.

Abbey spoke on, explaining more of her situation and, as she did, Barney followed every turn of her lips, listening to the words and interpreting their meaning, both stated and implied. He also embraced every movement of her eyes which reflected every thought and expressed subtleties otherwise impossible to convey. Laughter between them was frequent.

Marcel polished the glasses for a second time, glazing each with his breath before applying the cloth and, when they ordered another round of drinks, he selected two he had just polished.

They stayed on till one o'clock wholly absorbed in one another. Abbey then excused herself, insisting that she return home before she was missed. Just as she was about to leave she leant forward. Barney felt her warm breath on his cheek. She then whispered, 'Tonight, at midnight, behind the stables.' And within moments of having spoken she disappeared through the front entrance.

CHAPTER 28

Barney kept the important appointment, arriving and hiding himself in the shadow of a thicket a few minutes before midnight. He was afire.

Abbey, with nervousness more pronounced than ever before, parted the sheets of her bridal bed soon after the clock had struck its chimes. As silent as an apparition she stole away from Michael's side, passed through the doorway, crossed a ribbon of moonlight on the verandah and descended the stairs. She then followed a moonlit path that led about a hedge and to the gazebo. From here she moved along a hedged walkway, cutting across eerie shadows. Hark! The mournful cry of a solitary curlew broke the stillness. There, again, another wail from the night bird, following on the lingering note of the last. At the picket gate, the last obstacle to her escape, Abbey fumbled with the gate latch. She let herself through without a sound but when replacing the bar it slipped from her hands and fell into the metal keeper with a clunk. Peter's stallion heard the noise from his stable. He returned a short whinny then began to fidget. Abbey waited by the gate post, hoping that he would settle, but there followed another then another of his knowing whinnies, which were bound to wake Peter. Indeed, that is what happened. Peter awoke and, after lying about for a time, left his bed. Abbey stayed by the gate, apprehensive and fearful till, suddenly, Barney appeared from the thicket.

Within a flicker of time Barney was there, taking her into his arms and pressing his lips to hers. There was no need for instruction: the 'when' was immediate and the 'how' taken with a rush. Abbey's nightdress and Barney's clothes fell in a pile on the ground. They hugged their burning bodies together, caressing and kissing shamelessly. In feverish excitement they went to join, with Abbey leaning against the fence.

The joining, swift and incisive, impaled Abbey against the fence. She gasped, then begged for more. Barney responded, thrusting hard to satisfy the needs of both. Exhilaration reigned, swirling them towards fulfilment. With a cry Abbey gushed, coming to a climax while hugging Barney tightly. Barney, within moments of Abbey's release, let loose with rapid jerks. Time stood still till the pulsing subsided and left in its place a calm, a consoling sway which, in a strange way, complimented the fury of moments before. They then, while holding hands and kissing, spread the clothing to form a blanket. Abbey lay on her back on the makeshift bed and Barney snuggled close.

They rested and exchanged whispers that would never have passed their lips if the union had not taken place. The lull carried them forward to recovery and soon Barney began to trace Abbey's nude form with his finger tips: those tender lips, the steep of her nose; now a moment aside for another kiss; her breasts pale and full, nipples excited by his touch and further, beyond her navel to fondle her crotch. Abbey roused to his touch, nestling in close, rubbing his chest, joining her lips to his, passing her fingers through his hair, running her fingertips from his chin to his thighs, caressing him all over. Barney told a love tale and in return Abbey promised, 'Forever darling.'

Barney then lay on her, spread full length, and gave rebirth to the union. Abbey mastered the rhythm, moulding her movement to suit. 'Slow and deep,' she whispered, while squeezing his thighs tightly. Without care they indulged again with Abbey being the first to cry out passionately. Then a second time soon after. She hugged him dearly, groaning and writhing as everything burst into chaotic bliss. She then became limp and tearful and allowed Barney to prey on her body. With no thought to consequences Barney took of her, bringing himself on with careless regard. Slavishly, Abbey yielded to his pressure, opening her legs even wider. Barney continued relentlessly, having his way till, suddenly, his whole body stiffened as he stained her again.

Another period of calm followed while the panting and quivering steadied and the cool air dried sweat from their skin. Barney was the first to recoup and roll across. He suckled Abbey's breasts, one then the other, taking as much of their fullness as he could. Abbey lay with her eyes closed, wavering between want and fatigue, leaving it to Barney to decide. Barney cuddled close, pressing his body to hers. His pulse strengthened. Nothing of his desire had been tamed. He was on the rise again. Abbey stayed quiet, content to be passive; but when Barney took her again and his weight firmed she gasped, 'Oh darling ...' The sensory nymph was again at play, compelling her to join to the fullest. She was soon overcome, riding high with the feeling sweeping her senses. She surged to a climax on the fourth try and then with little more than a pause burst into another frenzy. Barney imposed on her to try again but Abbey was finished, unable to hold her position. All she could do was squeeze his hand and whisper, 'Thank you, darling.' She then lay still and quiet until he satisfied his craving once again.

They lay, hand in hand, drifting, till the lonely curlew renewed its lament. Something of its plaintive cry drew Abbey's notice, reminding her of the lateness. She roused and explained to Barney that she must return indoors. He understood and after setting a time to meet again they rose to dress. At this moment neither was aware that Peter had left his bedroom and was nearby.

During much of the time of their engagement Peter had been standing on the verandah that faced their way. He had been in one of those easy, carefree moods. He had heard nothing of their antics and had lingered there simply because sleep would evade him for at least another hour and the night air was fresh and pleasing. No wonder that, on seeing their heads and bare shoulders rise above the picket line, he suddenly jerked into life. His pulse leapt and his temper flared. He was astounded. It was no trick of his imagination; it was they, Abbey and young Simpson, canoodling while helping each other to dress. He witnessed the robing then watched incredulously as they embraced before parting. He wanted to intervene, to break Simpson's neck and deal Abbey a hiding. He almost stepped from the verandah but an invisible hand held his intent. He stayed hidden by the cover of the shadows and observed with disbelief. He watched, shocked and dismayed as his dear sister re-entered the garden, followed the pathways to the house then crept up the stairs and into her bedroom. Peter was at a loss. Even with all the power of his reasoning he was unable to comprehend why Abbey would engage in such indecency. Peter slept no more that night. He wandered the garden till dawn trying to disclaim the truth of what he had seen.

The next three weeks passed very slowly for Abbey. Every hour dragged on with each day and each night taking forever to pass. There seemed to be no transition, no passage of time, no changing from one situation to another; eternity, it seemed, was locked into one lasting moment. Try as Abbey did she was unable to lift herself free, to move ahead, forget that night and the memory of that scarlet encounter.

This morning she sat alone and quiet in the gazebo. Her awareness was numb; the sunflower blooms, standing high and so near, went unnoticed and the harbour, glinting beneath the tropic sun, brought no warmth to her cold heart. Life was without meaning, its purpose no more. The smiles, the compliments, the merriment, all the things that used to bring pleasure, had vanished. The routines, the rituals, the unexpected, all those happenings that provided both stability and spice to life, had ceased. The small interests—her attention to neatness, careful placement, orderly arrangement and other matters of detail—were now unimportant. Her attention to self—the grooming, the dressing, the poise, the style—was sorrowfully neglected. Every facet of her life had been stalled since that night of infidelity. She was on hold, chained to a standstill. There were no expectations, no future, no hope, just a treadmill on which to mark time. Round and round the same thoughts ran; over and over she tossed the doings of that night. It was in this context that Abbey sat sickened by contempt for which she could find no remedy.

Each new day brought the same. Nothing could stir her interest. Try as the other members of the household did, Abbey stayed unresponsive and reclusive, retiring to the solitude of the gazebo daily and for hours at a time. No one was to disturb her; this had been tried to no meaningful end. Abbey preferred to court loneliness, despondency and destitution. There were no sweet dreams, only nightmares that plagued her by day and by night. Nothing appeared negotiable or alterable. All possibility for change had ceased on that fateful night. Her thoughts lacked clarity and her every attempt at evaluation only caused more conflict and pain. Each day was damned from the very start. She could see no prospect, no likelihood that any day would be different from the day preceding. She saw, all around, nothing but worthlessness, uselessness and hopelessness. Life, to Abbey's altered perception, was now odious, intolerable and not worth living.

Today was no different with no reprieve in sight. Up to the time of her undoing by the garden gate Abbey had deluded herself. She had not foreseen such consequences, nor had she thought it possible that, in any event, a single act of unfaithfulness could drag her to a depth so low. Abbey had entered the arrangement with smug disregard. From the outset, from the time of her initial flirtation with Barney, she had maintained to herself that she was in control. However, that had now been proved otherwise. Nothing of the bitterness now commanding her heart had been anticipated. The thoughts of sadness now barring her every step had never been contemplated. Her mind was in pathetic disarray. Who could imagine that a plight could be so terrible as to wrench purpose from one's breast and leave only emptiness? To her it was inconceivable that she could have erred by a margin so telling. That one false step could lead to a future so cruel and ugly, that retribution could be so damning, was all beyond her consciousness. The cries of pain from within, though audible only to herself, rang of torment too gruesome to describe. On her own life Abbey would have sworn that this would not be the outcome.

But what of these fits of mind? Will they pass? Are they curable? Is it at all possible that by some fortuitous occurrence or intervention the malaise will be put to rest? And how, if no kind adjustment is forthcoming, will Abbey cope? Is her life to be one of perpetual distraction? Thus was the nature of Abbey's condition, a life now ruled by guilt.

Abbey did not meet with Barney Simpson at the Outpost Cafe as planned and had no intention of ever doing so again. Barney experienced no serious upset. His initial feelings of rejection at Abbey's non-appearance gradually shifted to a disappointment that still lay unresolved. The sowing of his seed had been sufficient to quieten his lust for conquest. In this way Barney walked free, leaving Abbey to bear the burden of the aftermath that, with the passage of time, would prove to be significant.

CHAPTER 29

'Fire! Fire! There's a fire!' sounded the shouts, piercing the still night.

'Fire!' The alarm sounded along Charlotte Street, punctuating the galloping hoof beats.

A lone horseman with bloody spurs galloped at full fury to the intersection of Furneaux Street then swung uphill to the Church of England where he forced his horse to hurdle the church fence. Here he sprang from the saddle, grabbed the bell rope and heaved at the knotted tail.

The clanging tolls filled the air, reaching everybody in Cooktown. Peter Britfield bounded from his bed in the two o'clock darkness. From his home the flames could clearly be seen.

The Church of England priest stumbled down the rectory stairs in a stupor. 'What is it? Where's the fire?' he cried.

'The Roarin' Meg! The Roarin' Meg's burning down!' came the frantic reply.

Father O'Gorman also rushed down his stairs and set his church bell peeling. Shouts and whinnies, together with the sound of galloping horses and speeding sulkies, cranked movement into the town. Those at the Cavalier, including Eli, rushed to the blaze. The police barracks had emptied. People from as far away as Two Mile Creek hurried to assist. Dozens of Chinese congregated in a mob reminiscent of the night of the riot.

Peter Britfield and Michael O'Reilly galloped down the hill, sparing nothing of their mounts, driving them all the way to the fire. Peter's stallion snorted and reared in the hot glare, cutting a sharp silhouette against the consuming flame.

The rear of the top floor of the hotel burned fiercely. Tongues of flame licked skywards, lighting the surrounding buildings. Five hundred or more people milled in shock. The situation lacked organisation. Nobody held command. Peter's horse plunged when he fired a second shot from his revolver. Sergeants Bill Frazer and Alistair McDonald, together with other troopers, ran to his side.

'What's the position?' Peter roared above the commotion.

'Don't know!' yelled back McDonald.

'Who's inside?'

'Haven't a clue. I saw the mulatto heading around the back!'

'Alistair, get the boys organised on the buckets and put the Chinese to work. Bill, you go and help the mulatto. He's probably after Meg.'

The jack pumps and windlasses were hopelessly slow. Soon, the water brigade used buckets attached to ropes, tossing them down and hauling them aloft by hand.

The saloon bar ignited. Its iron roof buckled from within. A creaking then crashing sounded when that part of the roof gave way, spraying sparks and littering nearby buildings, threatening Fuller's establishment on the corner and the barber shop adjoining the other side of the hotel. The scorching heat and blinding smoke hampered the men's attempts. Their hats and neck scarfs raised across their faces afforded little protection from the heat. They had difficulty identifying others in the thick smoke.

Suddenly, a big man shrieked.

'Fuller's place is alight!' Fuller's merchandise, a corner shop, was aflame.

Men dashed to save what they could of the stores inside.

'Leave it go!' bawled Peter. 'Let it go! Rip the barber shop down o'wise we'll lose the whole block! McDonald! McDonald!'

'Yes, Sir!'

'Get a bullock team from Lee's and tear the barber shop down.'

'Right, Sir!'

Angelique, Meg Challistine's senior assistant, groped through the crowd to Peter's side. She gripped Peter by the thigh.

'Meg! Meg!' she wailed. Peter leant over and pulled Angelique close.

'Where is she?' exclaimed Peter.

'Inside. She's inside!'

'Can she get out the back?

'No. The window's barred!'

'Who else is in there?'

'No one. She and I were the only ones!'

'Are you sure she's in there?'

'Yes. She kept screaming. I couldn't get her out!' Angelique then spluttered, 'Gunpowder—'

Peter shook her violently. 'What gunpowder?'

'I smelt it. Gunpowder and kerosene. It's Gunther. He's murdered her!'

Angelique's voice withered. She released her grip. Peter let go dispassionately, allowing her to crumple to the ground in delirium. There was truth in the old rumour linking Peter and Meg in a secret liaison. Peter could have crumbled but the call to duty deadened his sensitivity for the present.

Eli's hands bled from hauling well ropes. Barney stumbled from exhaustion while carrying buckets of water to those trying to douse the fire. Michael O'Reilly with a scarf covering most of his face worked furiously, shovelling roadside gravel against burning walls. Prue and Laura clutched each other in dismay. Father O'Gorman prayed for those who might be trapped inside. Some men, attempting to rescue Meg, axed down the front door but flames on the staircase drove them back. Sergeant McDonald raged with fury, driving the men demolishing the barber shop.

'Hack the studs down! Back that team up! Wrap the chains around! Move, damn you!' he commanded above the roar.

The attempt by Nicholas and Frazer failed. Gaping holes, billowing with flame and smoke, thwarted their efforts to reach Meg's bedroom from the rear. Frazer half led, half dragged the choking Nicholas back to the crowded street. Then, within moments of being left alone, Nicholas tried to re-enter the building. He took to a nearby balcony post and began grappling his way upwards towards the balcony.

Prue screamed an alert. 'Somebody, stop him!'

Peter responded, pressing his spurs to his horse's hide, going in for a rescue. When beneath Nicholas he reached high from the stirrups but Nicholas had already taken hold of the hot iron railing and pulled himself clear.

Nicholas confronted the searing heat. Those on the street watched helplessly. The balcony by the saloon bar hissed and roared with fire. Flames gushed from the hallway entrance. The glass doors fronting the gambling saloon cracked and popped. Nicholas defied the flames. He drove a fist through the hot, brittle glass of the gambling saloon. A slice of glass pierced his forearm, letting blood. He then kicked with his boots, shaking the concertina door, scattering more glass.

Prue cried, 'Help! Someone help!'

Frazer took up the call. He pushed through the crowd, took Peter's horse by the bit then shouted to Peter, 'Toss me aboard and take me in!'

The horse held firm while Frazer swung up behind the saddle. Then, at Peter's command, the horse took them in, chancing the danger.

The horse propped by a corner post where Frazer took hold of the column and dragged himself clear of the saddle.

Forty minutes had passed since the first alarm. The rear roof had collapsed, the walls were crumbling, the balcony floor was splashed with flames and the whole structure was beginning to lurch.

Frazer fought upwards, scrubbing at the post with his boots for grip. He scrambled onto the balcony without concern for his own safety. Then, without hesitation, he rushed to Nicholas' side, took hold of him, shook him and bellowed, 'For Christ's sake! Man, let's get out of here!' Nicholas remained limp and unresponsive, unable to reason. He was distraught, past caring. His lot was about to end. He met Frazer's shouts with a glib indifference.

'Out! Out! Out!' ranted Frazer, manhandling and shoving Nicholas to the railing. Frazer wasted not another second; he took full command, lifting and sliding Nicholas over the railing. He held Nicholas by the hands, easing him part way, then allowed him to free-fall to the roadway. Frazer followed quickly, sliding down the nearest post with molten paint smearing his tunic. One officer rescued Nicholas while another doused Frazer with a bucket of water.

Sergeant McDonald had lost the barber shop to the fire and he now strove to down the lolly shop next door.

'Back your bullocks up further, Tommy! Push 'em up!' he ordered.

'More chain!' howled a man on the shop's roof, caring not about his scorched soles or blistered hands. Inside the shop the heavy pounding of axes shook the walls. The wall nearest the barber shop caught alight, exploding like tinder.

McDonald raced inside. 'All out! We're goin' to pull 'er down!' he hollered repeatedly while pawing through the suffocating smoke to tap axemen on the shoulder. He followed the last man out then gave the signal to pull. The bullocks took the strain, leaning into the yokes.

'Move back!' yelled McDonald. 'Give 'em room to breathe!'

Again and again the willing beasts strained, drawing blood from their callused shoulders and all this time, during their unsuccessful attempts, the flames slithered on across the wooden shingles, hungry to reach the next building. The wells were dry, the men were spent. It was clear that if the fire was not contained here then the devastation would be complete, sweeping away the town's centre of commerce.

Peter suddenly shouted in desperation, 'Pitch in! Everyone pitch in!'

Tired men rushed the chains, grabbing the hot links, heaving as never before. Others joined the pairs of bullocks and buried their shoulders into the yokes. To repeated cries of 'Pull, pull, pull,' every man gave his best, straining in unison, determined to save the town.

Every man felt the first slight movement, the small gain and then another inch, followed by another in quick succession. The progress quickened; half a pace then a full pace, then another, sliding the lolly shop from its foundations and on to the footpath. Flames flared anew. More sparks flew, showering the men and bullocks with hot ash. What had, only moments before, seemed impossible was now being achieved; the carcass of the lolly shop was being towed well clear. When at a safe distance the bullocks were unhitched, leaving the crumbling structure to burn harmlessly on the street.

While the trashing of Fuller's store, the barber shop and the lolly shop was disastrous, their combined loss bore no comparison to the hurt inflicted by the collapse of the Roarin' Meg. Something of the charm of Cooktown was gone forever. Life, with its ambitions and doings, was finished for Meg Challistine. The certainty of death had won over the dream of immortality. Her charisma and spirit would be seen no more. Nothing, apart from memories, remained.

Nicholas refused to abandon the site. He mourned loudly and woefully, gibbering and crying out in a confused and hysterical state. Eli took charge as Eli would, allowing Nicholas the freedom necessary to grieve and purge. With his amorphous capacity he remained at hand, shouldering Nicholas' verbal abuse and chaotic rants. His knowing comfort, in a very individual way, was eventually accepted and, soon after daybreak, Nicholas allowed himself to be escorted home.

CHAPTER 30

Nothing would placate Nicholas. He refused to rest. On arriving at the Cavalier he stepped aside from Eli and leant against the feed shed wall, wailing and beating the heels of his clenched fists against the timber slabs. He wailed in two languages, English and Jamaican Creole. He cursed himself repeatedly for not having been with Meg last night and raved of vengeance against Gunther. He grieved violently, shouting and thrashing the wall, pouring out wild agony. He cared not who heard his laments and threats that lit the courtyard with interjections for nearly three hours. It was not till he began to take fluids—one cup then another—that some sensibility returned. Shaped by thoughts of retribution his whole focus then descended upon avenging Meg's death. He would not listen to reason; Barney, Prudence, not even Eli could persuade him not to go in search of Gunther. Blinded by grief and revenge he brushed Eli aside and stumbled through the gateway. He found his way to May Street where a child told him that a man fitting Gunther's description lived in the unpainted cottage at the southern end of the street. He raced to the cottage gateway, flung the flimsy gate aside and entered the open doorway. The owners, a poorly boot maker and his wisp of a wife, were startled at his sudden entry to their kitchen. They cowered before Nicholas' threats and demands. They were frightened and unable to speak. The wife, with her ginger hair, freckles and tight skin, held tightly to her chair while the husband, an insipid little man, sat erect with his forearms clutched against his chest.

'Where is he?' Nicholas demanded a second time, the corner of his mouth twisting.

Neither answered.

He kicked the table, shattering it to pieces. He then charged off to search the bedrooms. The trembling couple stayed silent and fixed while he ransacked the rooms. At his re-entry to the kitchen the wife tried to explain that Gunther had fled when the police had arrived earlier but Nicholas chose not to believe her. He reached for her, took hold of her withered breast and drew her beneath his heaving breath.

'Where did he go?' he pressured, tightening his grip. The woman began to cry and sobbed, 'I don't know. Ask the police. They'll tell you.' Her wimp of a husband uttered a feeble plea. Nicholas answered him with a shove that threw him to the timber floor. On releasing his grip of the stricken wife she fell to her knees and begged to be spared. The pathetic sight of the cowering couple dissuaded Nicholas from further interrogation.

Nicholas headed for the police station, hastening back along May Street then lengthening his pace on the downhill slope of Furneaux Street. The duty officer was taken aback by Nicholas' abrupt entry and even more upset when Nicholas' bandaged forearm left a patchwork of blood on the counter. The officer confirmed that they had made a visit to the address in May Street and that they wished to interview Gunther but more than that he refused to say. 'Police practice,' he told Nicholas in reply to his question. Nicholas, though singed and near to fainting, maintained his adamant stand. He abused the duty officer till the officer produced a loaded shotgun from beneath the bench. Its muzzle, dark and menacing, discouraged Nicholas and turned him away.

Nicholas visited twenty or so drinking houses in and about Cooktown. He also called by the Independent Billiard Saloon, one of Gunther's favourite haunts, but found no trace. He tried the Commercial Hotel and here the proprietor's wife, Mrs Larsen, managed to entice him to eat a meal in-between his rum drinking. He stayed on, comforting himself with alcohol, till he could take no more and then slumped, unconscious, across the bar. Augustus Larsen delivered him to the Cavalier in a buckboard soon after supper time.

For Nicholas, the night was full of horror and seemed to be forever lasting. Nightmares, plagued by images of Meg's death, haunted his every moment of sleep and when awake, in a semi-delirious state, real thoughts and ones no less bizarre than his dreams held him in torment. Dawn brought no real reprieve, only a reminder that he was alive and that Meg was dead. He was frail and hardly able to take the sweetened drink Laura brought to him.

A sad gloom encrusted the town and as it came nearer to eleven o'clock, the scheduled time for Meg's funeral service at the Church of England, more visitors called at the Cavalier to offer their condolences.

Two horse cabs were hired for those at the Cavalier, Eli, Prue and Nicholas in one and Barney, Laura and Cherie in the other.

Never before had there been such a large funeral in Cooktown; more than one thousand people crowded the small church and surrounds. It was most fitting that the hymns, sung by those inside the church and outside and to the accompaniment of a piano, drifted across the still townscape and could be heard at the desecrated site of the Roarin' Meg Hotel. The sermon was delivered in noble praise by the minister. He dwelt upon Meg's story of the Eureka flag, her father's involvement with its struggle and the pride with which she had related the heroic deed.

The Britfield's household was represented by Peter, Abbey, Madeline and Ces. Michael O'Reilly had intended paying his respects but, when it came time to dress he decided differently, saying that he would care for Juliette at home. Both Barney and Laura had exchanged glances with Abbey when she ascended the church stairs and now, as Abbey and the others filed from the church, Laura clasped Barney's hand with both of hers. Abbey fixed on both their gazes just sufficient to question Laura's possessiveness and Barney's loyalty. She then hurried ahead, appearing upset at the discovery.

The funeral cortege stretched from the church to the junction of Furneaux and Charlotte Street and further along Charlotte Street to the West Coast Hotel. A horse-drawn hearse led the way carrying the wreathed coffin of Meg Challistine. Behind this came men, women and children on foot. Carriages, coaches and buggies filed after them followed by those mounted. Sergeants Frazer and McDonald and several troopers brought up the rear.

Nicholas was awash and lent forward on the seat of the coach with his head in his hands. Prue sat between him and Eli with one gloved hand resting on Nicholas' shoulder and the other wiping away tears. Eli sat quiet and pensive.

The cemetery presented a forlorn setting; so many graves dotting the earth and so many sorrowful inscriptions citing seemingly unnecessary and untimely deaths. The townspeople, dressed in everything from gabardines and spurs to suits and bowler hats, congregated humbly before the open grave. Most present had attended for personal reasons, some of which would remain secret forever. Peter Britfield, in particular, carried a cherished memory of an intimate relationship with Meg from an earlier time. Ezra Cowan, manager of the Gold Bank, blamed himself for Meg's death. Meg had returned to him a large part of Archibald Hicksbury's outstanding debt to the bank and he was convinced that it was Hicksbury who set the Roarin' Meg alight as retribution.

A gusty breeze suddenly sprang from the south-east. It descended from the cool heights of Mount Cook like an omen. The minister remained silent while the eerie phenomenon flicked the pages of his bible. Others also felt the presence. Some even thought it to be a spiritual visitation. The gusts gave way to a steady breeze and when the leaves settled on the ground the minister turned the pages to the chosen psalm and began.

Prue and Nicholas stood arm to waist and with their heads inclined together when the final prayer was said. Then, when Peter Britfield and the other pall bearers lowered the coffin, Nicholas' restraint gave way. He sank to his knees and beat the earth with his fists, wailing in the language of his native Creole. Others wept and those with a kinship put an arm about their partner. This sad prelude to the final act of interment hovered till Prue composed herself enough to assist Nicholas. She knelt beside him and took his forearm. With bewildered eyes he gazed at the bunch of yellow wildflowers she offered. 'Take them. They're for Meg,' she whispered. They rose together, then, in the tender care of her arms, Nicholas was ushered by Prue to the grave. Nicholas, shaking his head in disbelief, beheld the fresh earth, the grave walls and the coffin deep below. The flowers quivered in his trembling hands as he said goodbye. He then let the tribute fall to rest with his love.

When others moved forward to pay their final respects, Laura shared more of Barney's space. She laid her head on his chest, closed her eyes and hugged him affectionately. Barney held Laura loosely, feeling the embarrassment of public display, especially with Laura's pregnancy now clearly showing and the label of father attaching to him by his association with her. Without looking Abbey's way he was aware of her watching him. He sensed her attention. He again thought of their estrangement, their affair followed by their alienation. Hope and despair, the consorts of love, revisited him: hope that he would be able to muster sufficient courage to look her way, to go to her side, to speak with her, and the despair that his slightest gesture might be cut short by a cruel rejection. For Abbey's part the situation remained as she had stoutly vowed; the affair was finished and, in spite of the misery in which she found herself, it would never be rekindled.

Peter, for his own bereaved reason, was anxious to quit and with Ces Bean at the reins their carriage was one of the first to leave.

Barney and Laura left soon after and all the way back to the Cavalier and later, while in Laura's bedroom, Barney's mood remained depressed for reasons that Laura only partly understood.

Nicholas' return to the Cavalier was marked by its brevity. The old Nicholas Hart, the vagabond, re-emerged and he set out on the town where, apart from becoming drunk, he learned that Gunther had fled to the Palmer River goldfield.

Never again did Nicholas sleep at the Cavalier Hotel. That night he slept on the ground in an alleyway. On his return to the Cavalier at breakfast time he stuffed his meagre possessions and some rations into a chaff bag, said a quick goodbye, then left. Prue, Eli, Barney, Laura and Cherie felt they had lost a member of the Cavalier family as they watched him trudge away, heading towards the Palmer Road.

CHAPTER 31

Although Peter Britfield considered himself above emotional attachments he was unable to turn aside the memory of Meg Challistine, the one with whom he had shared embraces during his early period of command in Cooktown. Since the funeral his memories of her had burnt fiercely both by day and night. Thomas Storm, police secretary and close confidant of Peter, made what amends he could, excusing Peter's unsettled mood and oversights. A most telling scene occurred when the party which had been sent in search of Gunther returned with a negative report. The senior constable in charge reported that his troop had searched the Palmer track between Cooktown and Laura and found no evidence of Gunther except for one possible sighting made by a shanty keeper along the way. Since the sighting was not far from Cooktown and none other had been made further west the constable had presumed that Gunther had not ventured to the Palmer. However, Peter's instruction had been that the contingent proceed all the way to the Palmer to make a thorough search. Peter became incensed when told of the officer's decision. He took no account of his bias in the case and delivered a stinging reprimand to the unfortunate officer. During the interview Thomas Storm stood aside, disassociating himself from Peter's view. Under normal circumstances Peter would have concurred with the constable's initiative but evenness of temper evaded him on this occasion. Thomas Storm was further surprised when, upon the constable's release, Peter announced that a patrol comprising himself, Bill Frazer and Ces Bean would leave for the Palmer the following morning. His mention to Peter that the return journey would take at least a week seemed not to count; priorities had apparently been rearranged.

That evening Peter remained quiet, preferring to eat in silence and retire to his study at the first opportunity. While he sat, shadows of the past flickered through his mind, inducing a thoughtful mood. He took his diary from the desk drawer and leafed through, reading old passages and becoming more absorbed as each recollection brought alive more of the past. He harkened back to the nights spent with Meg, reliving the intimacy that had bound them. It was all gone now, sorrowfully, forever, never to be recaptured except as memories. If Peter were to die, what then? There would be no recorded memory? In answer Peter dipped a pen in ink and wrote in the diary as follows:

In the event that I meet with some unexpected demise I wish to record something that is both very dear and sorrowful to me. On this day the 23rd of June, six days after the death of Meg Challistine, I confess that she and I were lovers. Within three months of my arrival in Cooktown we became intimate and remained so for one and a half years. How often we met and where is not of importance except to say that the relationship was sporadic, with meetings being more frequent at some times than others. By my pen I make the admission that there have been times when, without Meg's support, my command of this post would have been tenuous. She understood me in a way no other lady ever could. My only regret is that I resisted her wish to make our relationship public. Had we done so she would have had no reason to forego me in favour of another and would probably still be alive today. As to the other man, a mulatto, I must admit ...

The confession, though brief, conveyed a revealing story, leaving a durable record of his regret. The abrupt finish to the entry suggests that things were left undone between them, that Peter would remain unreconciled for many a year to come. Peter inadvertently or otherwise left the diary open on the study desk where Abbey often sat.

The next morning Ces Bean arrived at six o'clock and had breakfast with Peter. Michael had left for the police camp while Abbey, herself in a wretched state, attended to Juliette's needs. When it came time for the men to depart it was difficult for Ces and Madeline to separate but Ces drew strength when Madeline assured him, 'It won't be forever, darling. Once we've saved enough you'll be able to leave the force.' Madeline then waited on the verandah till she saw the three men riding out along the Palmer road. She called Abbey and together they watched glumly as the three men, mounted and with a pack horse at heel, rode past the cemetery then disappeared from view. Abbey then went to the study and sat in Peter's chair. The open diary immediately caught her attention, beckoning her to read. Abbey, for some instinctive reason, took the open page to be addressed to her. She read, quizzically at first, but then reread, gleaning more from the hitherto unknown affair. Abbey pondered about Peter and his life. *This man who is chained to duty, what is he really trying to tell me? What is it of himself he is trying to express? What of me?* She became absorbed, focusing on the good in Peter and wanting to be near him. Without conscious thought Abbey took up the pen, dipped the ink and penned the following lines beneath Peter's entry:

Shamelessly I read your passage and now with respect I write in your diary. I feel no hesitation in doing so. Quite the contrary, I sense your approval. Dearest brother, for ever so long I have wished to be near to you and now, from your own words, I know that we can share. I have sought the warmth of another. Only briefly but with lasting consequences. Please be accepting when the signs become apparent.

No signature was necessary, the authorship was clear. All that Abbey hoped for was that Peter would accept her plea. She returned the diary to its rightful place in the bottom drawer of the desk.

The mounted trio, travelling light, skirted the upper reaches of the Endeavour River then headed west, following the miner's track to the Normanby River. They passed miners, packers and teamsters most of whom were tattered and worn. For them many a dream had been shattered, many a spirit broken and many a life lost. Only a few could honestly say that life on the Palmer had come their way. Here they set camp with all routines of feeding and bedding in place before the lengthening shadows gave way to the threat of darkness. The horses, closely hobbled and with bells silenced, sensed the danger and stayed close. This hostile country allowed no complacency; each took his turn at night watch, hearing noises both real and imagined. The slightest stir invariably slid the guardsman's hand from the carbine stock to the trigger. Just before the break of day Peter wakened the others with a touch, signalling them to be at the ready when the light of day cleared the way.

The horses again felt the girth straps tighten and before the day breeze had risen the camp site was left far behind. The troop forged ahead to the Deighton River where men and horses rested for a short while. From there they left the main track and took the Douglas track, a shorter but more dangerous route to the Palmer. They pressed on through barren country till late that afternoon when they arrived at the Laura police camp. This camp, in comparison to other police outposts, was well established. Straw gunyas, made from boughs and sheaves of native grass, housed the native troopers while slab and bark huts sheltered the whites. On their arrival Sub-Inspector O'Connor, the commanding officer, extended a hearty greeting.

Inspector O'Connor knew well his responsibility, with this police camp being the most strategic of all police outposts in the colony, and that he commanded the largest contingent of native mounted police ever assembled in Queensland. The duties of this station were to disperse wild natives, keep the peace and escort gold consignments. There was no certainty. The threat of death was ever present. There were always shortages of manpower, horses and supplies. Time was at a premium, with the result that law enforcement was oft meted out where, when and how the officer in charge thought fit. Thousands of lonely graves littered the region; lost hopes buried in the crib of an unrelenting land. Place names on the frontier rang with savagery: Battle Camp, Murdering Lagoons, Cannibal Creek and Hell's Gate told ferocious tales.

And of the native troopers stationed at the outpost? What thoughts flooded their minds? Aboriginal men in their prime, mostly coerced or hoodwinked into service, taken away from their tribal ties, tossed into a wild frontier, risking their lives for a cause foreign, knowing not where their loyalty lay; confused, aimless and hapless and all for what? Nothing more than basic rations, a few pence and an occasional beating.

Only one night was spent at the Laura camp and when departing O'Connor tapped the butt of Peter's carbine and warned, 'Watch out for the Myalls at Hell's Gate!' The party held a southerly direction, following upstream along the Laura River valley. Many signs of recent native presence were seen but they met with no incident. As there was no water on the plateau above Hell's Gate a camp was set beforehand on the Laura River. Routine procedures were again taken to secure the camp throughout the night. They had little sleep. There was movement during the night and Hell's Gate lay ahead. They set out the following morning in fear. Eeriness, pock marked by the cawing of crows, hung over the troop as they approached the Conglomerate Range and Hell's Gate. At the base of the escarpment each man drew and held his carbine at the ready. Every movement of the saddlery, each clink of a horse's hoof—even the laboured breathing of the horses—seemed to ring loud during the hard climb. They approached Hell's Gate and paused before the sheer cliff face and the narrow defile through which they had to pass. All knew that once entry was made into this trap there was no room to turn a horse about, and that once in there a cascade of hardwood spears might be tossed by whooping natives standing on its heights. Peter, knowing well that to dally could lead to folly, led the way with a touch of a spur. Bill and Ces waited back within carbine range, risking one rather than three lives. Peter proceeded through this gloomy pit of carnage, gauging each moment as possibly his last. Step by step he ventured, maintaining a metered pace, fighting the anxiety to make a dash that could lead to a fall. Finally, and with immense relief, he crossed the far threshold, stepping to the open. The others then did likewise, marshalling the discipline necessary to make an orderly manoeuvre. The plateau they then traversed held no joy; the countryside remained desolate and disconcerting till they reached the far side where they beheld the vista of the Palmer River basin. The enormous river system stretched away, hiding within its folds the activity of thirty thousand miners. From here they descended to the valley floor then twisted about the meandering ridges to arrive at Maytown which was sited on the bank of the Palmer River.

Maytown, the capital of the Palmer goldfield, bristled with activity. Gaunt men, underfed and scantily clothed, toiled, working all day every day, halting only when darkness fell. From as far upstream as Buyerstown and downstream to Palmerville and beyond they employed every conceivable means to win the gold. Death was commonplace with many burials passing unnoticed. The field was no stranger to murder. Only a few days earlier a new chum, hardly acquainted with frontier ways, met his death by gunshot at Disraeli Bend after squatting on what he thought was a forfeited claim. More recently, bands of Cantonese and Pekinese with claims along Chinkee Creek attacked each other's camps, swinging shovels, sticks and knives, settling a dispute in a traditional manner. Nor were the police averse to brandishing weapons; law enforcement was readily dealt from the muzzles of carbines. It was common knowledge that detainees, marched to police headquarters in chains and shackled to trees for several days, found their dispositions quite altered by the time of their release.

The government officials stationed at Maytown were surprised but well pleased with the unexpected arrival of the inspector and his party.

Tom Clohesy, the police officer in command, was caught with his beard untrimmed and a sweat-stained shirt cladding his back. There was much business he wished to discuss and soon he and Peter were engaged in discussion.

Mrs Sellheim, the mining warden's wife, kindly invited the inspector to dinner. He arrived at eight o'clock to be entertained with a style seldom seen on the field. A wholesome meal was had, and later fine liqueur was served on the verandah by a Chinese servant.

Peter slept well that night and shared breakfast with Tom Clohesy.

Tom had attended to his appearance and now, with his beard tidy and wearing a clean shirt, he appeared more as a man of authority. At mid morning a constable reported that Jeremy Tweed, proprietor of the Caledonian Hotel, could supply information about Nicholas. Tom and Peter visited Jeremy's bark-and-tin shanty at the river end of Leslie Street and asked him some questions. Jeremy told them that a mulatto fitting Nicholas' description had called and asked the whereabouts of a man named Gunther. He further advised that Nicholas had revisited the Caledonian that same evening and, during the course of having several drinks, confided to him that his intention was to take the track southward to the Hodgkinson goldfield then travel east to the Mossman River where his brother was settled.

The most curious of all Peter's initiatives while at Maytown was his interview with the clerk of the court who was also the registrar of deaths for the goldfield. It was difficult to hear through the panelling of the closed office door but enough was heard by the court assistant to prompt his speculation. He pieced together the snippets heard and puzzled, *Why would Inspector Britfield make strenuous representation to persuade the registrar to falsify a death certificate? Further, to whom did the certificate refer and for what purpose? What motivation could there be to substitute the death of a deceased for that of a person not yet dead? How was it that the registrar agreed to the unlawful request?*

Peter dined at the police barracks that evening, moving about, listening to the troopers' stories and boosting morale. He and Tom

Clohesy then sat till very late by the glow of a dusky lamp, deliberating, making decisions and framing strategies. Breakfast was early and soon after he, Bill and Ces started on the journey homewards with the horses eager to retrace their steps.

They maintained a medium pace, climbing from the river valley and crossing the plateau in good time. At Hell's Gate they were able to mount a reconnaissance and clear the area from the upper tableland side before negotiating its treacherous corridor. Once clear of this ugly stretch the men became more relaxed and allowed their thoughts to wander. Bill fancied what epitaph would be inscribed when his time finally came. Ces' imagination was full of dreams of Madeline. Peter tossed about, cogitating one then another of his varied concerns. They reached the Laura River before sundown and secured the same camp site as before. A spiral of smoke about three miles upstream curled its way ominously into the evening air. As a safeguard the men, in addition to normal night watch, unrolled their swags by the fire but slept elsewhere beneath the cover of bushes. When piccaninny daylight brought the first glow of sunrise to the ridge tops the men stood to, guarding their position as dawn sculpted the landscape. Then while Ces prepared breakfast Peter and Bill went with carbines and bridles to catch the horses.

The going was rough and it was some time before they located three of the four feeding in a soak. Peter's stallion was missing and it was with reluctance that Bill agreed to Peter's searching further and his returning to camp with the pack horse and two saddle horses. Peter headed off and not far on found the horse's tracks. He followed the tracks, winding further away from the camp. The creek bed he traced led him to a tight bend where the embankment on his left stepped into a ridge. Here by a small rock pool he found his horse, unhobbled and tied to a tree with a makeshift halter. Peter was alarmed. He immediately sensed that he had been led into a trap. He put both hands to his carbine and pointed towards the high ground. A terrible feeling stirred within; to be so vulnerable was terrifying. To escape would be nearly impossible. To fire a shot to warn the others was foremost in his mind. He scoured the ridge, sweeping its crags and pockets for any sign, any movement that would warrant his first shot. Suddenly, from somewhere high above, a rock was tossed and fell to the ground nearby. Peter aimed nervously, ready to shoot. There followed another, then another and another, all pitched from different places and falling close but not too close to his position. He swung the barrel this way then that but saw no one. More rocks came his way, now smaller ones and many of them; the spookiness of it unnerved Peter. He became frightened and sweated. He could try to run but dared not, for any attempt would surely fail. Never before had he encountered such an ambush. *What's their game?* he thought. *I must play their game. It's my only chance!* With that he lowered the barrel of his carbine to indicate surrender. He then heard a native command shouted from the shelter of an outcrop, a singular word, repeated twice. It put a stop to the rock throwing and left in its place a maddening silence. The only movement was from the horse. It snorted, pawed the ground and tugged at the halter, trying to set itself free. Peter was amazed when, on the highest point, there appeared a tall, lithe native with spears and woomera. His example was soon followed by another and another till a full troop stood against the skyline with spears at the ready. Peter made not a move, not even a twitch that might cause the launch of a flurry of spears. He waited. The initiative was theirs. Nothing could be done except fawn before their strength. The horse detected their next move. He lifted his nostrils to the air, then, with ears pricked in the direction of a bushy crevice, he snorted a warning. Peter watched as the leaves of the shrubbery parted and two natives stepped forth with spears. They seemed unaggressive and carried the spears at ease. The younger of the two, a lad of no more than twenty years, was relaxed and led the way. Peter lowered his carbine further, resting its muzzle on his boot as display of treaty. The two came within a spear length then halted. Each party searched the other with curious looks. It soon became clear to Peter that the stand was of a peaceful nature and he set to establish empathy, some accord that would save his life. He forced a smile and gestured friendship by extending a hand palm upwards. To this the young native nodded and grinned. Peter ventured further and spoke.

'Me,' he opened, pointing to his chest, 'me policeman from Cooktown. Come to find my horse,' and he pointed to the mount.

The young native was quick to reply. 'Me, Pompo, longa Mitchell Vale,' he said in broken English.

Peter was astounded. Here, in the wild, a naked native who could speak English! He strove to keep the relay alive. 'You speak English?' he asked.

'Me bin Christie's mate,' replied Pompo, not understanding Peter's question.

Christie Palmerston, thought Peter, *and his black boy, Pompo*. He struggled with the thought.

Pompo then stated something even more incredible. 'Christie,' he said, 'he longa dere with Myalls. He say, Pompo, you bin trick dis big fella policeman. You bin bail 'im up and throw 'en plenty stone to gib fright.' Pompo then broke into laughter and set his companion giggling.

Peter smiled in return then asked, 'Is Christie truly up there?'

'Plurry oath. He bin dere,' confirmed Pompo.

Peter was tempted to shout Christie's name to summons his help but discretion had him stay calm and follow the lead that was set. 'Whereabouts?' he asked.

'Up dere,' answered Pompo, casually and without showing any inclination to include Christie.

From the to and fro that ensued Peter deduced that this was Palmerston's means, eccentric as it might be, of reporting back to him and showing that he had pacified at least some of the natives as per their agreement.

Peter asked Pompo again, 'You say that Christie is here?'

'Yeah.'

'Then you ask him to come down.'

'No. Not dis black fella.'

'Why?'

''Cause boss say.'

'What does he say?'

'He say: Pompo you tell policeman dis black fella place. Tell policeman to fetchim horse and bolt. Go longa Cooktown where belong.'

Peter was not about to argue. He set to shorten the meeting by seeking approval to untie his horse then, with more gestures, he excused himself and left with the horse. Peter was at a loss to know how Palmerston had been informed of his travels, particularly the timing of his stay on the Laura River. His nearest guess was that word of his movements had reached Christie by native relay. Although Peter wore a forage cap rather than his pith helmet to disguise himself his chestnut stallion was clearly recognisable.

The men left their camp within the hour, riding with carbines drawn. The remainder of the trip to Cooktown was uneventful, giving Peter time and space to ponder. Palmerston stayed prominent in his mind. Something of this cavalier bushman and his ways dug deep into Peter's consciousness. He asked himself several times, *How is it that Palmerston can do what he does; one day in the company of the whites and the next roaming the ranges with the Blacks? How does he maintain the loyalty of members of both sides? Will he be able to stop the hostilities?*

Peter also dwelt upon Palmerston's capacity to lead, adding more to his image of the man, granting that Christie may be a man destined to serve some lordly purpose; that he might be the messiah the frontier needed. These few days of relative solitude and introspection induced a shift in Peter's thinking. He realised the shortfall of his strategy of guns and gunpowder and acknowledged the gains to be had from talk and compromise. On returning to his office the first duty he attended was to rescind the warrant for Christie's arrest.

CHAPTER 32

Now that the Roarin' Meg Hotel was destroyed Archibald Hicksbury found other places to gamble.

Archie had, of late, bottled himself in the Cock's Spur Tavern where the rules of the house were few. On this night the usual number of obliging harlots sprawled about the bar room. Sassy, the lead girl and a buxom wench, was willing to make herself available against the bottle rack out the back for five shillings or a few pennyweight of gold. The barmaids, brash and bawdy, also solicited for business. The frontier men took their chances: drinking, gambling, fighting and fornicating and very often ruining their lives.

Hicksbury was engaged in a two-man game of poker at a small table by one of the bar windows. The lamp above, little more than head height, cast a moderate show of light on the hands of cards being played. His opponent—for Archie always regarded a challenger as a foe—was a surly seaman who captained a fishing boat named the *Sea Rover*. He was a most offensive man with matted, shoulder-length hair and a thick beard waxed with grime. He smelt as unkempt seamen do, arousing even the most insensitive of nostrils. Since sitting down as adversaries two hours earlier, their cross-table antagonism had become apparent to bystanders. Hicksbury had lost heavily, argued incessantly and now accused the captain of the *Sea Rover* of cheating.

'You swine!' he declared. 'You've been switching cards every time that dame gets near you!' Hicksbury was referring to the captain's woman who had accompanied him ashore the previous day.

She had, since play began, engaged in a range of ploys that allowed her to slip him a card that gave him a winning hand. The captain's response was immediate and noisy.

'You scum!' he shouted, slamming the table with a heavy fist. 'Accuse me of cheating, do you? I'll give you cheat!'

Hicksbury was momentarily bluffed and reduced his assault to cusses about the woman switching cards. But within a few breaths his aggravation gave way, leaving him unrestrained.

'That bitch!' He pointed a shaking finger at her bare midriff. 'She ought to be lashed to the main mast for the crew's pleasure!' He then rose to his feet in a threatening rage.

The accused woman stood firm with hands on hips and spat denials. She then urged her man to tear out Hicksbury's throat.

The confrontation turned the heads of those in the bar room. Snide remarks, alluding to the girl's sensuous form and Hicksbury's suggestion of her best use, became their amusement. One suggested taking her now. Another announced that he would be first. Another asserted that the captain was too old and should be put to sea alone. Yet another called for her to be stripped and made to dance naked on the bar before anybody laid claim. The barmaids delighted in the frolic and dared their favourite men to be first to tear a stitch. The publican, attending to his own interests, cleared away bottles of liquor and glassware.

The sea captain had no wish to brawl. He wanted further card games while in port. He ignored his girl's rants for revenge and, instead, began stuffing one-pound, five-pound and ten-pound notes into his pockets. Hicksbury was aghast and, mistakenly, grabbed for a share. A thunderous blow from the captain's fist crushed his wrist against the table causing him to shriek and pull back. The sight of the disappearing money, all those notes, the last of Hicksbury's hopes, fractured his sanity. He reached across the table, grabbed the captain by the head and slammed it downwards, cracking his forehead hard on the table. The girl screamed, 'Murder!' then attacked Hicksbury with her nails. Hicksbury reeled, releasing his hold to shield himself against her ferocity. Others, inflamed by the strife, shouted for her to claw him more, to shred his face. The girl, a Malay of about thirty years, who had been raised on junks in the South China Sea, gave Hicksbury no room, clawing him severely about the eyes. The ship's captain regained consciousness amidst the blur of the commotion. In a whirl of crazed anger he bumped around the table, pushed the girl aside then struck for Hicksbury's throat. Hicksbury gasped and pounded wildly with his fists as the squeeze tightened. It seemed that his bloated face would explode before all breath escaped him. Its redness turned to blue then purple. His terrified eyes popped beyond their lids. The girl wrenched the lamp from its holder and took her revenge by pressing the hot glass to Hicksbury's face. Without a flinch she held the cruel instrument hard to his cheek, burning the flesh. If it had not been for the intervention of bystanders Hicksbury would have met his death pinned to that table. The seaman was forcibly pulled aside by two burly onlookers while a strapping buck drew the girlfriend's ire by stripping her skimpy blouse clean from her bare breasts.

Hicksbury was a done man. His face was scarred forever. The last remnant of his dignity gone. As a broken man he staggered to the front doorway then stumbled to the footpath. His mare trembled in the sulky harness with his rowdy approach. While holding the reins hard against the bit he hauled himself upwards and clambered to the driver's seat. He fumbled for the whip, felt the power of its handle in his grasp then flogged the mare.

This was to be Hicksbury's last ride. Beneath a pallid moon he wielded the whip incessantly, striking a maze of cuts across the mare's rump. The solitary mood of the street was shattered by his cries and whip lashes. The mare bolted, taking the steel bit between her teeth, cutting through the midnight air, heeding not what lay in her path. Her pace gathered till the shapes of the buildings along Charlotte Street flashed by as foggy facades. The breastplate remained taut as the runaway mare swerved about the curve leading to Chinaman Creek. Without yielding the mare held her pace, thundering by the cemetery, shaking the earth on Meg Challistine's grave. Away and away she galloped, distancing them from civilisation, disappearing into lonely bushland.

Hicksbury had been driven insane by alcohol and greed. He hurtled headlong into Judgement Day. Chaotic thoughts fleeted through his mind: *The world has wronged me! A man of stature cheated of his just entitlement! Ignorant culls, all of them ...* He shouted into the night, raising sufficient alarm so as to be heard by households along the way. 'Where's the justice! Where's the justice! Where's the justice ...' The repetitive howl sooled the mare harder, clicking the leather harness loudly against her hide. The sulky tossed and bounced, tilting precariously. At the approach to a shadow on the road the mare shied to the left and the strain on the harness tore the stitching, sheering the breastplate in two and allowing her to gallop free. The sulky capsized, entangling Hicksbury as it went. It came to rest upturned beside the roadway with Hicksbury pinned to the ground by the wheel. Archibald Hicksbury's life had finally come to an end.

CHAPTER 33

Ces Bean thought the inspector took a curious interest when investigating the circumstance of Archibald Hicksbury's death. The measure of his personal involvement struck Ces as inordinate and uncharacteristic.

Peter Britfield had been taking breakfast when Ces, presumably pursuing his courtship of Madeline, arrived at the house with the first word of Hicksbury's accident. Peter immediately detailed Ces to saddle his stallion. Following a quick meal, Peter and Ces cantered down the hill, joined Charlotte Street then henceforth to the police station. Hicksbury's body, covered with a canvas, and the retrieved sulky harness lay in a buckboard. Peter bypassed the open door of the duty office and drew rein abreast the constable minding the corpse. To Ces' surprise and later his horror Peter instructed the constable to draw the wrap fully aside. The sight of the body drew reflux to Ces' throat, forcing him to gulp to avoid being sick. Hicksbury's prostrate figure had already begun to decompose, with his limbs rigid and his skin tight and tinged. His face was contorted in the most hideous manner, clearly portraying the gruesomeness of his death. His pin-striped vest, the hallmark of his presence, lay open, torn and stained with blood. Ces moved away to contain his nausea and on returning he found Peter inspecting the wrecked harness. Peter seemed distracted, absorbed in thought. His preoccupation was interrupted only when the attending constable suggested the corpse be covered.

A senior constable had taken charge and was preparing notes for his report when Peter entered the office and, with few words and no explanation, told him that he himself would attend to the report. The senior constable, though not perceiving the instruction as a slight on his ability, was nonetheless mystified as to why the inspector would concern himself with such a routine matter.

Without delay he and Ces then proceeded along Charlotte Street to Hicksbury's office. The professional notice in the window, the one Barney had read so often, took on the meaning of a strange epitaph; words and advice of learned and respectful magnitude ascribed to a man meeting his death in disrepute and destitution—indeed a testimony to the need to limit trust in others. Their access to the office was blocked by a locked door and windows until Ces smashed a window pane, flipped a catch then scrambled through to unbolt the rear door. Ces had almost invariably been Peter's aide during searches but in this instance and to the arousal of his curiosity Peter stationed him out front with the horses and conducted the investigation alone. While waiting Ces noticed Barney Simpson loitering across the street, looking towards the office. He recalled Barney's association with Abbey but attached no significance to his being there on the street.

Peter found the office in a shambles. Everything lay in disarray with files, papers, office requisites and personal oddments scattered haphazardly. Peter pulled aside a shabby curtain screen revealing boxes upon boxes of documents most of which were outdated or superfluous. He pawed through these without respect, strewing the contents about the floor after quick perusal. His involvement with this archive was lengthy and the tin roof began to creak before he tossed the last file aside. In his continued search for information relating to Tom Simpson, Peter pulled the desk drawers from their slides, then the draws of a wooden file cabinet. He discovered nothing pertinent till he sorted the bottom drawer of the cabinet. There, he found a bulky file clearly marked 'Thomas Simpson'. Its contents were exhaustive, everything from wanted notices to correspondence with the police departments of New South Wales and Queensland, and an assembled history of Tom Simpson that read almost as a personal memoir. Peter remained totally absorbed while scrutinising this file. He then paused in reflection while casually studying the desk items, fingering the sealing wax, testing the sharpness of the pen nibs and tapping the brass letter opener on the blotting pad that lay central on the desk. The annotations scribbled on the pad's margin captured his notice. This, then that, then more, till suddenly a cursory glimpse detected the entry: 'The witch must go'; and near to it and written in an angry fashion, 'M.C. must go'. The realisation that 'M.C.' probably referred to Meg Challistine stunned Peter; the possibility that Hicksbury may have set the Roarin' Meg on fire had him clench his knuckles. *Where, where can I find corroboration, further evidence to substantiate my suspicion?* His mind reeled at the thought, and he cast about quickly for anything he may have overlooked. He impulsively upended a kitchen chest, spilling cups and spoons to the floor, then ripped up the train of red carpet leading to the front door. He even tore the calico lining from the ceiling in search of concealed compartments. His failure to find evidence agitated him, biting at his temper until he heaved the heavy oak desk onto its side. A leather-bound book fell to the floor. He grabbed it, flipped the pages feverishly and discovered that it was Hicksbury's diary!

He scanned the diary. The first entry was dated three years ago. He found dealings, involving deceit and illegal conduct both in Cooktown and elsewhere, that told of a man wholly unprincipled and undeserving of the society in which he lived. The crimes were sufficient to have him jailed for life or hung—whichever the judge chose.

With respect to Tom Simpson, there were numerous references to contacts made with investigative agencies, information received and, in a most recent entry, the assertion that the suspect was residing in Cooktown. Pending advice from Sydney, an arrest was soon to be made. This entry of only two weeks earlier also alleged that the fugitive had an alias. However, it did not reveal the assumed name. A margin note indicated that Hicksbury was unprepared to divulge the suspect's alias for fear of being cheated of the reward. His caution was so great that he refrained from even penning it in this secret volume. Further, it was clearly implied that the wanted man was being aided and abetted by a senior officer of the police force in Cooktown, one so senior that the arrest would have to be initiated from police headquarters in Brisbane. However, nothing indicated that the authorities in Brisbane had been informed and, knowing Hicksbury's obsession with secrecy, Peter thought it improbable that this particular would have yet been disclosed. In addition to these discoveries Peter sighted references that confirmed Hicksbury's knowledge of Barney Simpson's presence in Cooktown and his relationship to Tom Simpson.

Peter opened the windows, allowing a draught through the hot room before examining the diary further.

The puzzle of the reference to 'M.C.' now held his attention. Peter recalled the specific date of Meg's death, opened the diary at that date and studied the page which was crowded with details of the fire. Though no incriminating mentions were made there was, at the bottom of the page, the notation, 'M.C.—addendum'.

Peter carefully turned the unused pages towards the back of the diary and partway through found the secret of secrets—an addendum detailing the darkest of Hicksbury's doings. Each of the entries listed were cross-referenced to the main diary by corresponding dates.

A suffocating anxiety seized upon Peter as he proceeded to read and interpret:

17/6/77: M.C. robbed me of £120 in the last six months. She preyed on me relentlessly. She took no heed of my warning. She had to be stopped.

The message was clear to Peter: Hicksbury had burned the Roarin' Meg to murder Meg.

Peter sat in Hicksbury's chair and lapsed into a state of remorse. He thought, *Had I not been so rigid, had I not let Meg slip from my life, this would never have occurred. If I were easier to talk with she would have confided in me. And if ... if I hadn't been so stubborn, I would have allowed our association to be known publicly and then no one would have dared trespass upon her. What a blind man you've been, Peter Britfield. So self-centred as not to be able to accept that others might be right. Oh, how could I be so blind as to let this happen?*

Peter blamed himself for Meg's death. *If only* ... he chastised himself over and over again. He stared at his open hands in criticism for having failed to act wisely. His measure of himself was reduced.

Peter was confused. He lamely rose from the chair and cast about the still room. Then he left the office, taking with him the diary and the Simpson file. He gave Ces instructions to bundle and burn every shred of paper in the office. He then rode to the cemetery where he stood by Meg's grave. He was now alone, away from others and their scrutiny. He allowed himself to grieve openly and honestly before Meg's grave.

CHAPTER 34

Barney had slept well and woke in a contemplative mood, so much so that he slipped away from the Cavalier Hotel before breakfast to extend his moment of solitude. At the base of Grassy Hill he left the roadway and began the ascent, leaving traces of his footprints on the dewy ground. He settled himself on a rock on the lee side of the hill overlooking the harbour. He was very much at peace and let his thoughts wander.

Gradually, a new understanding winnowed his thoughts, letting the light chaff of thoughtless nothings float away on the breeze and leave before him a clear view of life. Never before had Barney found himself so absorbed in thought—the past, the future and the present all linked together.

He considered his mother and her neglect of him as a child. He realised that much of her life had been beyond her control. He now saw her as a child herself, denied adequate parenting, thrust from the cradle and left to fend for herself. He visualised her as a sad and destitute person, one to be pitied and, if possible, to be forgiven. Gentleness from within called on Barney, petitioning him to understand and forgive. He accepted this plea and, in doing so, allowed the softness of love to erase pain from his heart.

As the sun rose higher and broke over the crest of the hill thoughts of Abbey O'Reilly and his intimacy with her came to mind. He came to the conclusion that in essence his affair with Abbey had been little more than a desire to tag her with his manliness. From the outset his advances had been a conquest, a sort of game. Now, in retrospect, he realised he should never have become involved. He accepted that a fancy is admissible but to maul and to stain was beyond the bounds of acceptable conduct—particularly a woman stationed both in wedlock and parenthood. For Barney a touch of regret shadowed his thoughts but nothing of real reproach found a place of significance.

A young bird perched in a tree above began calling for its mother. Again and again it called, crying for her attention. Barney was suddenly struck by the need for commitment. Laura already carried responsibility for their child and soon, only two months hence, it would bare itself to the world and cry for his help. Barney's thoughts became serious: there could be no return to those careless, flippant days of earlier life. A future defined by commitment lay ahead.

But while Barney sat on the hill winnowing his thoughts the situation at the Britfields' home was otherwise. Abbey had been crippled by guilt since that interlude by the garden gate and now, two months later, no reprieve was in sight. Members of the household tried to reach out to her: Madeline placed herself at Ma'am's disposal, fetching and fixing; Peter became more understanding and sidestepped all contention; Michael displayed more affection.

Father O'Gorman, a close family friend, had become involved. Abbey's impoverished state became clearly apparent to him soon after that wretched event. Since then he had made regular visits and, if nothing else, endeared himself by consoling her with his presence. This morning he arrived to once again take tea with Abbey.

Madeline, a wonderful lass in every respect, greeted Father cheerily at the picket gate and accompanied him to the verandah. She then went to Abbey's bedroom where she found her mistress seated quietly before the duchesse. Abbey viewed Madeline's entry by the reflection in the mirror but made no movement, not even a flicker to wipe the gloom from her face. Not until Madeline placed a caring hand on her shoulder and announced, 'Father's here', did Abbey respond. She raised a hand to touch Madeline's, thanked her with a nod then rose from the stool.

Abbey stepped from the hallway, bid Father a restrained welcome then invited him to be seated. Abbey customarily took Father's hat but today it was left to Madeline. As he passed the hat Madeline noticed the quiver in his hand, a slight tremor over which he had no control. Abbey and friends were aware of the condition that Eli had diagnosed as a nervous system disorder. Madeline waited till they were comfortably seated then excused herself to prepare a pot of tea.

Abbey spoke only a few words then fell silent. Further thoughts were stalled. Nothing worth mentioning would come to mind. Father found it difficult to make conversation and was pleased when Madeline served the tea. He poured tea for two then handed Abbey a cup, forcing her acceptance and a 'thank you'. During the next half hour Father did most of the talking, trying to get Abbey to discuss the problem, but she remained largely unresponsive. Madeline then brought a fresh pot of tea and when Father went to pour himself a cup his hand trembled and some spilt in the saucer. He tried to dismiss the slip with a short apology but this small mishap bore maddening ramifications.

Abbey, aware of his failing health, suddenly became distressed and burst into tears. She held her head in her hands, trying to contain her sobbing. Father waited a while and when she did not stop he addressed her directly and asked what the problem was.

Abbey raised her head and began to speak, allowing her hurt and shame to surface.

'The tears I shed might well be my blood for all I now care about life. What use, what purpose ... Tell me, Father, why persevere with an existence so ragged, so painful as to be unbearable? Father, I must be honest. I will be. I have tried to be faithful to the Church and its tenets but how ... What hypocrite am I to say I believe when belief has been replaced by doubt? Father, I no longer believe!'

'No! No! Abbey please,' uttered Father, 'no more.'

'Yes, Father, I have been tempted and misguided. I have been weak, hopelessly weak. My will has been reduced to that of a suckling, blindly feeding on the senses and nothing more. Father, I have breached the cardinal laws and there can be no redemption.'

'Abbey! Please, please be silent! You know not what you say! Whatever it be has stricken your senses!'

'Father, I beg you not to distress yourself on my account. There is your health to consider. You can't jeopardise yourself on my behalf. Please let go for your own sake. Please leave. Leave to save yourself.'

'Never! Never will I desert you! You're too precious!' retorted Father with forthright rejection. 'Abbey, I cherish you as God's child. Here!' and he took her hands and squeezed them with all the sincerity he could muster.

Abbey sniffled, interrupted the tears, and took notice. Her blue eyes, now almost steel grey in colour, pleaded for help. Father understood and asked her to join him in prayer. Even though Abbey did not confess they prayed together, seeking forgiveness. Abbey's composure slowly returned and following prayer Father reassured her that there was nothing she could have done that the Lord could not forgive.

It was then that Madeline, with astute timing, came to their attendance and suggested that, since it was nearly noon and the men were away, Father may like to join them for lunch. He accepted graciously then immediately enquired of Juliette. It required no more than a single call to bring Juliette scurrying along the verandah to occupy her favourite place on Father's knee.

Father O'Gorman had a companion at the church. Oh yes, for the past two years the twosome had resided happily upon the same plot of consecrated ground in an atmosphere free of dispute and almost always an air of co-operation. Everybody was aware but no one complained. All were happy with the arrangement and the upkeep. The children could find no fault with the one Father had selected and oft, after school or morning service, they slipped away and could always be found in his friend's company. Jack Straw, the aged saddle horse, was a most lovable equine. As to being named Jack Straw, the texture of his straggly mane and tail was clear evidence. Numerous children, both of the faith and others from without, attended to his grooming but Jack Straw he would forever be.

Since yesterday's meeting with Abbey, Father had devised a plan. The new prospect excited his mood. He bustled through the morning's chores then briskly made his way to the Cavalier Hotel. His call on Prudence in this time of need was not ill considered; Prudence, though not attending church regularly, was nevertheless a staunch member of his faith and most dependable. In the privacy of her office they discussed Father's proposal and reached agreement regarding the assistance she would provide. With this in place he hurried off, as quickly as he had come, to lay open his mission.

Jack Straw, a most gentlemanly horse, stood quiet while Father fitted a bridle and saddle. With hardly a pull to the reins he followed to a railed fence where Father, with his short legs and rotund middle, made use of the rail to mount.

At a walk then a jog Jack Straw and Father Patrick O'Gorman headed from the town, leaving behind the houses and their people. Into the bushland they ventured, with each furlong, each mile, bringing them nearer to the police camp that lay six miles upstream on the Endeavour River. Good fortune accompanied them all the way, even to finding the gate of the police paddock wide open. A meandering track, no more than a buggy in width, marked the way to the camp. Thickets of tea-tree and wattle flanked the path. A flight of sulphur-crested cockatoos lifted from a tree, screeched their way skywards and winged to the south. Two grey kangaroos bounded from a patch of thick grass, hopped across the road and startled both Father and Jack Straw. This was Father's first visit to the police camp. Never before had he travelled this track, such a long distance for a man in his state of health. He estimated that the camp must be near and, once again, retraced what he knew of Michael O'Reilly. The detail, at best, was incomplete. That Michael was a competent shoeing-smith and that he had arrived from Sydney some two years earlier was readily known, but apart from this his past was a mystery.

Even Abbey had admitted to having a vague and far from complete knowledge of Michael's pre-Cooktown era. 'He just won't speak of it,' Father recalled Abbey saying. Abbey also confided that it was certain that, whatever his history, it undoubtedly had been unhappy. 'I see the pain in his expression when I surprise him alone. He's forlorn and broods but is reluctant to admit so. It's as though he's anonymous—no mail, no family, no hint of earlier years. He's severed himself from his past but, hopefully, for Juliette's sake, he will one day tell his story. All we can do is be patient.'

Father dismissed doubt that questioned his judgement. After all, for all he knew, Michael may have always been a man of honour. Who was he to judge? Peter Britfield, too, avoided making comment about his brother-in-law. Not even in his diary had he made reference to Michael, no note celebrating his marriage to Abbey, no inkling in his daily entries that here dwelt with them a living man. In fact, nowhere was there any mention of a 'Michael O'Reilly' or a 'Michael'. These omissions, which should properly form part of a diarised record, prompted the question: why the secrecy? The marriage was on public record. The couple lived as husband and wife. They had between them progeny by the name of Juliette O'Reilly. They all live together in the same home. Why then did not Peter Britfield, inspector of police, acknowledge these salient aspects of family life? A curious shroud had been in the making. Peter Britfield, for some personal reason, had been shielding those of his household. While Father O'Gorman had no direct knowledge of the diary he had, on various occasions, noted reluctance on Peter's part to speak about family.

Father's thoughts were suddenly interrupted when, around a sharp turn, the camp came into view. Jack Straw quickened his pace at the sight of the camp horses. Beyond the cleared area at the foreground, buildings, clearly segregated into two groups, evidenced the racial nature of colonialism. Near the heavily wooded river frontage stood the dome-shaped gunyas of the native troopers. These small, flimsy humpies were made from saplings, palm leaves and strips of bark. Each could hold two people and to enter they had to crouch. All of life's living, apart from sleeping, was conducted outside on common ground. In contrast the European officers, varying in number from fifteen to twenty-five, were housed in more substantial buildings and distanced further from the river and its mosquitoes. Unlike the native gunyas the white men's quarters with high, bark walls and tin roofs provided waterproofing and ventilation and allowed for freedom of movement. They lived four to a hut, enjoying indoor living and the company of lantern light by night. Beside the officer's clustered fortifications lay the stores and kitchen facilities and beyond this, and further again from the river, another track led to the saddlery shed. Another building set farther on but well within carbine range did not conceal its purpose. The lock-up, secondary to the one in Cooktown, was divided into six cramped cells. Its stark presence stood as a humbling reminder of the harsh administration of frontier justice.

More pleasing to the eye were the horse yards and smithy shop situated across the way near the road's end.

The horse yards were busy. Thirty or so of the one hundred and ten remounts recently bought from Lyndhurst cattle station were being introduced to the bit and police service. Leathery horse-breakers with buckled hats and goose-necked spurs roped and saddled the wily youngsters. Their curses, loud and blasphemous, rose above the general commotion, reminding Father that little had been learned and much remained to be taught before the Lord would be satisfied. Fortunately Father, who wore no distinguishing garb, did not hear when one lanky stockman by the name of Shotgun asked his bushman mate, 'Who's that podgy old codger that's come visitin'?'

Father dismounted and tied Jack Straw to a tree. He felt empowered by his belief in God and with this confidence he invited himself into the smithy shop where Michael was forging a set of horseshoes. He waited patiently while Michael shaped the shoes then, as a courtesy to the others present, he asked Michael aside. They moved to the shade of a tree and there Father expressed his concern for Abbey. He found Michael sympathetic and willing to listen.

'She was in a terrible state yesterday, just dreadful. She is beyond making any promises to herself; determination is beyond her reach.' Father continued, 'I first noticed it weeks ago, before Peter went to the Palmer. One week she was fine, the next I found her in near desperate circumstance. Knowing a little of the problems women experience I waited, thinking that, whatever the ailment, it would pass. I waited the first week, then the next and the next ...

'Sorrow, Michael, lasting sorrow is brought about by unresolved grief or remorse. It's different from mood swings brought about by, if I can put it this way, by nature. While those are commonplace and upsetting enough they are nothing compared with the lasting agony of an upset that strikes at the very heart. I know. I've experienced it and I can tell you, it's frightening. You yourself, I would guess, have felt the same. Honestly, when we were first introduced, just before your marriage, it was the hardship in your eyes that won my pity.

'And, being frank once again, the eyes are a storybook painted with telling pictures and each day, each hour, each minute and moment it's opened at a different leaf. Sometimes there's the child and other times there is the bold, the frivolous, the stern, the compassionate, the thinker, the adventurer; and then there is the sorry one, woeful and stricken.

'Michael, we must help Abbey; you and I and Peter must stay by her side, devote as much time and attention as possible, try to figure the cause and banish it from her mind. If we don't, then I'm afraid—' Father was interrupted by a sudden twitching of his right hand. He clasped it with the other to steady the shakes. 'She's a fine girl, a fine mother and I'm sure a fine wife. She's devoted to Juliette and it's occurred to me that possibly there lies the problem. Remember when you and she were first married, Abbey was always bubbling with vitality and enthusiasm, always helping—president of the Ladies' Guild and all that. She's let things slip, till now all she does is sit and at best read. Michael, Abbey's a strong girl both in body and mind but something sinister has possessed her. Will you help?'

Michael, tall, lean, raw boned and scarred from a life of labour was slow to reply. His reserved nature had him speak in general terms till detail of a specific incident focused his attention.

'Last Sunday, my day off, was the worst I've had. I decided to spend the day with Abbey, doing whatever might please her. She stirred a little after first light and I put my arm across to cuddle her; nothing out of the ordinary, just my arm lightly about her. At first she didn't mind but soon she squirmed about, took my arm and put it back on my side of the bed. It's hard to know what to do so I leant over and whispered that I loved her and that everything would be all right. It seemed to spike her. She pulled the bed covers over her head like she was trying to hide from something then began crying. She cried and cried. I heard Peter on the verandah and I'm sure he overheard. He must have been wondering what was going on. In frustration I sat up and told her we must talk. She ignored me, crying away and dragging the sheets closer. I sat there for a while, then, in desperation, I made each of us a cup of tea and tried again. I brought the tea in and sat on her side of the bed and talked on about nothing in particular. She just lay there not saying a word till I put my hand on her shoulder. It seemed to act like a trigger. She told me to go away. I asked why and this, I now realise, is the worst thing I could have said. She pulled the sheets from her face and looked at me with a blank stare. I'll never forget the look. It was frightening. She was a different person—not Abbey. I tried to talk again and she became almost hysterical saying, "Leave me. Leave me alone. Just leave me alone!" I should have taken no notice but I couldn't handle it. I dressed and went over to the horse stalls.'

As to what happened between then and later that morning Michael gave only a brief description, saying that Peter left for the police station soon after breakfast and that Abbey didn't leave her bedroom till nearly midday. He then resumed in detail.

'Father, I'd been sick in the stomach all morning, worrying and trying to think what to do for the best, then Madeline came to me and said Abbey had gone. We both hunted about and before long I found her sitting in the gazebo. I went over, thinking that being near her might bring her around. I picked a flower as I went but when I stepped to the decking the look on her face sent me cold. I stood by the railing just watching her, not knowing what to do. She sat upright and stiff with a book of verse in her lap. She didn't move. It was as though she didn't know I was there. She just kept staring into the hedge as though lost in another world. Father, you've no idea how I felt while watching her. It seemed that everything of our marriage was gone. I waited for a minute or two but I couldn't stand it anymore. I went up to her with the idea of putting a hand on her, to let her know I cared, but when I went to touch her she turned the other way. My hand froze where it was without touching. It's the worst I've ever felt. I think it was being so near yet so far that was so upsetting. I stayed there for a minute, wanting to scoop her up and hug her so tight but I couldn't. I don't know why but I just couldn't. All I could do was put the flower in her lap and leave.'

All the anxiety which Michael had been holding back was now freed. He told more, relating another two instances of Abbey's estrangement, both of which were equally sad and compelling. Father then added more of his assessment.

'We must spend more time with her, all of us,' he explained. 'And poor Madeline, bless her, most of the burden is on her shoulders and how—little more than a lass she is—how she copes is a wonder. My suggestion is that, with Peter's approval, we hire you an assistant; somebody familiar with smithy work and shoeing; preferably a keen lad looking for the prospect of an eventual trade. If we get the right lad you could, well, straight away cut your week from six to five days and then further as the lad gets a grasp of the work.

'I know there's the matter of earning an income but Michael, if I can take the liberty, the Britfields are very wealthy, apart from any salary or benefits Peter may gain as inspector. I'm positive they'd welcome your spending more time at home. Peter's a generous man and, most of all, Abbey needs you. She needs you, Michael, and now; not some time in the future but right now at this very moment. There's no stigma to working less than a full six days. Even riding to and from work, leaving at dawn and arriving home after dark is exhausting, without work in between. My belief is that family involvement should be given at least as much time if not more than that given to earning a living. The family is as important as bread on the table. There's no point having one and not the other.

'I've checked about. There's a young couple working at the Cavalier Hotel. They hope to marry soon and it would be good if the lad could get a trade. He's a reserved lad but one I'd put my faith in. As it is he shoes guests horses and apparently most satisfactorily. He presently works as yardman at the hotel but his employer, Prudence Swanson, the proprietor, says that she could comfortably let him work elsewhere two, maybe three days a week. She has another young chap, a kind of understudy, who she says will happily fill any gap. I haven't yet mentioned it to the lad but Prudence is sure he will be excited at the prospect. If you agree then all I have to do is confirm the arrangement with the lad and get Peter's approval and, once done, he could begin immediately.'

Father's careful presentation allowed Michael to accept the proposal without loss of dignity. Both elements, being a worthy worker and a caring husband and father, were preserved.

They discussed the matter in detail and Michael settled on a four day working week. They confirmed the meeting with a handshake.

Jack Straw lengthened his pace on the journey homeward but was disappointed when reined in at the Cavalier Hotel. Prue and Laura had waited all morning for Father's arrival. Father told them of the success, adding that all was well and that he would get Peter Britfield's approval the following morning, and for Barney to go ahead and present himself for the interview. Later that evening, in the intimacy of Laura's bedroom, she introduced Barney to the idea. He hesitated, saying that it was a long way to travel on foot each day but when Laura suggested the police might loan him a horse he agreed.

CHAPTER 36

As Barney walked to the police camp the next day he felt uneasy. He was anxious about the commitment that lay ahead and the responsibility awaiting him back at the hotel. Also, what of the implications of his being employed by the police force? Would this compromise the safety of his father? And another consideration, one Laura had referred to last night, a passing reference to the Britfields, burdened him further. He stopped at the gateway into the horse paddock and procrastinated, trying to sort these nagging thoughts. He mulled over the situation for a few minutes then decided he would proceed and view the camp from the safety of the forest before making a final decision. Before long he sighted the camp and its activity.

Two natives crossed the open space from the river carrying a pole laden with fresh fish. A third man in their company carried a bundle of spears. The attention of a group of fellow natives standing by a gunya was drawn by the catch. A few others, whom Barney could barely see, sat by a smouldering fire. Closer to hand, horse breakers were busy in the yards, roping wild horses, stirring dust and shouting. In another yard a mob of seasoned pack horses and saddle horses milled restlessly. Several pack saddles lined a railing beside the saddlery shed—probably in readiness for a patrol to depart later in the day. A troop of white officers sat at bush tables beneath a large tent fly, drinking tea. A grove of wattle trees hid most of what was happening at the smithy shop making it necessary for Barney to flank to the left to see clearly. The pole structure, with a tin roof and no walls, made for a breezy workshop. A native stood pumping the bellows while the smithy and a native forged hot steel. Barney, hidden by shrubbery, moved to within one hundred and fifty yards of the smithy shop. Here he knelt and watched. His focus settled upon the smithy; there was something distinctively familiar about his movements, but what specifically Barney was unsure. Was it Barney's love of the anvil and forge and hot steel, the characteristic setting? Maybe the association was wider, encompassing the whole camp with the smithy's function being central to the troop's operation?

No, he thought, *it's the smithy himself.*

He looked closer, gauging the smithy's stature and manner.

Somewhere, somewhere ... He paused again to study the smithy's stride to the furnace. The light of the forge fire flared with the pumps to the bellows, casting a brilliant show of light, but one confined to the furnace and not lighting the smithy's profile. This intense curiosity waived, at least for the moment, the purpose of his visit.

'Something, something, something,' he repeated aloud while watching the steel being heated then shaped. It was not until the smithy had completed his task and stepped outside to douse the hot steel in a trough of water that the unequivocal truth was revealed. Barney was stunned. He saw again when the steam dispersed and the smithy rose upright from the trough. Tom Simpson examining the work he had just forged!

Save me! Save me! thought Barney, grappling with near hysteria. He was stupefied. What he saw could not be true. Never could he have conceived such a situation. But the visual declaration was before him; he was seeing for himself.

By God. Can it be? The last two years, the not knowing.

Barney's search for his father had come to an abrupt conclusion. What now, what next, he knew not. Strange complexities, considerations never before imagined, began to draw his attention. *The—* He could not think.

One of the native assistants joined Tom and held the shoe while Tom wiped his brow. As always Tom carried a sweat rag in his rear pocket and as always rubbed his face to the right then the left and then mopped the nape of his neck.

Of all that had been or could ever be Barney was sure nothing could be more astounding than this. He stumbled for thought. *So, so close to everybody; to the troopers, the townspeople and—*

He recalled Laura's reference to the Britfields and realised. *Abbey. He's married to Abbey O'Reilly. How then ... Yes, it must be a false name!*

Barney's limited worldliness hampered his capacity to cope. Life's experience had provided him with few resources to draw on in times of crisis. The ability to make considered decisions in times of stress was beyond him. Instead, he habitually bumbled through without identifying causes or formulating solutions, often adding more to his baggage of dispiriting experiences. Barney struggled within these constraints. His dire necessity to be reunited with his father demanded he declare himself, but dread of the consequences compelled him to remain fixed.

The realisation about his father and the implications of his own association with Abbey O'Reilly were almost too much to comprehend. Also, what of Juliette, his half-sister? The existence of a sister, an only sibling, created more confusion.

Barney watched with a rigid gaze as Tom Simpson, alias Michael O'Reilly, sat on the trough and rolled a cigarette. Barney followed every turn of that well-known ritual, even to the way in which the match was flicked aside. The native at the bellows took up a halter and walked to the horse yards to catch another horse. Tom's other assistant returned to the shade of the shed. Tom stayed by the water trough and after a while lit another smoke.

Should I or should I not make myself known? If so, when and where? If I were to make contact what would happen? Is father content with his new life, and if so would exposure cause him harm? Could the secret be kept or would others eventually realise? If I marry Laura and stay in Cooktown and our baby is born, what then?

Suddenly, a loud barking from over near the horse yards jolted these imponderable thoughts. Barney turned and saw a big, brown dog poised and looking in his direction. Its rabid barking challenged the wind, piercing to every corner of the camp. Barney panicked. He crouched down and crawled back through the shrubbery. When at a safe distance he stood up behind a bushy tree. The dog had ventured no closer but Barney was not going to take a chance. He risked a final glance towards the smithy shop. Tom was standing, gazing directly Barney's way but unable to see him. After a wistful pause of farewell Barney left, cutting cross-country to avoid detection. The dog's barks followed him deep into the forest, fading more the further he went, till eventually the threat was left far behind.

CHAPTER 37

Father O'Gorman did as he said he would. He called at the Cavalier Hotel at mid morning to confirm Barney's intention and was pleased to learn that Barney had already left for the police camp. Father was most jolly whilst taking tea with Prudence and Laura then, presuming that Peter Britfield would approve, he went to the police station to tell Peter of his plan. He had arranged to return to the Cavalier to brief the girls of Peter's response and to lunch with them.

Thomas Storm, the police secretary and a man well practised in protocol, made good Father's request for a meeting with the inspector. He admitted Father with courtesy then closed the door leaving Father and Peter in private. No pretentious greeting was necessary. Father was family, even down to drying the dinner dishes, cradling Juliette to sleep and sitting on the verandah with Peter of an evening enjoying a chat and a malt whiskey. If anything of criticism could be said of Father it was his gregarious appetite for conversation. Sometimes he followed Abbey about the house and, in perfect harmony, related stories, some new, some old and some for the third time. Madeline, too, found that the simplest of tasks took longer to perform when Father assisted. It was his way, happy with the small blessings of life, finding interest in everything from English china to the small potted violet that graced the kitchen sill.

On entering Peter's office Father immediately became absorbed in Peter's interest at hand.

'What's this?' he queried, stepping around the desk to Peter's side to view the large map of Cape York Peninsula spread across the desk. Peter held a set of dividers in his hand which he used to mark off scaled distances.

'I'm trying to plot a new track to Normanton,' he said while tracing a finger along a pencil line that marked a course from Cooktown to the port of Normanton in the Gulf of Carpentaria. 'Since the fever wiped out Burketown, focus has been on Normanton. It's essential to the development of the gulf that adequate docking facilities be maintained in that area. James Mulligan's pressing this view and wants a better overland route across the peninsula.'

'What about the government surveyor?' asked Father.

'Alf Starcke may be a good surveyor but the government's too lame to move on this one. James wants to muster support for a private expedition. There are pastoralists who are prepared to provide backing and at least one mining company has expressed interest.'

Peter and Father both leant over the crude but best available map of the peninsula. Geographic detail was sparse and not necessarily to scale. Mountain ranges and many rivers were absent as exploration and mapping to date had been incomplete. Many thousands of square miles still remained unsighted by white men. The project was most ambitious and one which, if successful, would elevate both James and Peter to public recognition.

Peter's interests were diverse, another being his fascination for hoarding collectibles. All about his office lay unusual pieces, some so old as to be relics and others more contemporary. It looked more like a private museum than the office of the inspector of police. Items used in mining were the most numerous: pans, shovel heads, doleys, acid bottles, porcelain crucibles, to name but a few. In the corner to the left of the window a collection of skulls and other skeletal remains of native fauna gathered dust in the wake of the much popularised Darwinian hypothesis of evolution. High on the wall behind his desk was mounted a valuable array of firearms, everything from old muskets and pistols to the modern weaponry of rifles and revolvers.

Although Peter harboured a private dislike of the Chinese he displayed many artefacts from their culture: pots, pans, jars, coins heaped in eating bowls, chopsticks, banners, incense and even a bundle of fire-crackers still in their wrapping. Beside the door stood a bundle of Aboriginal spears, a woomera and a waddy. Most of all, and to Peter's expressed pride, was his collection of gold specimens displayed behind the glass front of a secure cabinet.

Peter also had the ability to infect others with his enthusiasm and before long Father was engrossed in the Cooktown to Normanton challenge to the exclusion of his own request. The talk of expedition inevitably led to talk of gold which prompted Peter to show a recent acquisition. He took from the specimen cabinet a striking sample of quartz gold. He handed to Father a lump of white quartz that was the size of a man's fist and which was impregnated with lava of molten gold. Its profound beauty, the lace-like intricacy of the pure gold set in the unblemished mass of quartz, impressed Father immensely.

'Where did you get it?' he asked softly, holding it closer to the light.

'From Christie Palmerston.'

'Palmerston,' murmured Father still mesmerised.

'Yes. He sent it with a note saying it was payment for three horses.'

Father, not being a man of business, was confused by the deal. He looked to Peter for further explanation.

'He borrowed three police horses weeks ago and apparently they have either perished or he's taken a liking to them. It's typical Palmerston. He has a propensity to covet things. He has difficulty differentiating between possession and ownership: he thinks one is synonymous with the other. That's what landed him in jail in the first instance. It's not an uncommon personality trait, quite prevalent really. In Christie's instance he's a dark horse about his past but there are always tell-tale signs. This is one of his.'

When Peter returned the gold sample to the locker Father introduced the subject of Abbey.

'I've come about Abbey,' he opened. 'I visited the day before yesterday and found her in a dreadful state. She seems ...'

Peter took his seat as was customary when he had something of importance to discuss. He motioned for Father to take the chair opposite. Peter stroked his bottom lip with a forefinger while Father related fully the details of his recent visits. Much that Father said brought nods of agreement from Peter. Even when Father told that he had implemented an, as yet, undisclosed plan to assist, Peter nodded tentative approval. Father was inclined to ramble when dealing with delicate matters. He spoke at length of the necessity for the family to be patient yet positive in helping Abbey through the crisis. He then elaborated his plan whereby he was arranging for an assistant to relieve Michael at the camp for up to two days a week and hence allow him more time to devote to Abbey and Juliette. Father's ongoing address of the situation was timely and pertinent, reminding Peter of the crucial, but oft overlooked, importance of family involvement. All of this was received well by Peter until Father innocently said, 'The lad I've spoken to is a Barney Simpson, the help at the Cavalier Hotel. He's out seeing Michael now.'

Without warning the foundation of Father's initiative crumbled. Father O'Gorman, the theologian, the man of human affairs, watched incredulously as he witnessed the transformation of Peter Britfield, the inspector of police. Something perilous had been uttered or alluded to in the words just spoken. Peter's face was smitten by the grave tidings. Life withdrew, leaving a man of marble: pale, cold and immobile.

'Peter! Peter!' urged Father in confusion. 'What have I said? What is wrong?' Father, thinking it may be the onset of a fit, reached across the table and shook Peter's clammy forearms. 'Are you sick? Tell me. I'll get the secretary!'

'No ... No,' Peter muttered through quivering lips. 'Wait. Just wait. Wait.'

'But—'

'No. Just wait. Give me a moment. I'll explain.'

Father sat back and clasped his now trembling hands on the desk. It took some moments for Peter to regain a semblance of order. He looked a wretched sight when he eventually began to explain.

'Father,' he said with a laboured tone, 'Michael O'Reilly is not Michael O'Reilly. He is Tom Simpson, the father of Barney Simpson. And he's wanted for murdering a policeman.'

Father gasped, 'Forgive me,' then retreated back into silence. He was overwhelmed. He stared blankly at the table top. Many seconds of absolute silence passed as he struggled to understand. He then sought excuses, casting about for anything that would support disbelief.

'It's not true,' he stated stubbornly without lifting his gaze.

Peter remained silent.

'It's not true,' repeated Father. He then raised his head and confronted Peter with moist eyes. 'Do you have proof?' A few seconds later he added, 'You don't, do you?'

Peter drew himself into a more upright position, trying to regain composure. His speech was still limp.

'Yes, Father, I have proof.'

'Where, what?' Father retorted more loudly, still refusing to believe.

'Father, and I say this respectfully, let me explain if you will. You'll recall how Michael first came to us. He first worked for Claude Henge, shoeing the garrison horses. Then there was the business of Abbey's pregnancy and her subsequent marriage to Michael. Now, at the time of the marriage I had no knowledge, not even an inkling that he was the said Tom Simpson masquerading under the alias of Michael O'Reilly. It wasn't until soon after Juliette's birth that I discovered the truth. The murder he's alleged to have committed was two years past by that time and, in accordance with normal procedure, I had received correspondence detailing all that was known of the fugitive. I add that there's a four-hundred-pound reward on his head.'

Peter collected his thoughts and now related fluently, 'As with all such reports they were received and filed under the appropriate name. It was an unassuming file, one that didn't draw attention. I never suspected until I saw an identifying mark. The file described a Maltese cross tattooed on the suspect's right upper arm.'

Father interjected, 'That's not necessarily proof!'

'Yes, Father, but it also had the name "Bess" tattooed beneath it.'

'Who's Bess?'

'She's Michael's former wife.'

'But!'

'I know, Father, I've agonised over the same thing.' He returned to the evidence. 'The tattoo has significance in that the cross was originally the emblem of Medieval Knights who assisted pilgrims and others on the island of Malta and elsewhere in the Mediterranean. It's carried on to the present as a symbol of valiant service. Now, the implication is this: even though Bess was irresponsible and promiscuous they said the ethic surrounding the cross typified Michael's attitude towards her. So much so that the New South Wales police were sure he would return and kept, and probably still do keep, her house under periodic surveillance.'

Father gradually accepted the reality of the debacle. He eventually nodded and sympathised with Peter. 'You must have been shocked at the discovery.'

'Very much so, Father. Michael never gets about without a shirt on and always with long sleeves rolled only to the elbow. I was passing his bedroom door one morning and spotted it.'

'Are you sure?'

'Yes. I made a point of seeing it again. And apart from that his whole profile, physical, occupational and social, fits the description. Another thing I noticed was his familiarity with police regulation concerning the keep and care of horses.'

'What's Abbey say about the tattoo?'

'Don't know. He's probably given her some story.'

'And the file. Is it hidden?'

Peter now took a firm grip of the situation. 'Father, in my business, if you don't like the evidence you burn it!'

'But it's not that simple, Peter. What will Michael do? Barney? And what about Abbey? Oh what a mess I've created!'

'No, Father. There's still time if we use our wits. I know Michael and I've met young Simpson. They're both street smart. This at least gives us a chance!'

The potential devastation to the Britfield name was incalculable. Vestiges of the scandal surrounding Abbey's marriage still lingered. How could their name possibly survive an onslaught of this magnitude? Peter still carried the standard of his old regiment in his heart and conduct. Every day he toiled to maintain position, to elevate status, to enhance his image and that of the Britfield family. How now could he cope with such a despairing revelation, an undoing that could leave the Britfields bare and vulnerable? The secret must, at any cost, be contained—the truth cloistered, discredited, denied—whatever it might take to protect the Britfields' standing. Peter rose aggressively then grabbed his revolver and cartridge belt from the top of the cabinet. He spoke quickly as he buckled it about his waist.

'You go to Prudence. Tell her that Barney may come home upset. If he does she is to try and appease him but not mention anything. You can tell her of his upset in broad terms but not a mention of his father. I'll head to the camp to see Michael. I'll see you later. I must be off.'

'But ...' Father's words were lost to the wind.

Father left the police station and went directly to the Cavalier Hotel. Prue and Laura were seated at a table in the far corner of the dining room discussing Laura's future when Laura spied Father coming through the carriage gateway. She pointed and said, 'Father's coming.'

Prue turned and saw him approaching with a faltering gait. 'He's not well,' she replied as she rose from her chair.

Together they hurried to the back door, took Father by an arm each and helped seat him at the table. Laura fetched a glass of water while Prue comforted him. He was very nervous and unable to speak till he drank the water. He then opened with, 'Please forgive me. I don't know where to begin. So much has happened. So much has been told to me by Peter.' He continued in a trembling voice. 'Peter's gone to speak with Michael. I have caused trouble, much trouble, more than I am at liberty to say. Laura,' and he leant her way, 'I feel most for you. Whatever becomes of all this remember ...'

Prue let him finish then spoke, 'Father, please don't be critical of yourself. I don't think it will help at this time. Tell us what Peter had to say. You know that confidentiality is assured. Whatever it is must be resolved and if not here then I will have to speak with Peter myself.'

At hearing her assertion Father grimaced and clasped his hands tightly.

'We will come to know, either way,' pressed Prue. 'Peter, I'm sure, will understand.'

'It's that everything is a mess,' said Father, agreeing to confide. 'All I can do is to tell you as it was told to me. If it had come from anybody except Peter it would be unbelievable.

'When I visited Peter's office less than two hours ago I suspected nothing. I thought Barney was ... But Peter knows more. He's known all along about Barney and the reason for his coming to Cooktown.' Father hesitated then continued, 'Barney's father is in Cooktown!'

Prue and Laura were spellbound as Father gave a full account of what he knew. When finished he looked at each of them, seeking approval. Prue broke the girls' silence by saying, 'Father, you were not to know of the link between Barney and his father and it could be beneficial that we now know. Somebody else has been enquiring,' and she glanced at Laura to remind her of Hicksbury's visit to the hotel.

Prue told of Hicksbury's visit then raised the issues she thought were most pressing. Father and Laura also gave their views and after a lengthy session they decided to wait till they knew the outcome of Peter's meeting with Michael.

During their discussion Laura had kept watch through the kitchen window but, as yet, Barney had not returned. Father was appreciative of Prue's offer to call a horse cab but he preferred to walk the distance to the church.

Peter's meeting with Michael uncovered no evidence that Michael had made contact with Barney. Following the meeting he made a hasty return to town and now rapped the brass knocker of Father's door.

Father heaved himself from his chair, took a deep breath then answered. Peter entered hurriedly, declined to be seated and reported, 'The implications of this are horrific. If that lad discloses his find then it will be the finish of us. I will be imprisoned for aiding and abetting and Michael will go to the gallows.'

Father listened intently then told of his meeting with Prudence and Laura. He followed with a very personal concern. 'Peter, I have officiated at a bigamous marriage. I should have been more careful. I should have checked first. And think further, Peter, of what else is implied. It makes Juliette an illegitimate child!'

Peter ignored his comment. He rose abruptly and stated loudly, 'We can't just let him wander the streets! It's all very well for you people to be considering Simpson, but there's more to it than that!' Unknown to Father, Peter was referring to his sighting of Abbey and Barney near the garden gate and Abbey's subsequent note in his diary, intimating she was pregnant.

He continued, 'The lad must leave Cooktown. That's a must. To continue here would be intolerable. Whether he takes the hotel girl or not is incidental. If need be I, personally, will see to it that he is shipped out. There's no compromise on that point: go he shall, back to Sydney if need be! Father,' and his voice sank to a growl, 'for the family's sake I'm prepared to protect Michael but as for the lad it would be a blessing if he drowned at sea.'

Father made a hasty rebuff. 'No, Peter, you are wrong. We all have failings, particularly the young. I've come to know the lad. He's all right and deserving of a chance. Please leave it with me. I'll visit Prudence again this afternoon and pass on your concern.'

If it were anybody else Peter would not have given them a farthing of a hearing but Father was not to be counted among other men. To Peter he was family. Before departing Peter gave Father an undertaking that he would give him time. He had twenty-four hours to have Barney Simpson aboard ship!

<h1 style="text-align:center">CHAPTER 38</h1>

Barney's discovery of his father reduced his mind to a mire of confusion. If he made contact then Tom might go to the gallows; if he stayed silent then they might never be reunited. Either way a tremendous sacrifice would be made. He wandered the bushland, avoiding human habitation and traffic-ways, knowing not what he would say if someone challenged him. After many miles of trekking through forest he crossed a stretch of sand dune mulga that opened to the southern end of Quarantine Bay. The fresh salt air, driven by a favourable breeze, welcomed him and brought relief to his troubled thoughts. He kicked about along the sandy beach, tossed driftwood to the surging swell, found diversion by following the flight of gulls then skirted around the seaward side of Mount Cook to enter Finch Bay. Here he waded across Alligator Creek then rested in the shade of a sprawling mahogany tree.

As always, physical exertion helped restore calm to Barney's mind. The monotonous, rhythmic beat of his long walk tempered his mood, allowing him to think. When darkness fell he sat on a sand dune and watched the moon heave itself from the horizon. At about the stroke of eleven he left the solitude of nature and re-entered Cooktown via Walker Street.

Laura had waited on the hotel verandah for Barney to return and now seeing him enter through the tradesman's gate her excitement swelled. She watched as he walked to his quarters at the feed shed. Without delay Laura went to the kitchen, took Barney's supper from

231

the warm stove, crossed the courtyard to his room and there, by the night light, coaxed him to eat.

With hardly any exchange of words Laura snuggled in close, hugging Barney while he ate. When finished she laid him on the bunk and began caressing his body. Barney was surprised but responded, fondling her breasts. Soon, they lay together fully naked and when Laura lay on top of him he helped her position herself. Laura wanted him so badly that she was prepared to give all. She set a natural rhythm and spoiled Barney till he satisfied himself. They then lay side by side on the bunk and rested. A sudden movement by the baby prompted Barney to say, 'It's a colt. I can tell by the way it kicks!'

This provided Laura with an opportunity and she asked, 'Barney, when are we going to get married?'

Barney remained silent.

'Come on,' she insisted, 'you can't wait till the colt's at foot. That wouldn't be decent!'

'Who says?'

'Me, Barney. Laura, your wife to be. You know that.'

Barney thought for a moment then said, 'It's not that easy. The job I went for this morning didn't work out. It's too far from town.'

'Well, that's even better,' Laura countered. 'Remember the thirty pounds that Eli and James Mulligan put into the bank for me?'

'Yeah.'

'Well, I've added to that and now have £32 5s. Enough for us to get married and shift to Brisbane.'

'Why the sudden rush?' he asked curiously

'Promise me you'll marry me.'

'Who have you been talking to?'

'Promise me, Barney.'

'What's the game?'

'No game, Barney. You know and I know.'

'Know what?'

'That you came to Cooktown to find your father and that you found him today and—'

Barney's body tensed, snipping Laura's words, but she quickly recovered. 'Barney, I love you, you know that. What's happened doesn't matter. I want us to get married, tomorrow, and leave for Brisbane. I have an aunt there, my mother's sister. She has enough room for all of us. Please say yes.'

'Who else knows?' asked Barney quizzically.

'The secret's safe. There's only Father O'Gorman, Ma'am, Eli and me.' Laura omitted to mention Inspector Britfield and his demand that Barney leave.

'Who found out?'

'Ma'am and I. That Mr Hicksbury, the horrible man, he came here one day saying things and asking questions. Ma'am got riled and told him to scat.' Barney waited for further explanation. 'Well, he didn't know for sure, did he,' added Laura, 'otherwise he would have claimed the reward.'

'There's more, isn't there Laura?' said Barney slowly. 'You wouldn't have sent me for that job if you knew that father was there. Somebody's just told you, haven't they?'

'If I tell will you promise to marry me?'

'Maybe—'

'It's Inspector Britfield. He told Father this morning. Apparently your father is married to his sister!'

At hearing this Barney's pulse soared to a runaway rate. Laura felt its pounding, passing from his chest to her bare breasts. She was forced to tell more. 'The inspector also told Father that he wants you gone from Cooktown within a day!'

Barney slid aside, sat on the edge of the bunk and pulled a blanket across his thighs. Laura did likewise, sharing the blanket and laying her head on his shoulder.

Barney was again confused, not wanting to talk. Laura accepted this and sat quietly with him till the chill of the northern winter had them reach for their clothes. Soon after, they hugged and kissed to confirm that all was well. Laura then left, crossed the dewy lawn, wrote a note for Cherie telling that she would be late in the morning, doused the light and went to bed.

CHAPTER 39

Unknown to Laura, Eli was awake, lying on the bed covers in Prue's bedroom, when she passed along the verandah to her bedroom. Prue woke at first light, rolled over, kissed him on the cheek and then asked, 'What fresh thoughts have you about Barney and Laura?'

Eli turned her way and began, 'Well, I think it best if it's left to Barney to decide. If we all input ideas he could panic and make a wrong decision.'

'But he's only young,' countered Prue. 'You can't expect him to make a decision like that alone.'

'Why not?'

'Because all wise men were once young themselves'

'What do you mean by that?'

'That we all become wiser as we get older.'

'That's true.'

'Then,' said Prue, 'I think we should be involved. Talk it through with him and Laura. Laura's level headed.'

'You're presuming that Laura can influence him.'

'Eli, they need to be loved,' said Prue. 'It's all very well to talk about individuality and responsibility but they're only young ...'

It became apparent that they differed about how the situation should be handled, Eli treating them as adults while Prue believed they needed nurturing. They talked on till they heard Cherie arrive for work.

Cherie discovered and read Laura's note. Little escaped Cherie's seemingly quiet disposition; she was one to observe but not to say. She had pieced together snippets and surmised that trouble of some kind was brewing. Prue entered the kitchen soon after, read the note then quickly set to work.

Father O'Gorman arrived at the hotel at mid morning. Apparently he had overslept and apologised for his lateness. His unbrushed hair and side whiskers evidenced that he had not slept well. However, Prue's warm greeting and the offer of a cup of tea seemed to relieve some of his stress. Cherie conveniently excused herself to attend upstairs duties.

From Laura's note Prue presumed that Barney had found his way home late last night and, like Laura, was still asleep. Therefore there was no new information for her and Father to discuss, so they reweighed yesterday's events until Laura descended the staircase. Her loose-fitting smock, though somewhat unbecoming was, nevertheless, appropriate considering she was so heavy with child. She smiled cheerily, showing an acceptance of self which, given her quandary, some would find difficult to understand. Most important of all was her air of expectation. Even though she reported to Prue and Father that no decision had yet been reached she remained confident that a solution would be found. 'Barney has a lot to consider,' she explained.

Father soon raised the matter of Peter's ultimatum that Barney depart that day. He said, 'While I'd like Barney to stay I don't think Peter will listen. There's a lot at stake.'

Laura railed against the urgency of the threat. She told Father unequivocally, 'The inspector will have to wait.'

Father pushed back with, 'Barney can get in touch with his father later.'

'No, Father,' said Laura assertively. 'Barney doesn't trust the people here, particularly that inspector.'

'I understand Barney's concern,' added Prue. 'It's his father and he should be allowed to decide.' She leant towards Laura and added, 'I'll support whatever you and Barney decide.'

Laura expressed her gratitude. 'Thank you, Ma'am. That means a lot to me and Barney as well.'

Laura then outlined how she had suggested to Barney they go to Brisbane but he was noncommittal.

Barney peeped about the hessian drape screening his doorway and spied the trio through the dining room window. It hurt him to think they might be discussing him and his father. He was depressed. He wanted to remain reclusive. The only exception was his want of Laura. More than ever before he longed for her, not for any base gratification, but for something far greater: for the unquestionable support he knew she would provide. Only Laura could allay the fear which beset his mind, only she with her knowingness and patience could free him from the uncertainty that held him imprisoned. He became increasingly agitated, fidgeting and sweating. He paced the room, up and down and round and round, trying to suppress the urge that called for him to break free and race off into the bush. His dread that he would have to depart Cooktown, leaving his father and Laura and the babe, stifled his every attempt at making a decision. He was under siege, driven relentlessly by fear towards a state of panic. The walls of the shed were closing in, squeezing him. He paced faster and punched his fists into his palms, trying to deal with a mind almost bereft of reason.

Laura intuitively sensed that something was wrong with Barney. This inkling firmed as the meeting progressed till eventually she excused herself and went to his room. She pulled the doorway sash aside and found Barney in a desperate state. Barney, at seeing Laura, stopped pacing. He stood stark and still. Laura, without hesitation, moved close, wrapped her arms about him and hugged him dearly. Nothing was said, neither murmurs nor soft words. Laura gave of herself, sharing her nearness with Barney. She held him in her aura till his sensibility returned. Barney raised his head, looked into Laura's eyes and saw the longing reflected in her gaze. He bent his head, put his lips to hers and kissed her tenderly.

They did not join as they had the previous night. There was no need in the light of the present understanding. Before long they sat on the bedside and, while holding hands, began to deliberate all that had happened during the past twenty-four hours.

Laura and Barney pooled their lot, wholly and unconditionally. They were now spliced together as one, inseparable, regardless of fate. They talked through the dilemma, seeking a solution that would save his father as well as reunite them. Their main concern was what would be best for Barney's father. Would he want to go to Brisbane with them? Did he want to stay in Cooktown? What of his relationship to Abbey and his daughter? How safe was he if he stayed?

The young minds tussled with these questions till well past the sounding of the lunch-time gong. They eventually reached a decision: they would abide by the inspector's directive, provided a sound guarantee of Tom's safety was given. With this decision made, Laura gave Barney a strong hug, made him promise that he would prepare himself lunch, then set to deliver the news to Prudence and Father O'Gorman.

Laura met Prue in the main corridor leading to the pavement. Here, by the staircase and in surrounds of doubtful privacy, she told of the proposal she had for the inspector. Prue, less optimistic than Laura, hedged her opinion by saying that it would be difficult for Peter to provide a guarantee. Laura was dismissive of Prue's concern and said she would go and tell Father O'Gorman.

Father was quick to answer the door when he heard the knock. Laura was puffing from the uphill climb and Father offered her a seat.

'Father, it's almost set,' she opened, then proceeded to tell of the plan she and Barney had made. While Father agreed with the plan he expressed doubt that it would be acceptable to Peter. 'There's no guarantee he can give,' Father said three times during the meeting. However, he agreed to be courier and since it was late afternoon and Peter was out of the office he promised to visit him early next morning.

CHAPTER 40

Peter welcomed Father into his office with a wry smile. Father took the seat opposite Peter, outlined Barney's stance and told of the proposition. Peter's initial reaction was antagonistic. He cited the undertaking he had already given and saw no reason for further justification. Father, while agreeing with Peter, put the view that, irrespective of the adequacy of the guarantee already given, it was imperative to do whatever was necessary to satisfy Barney.

'Damn young Simpson!' blurted Peter, thumping the desk and shaking the crockery, venting his frustration in a manner that choked Father's enthusiasm. 'Why so much attention devoted to him!'

Father stayed quiet.

Peter rose to his feet with a flush of blood colouring his cheeks. 'Proof he wants,' he muttered to himself. Then, with renewed anger, he declared, 'I'll give him proof!' He then spoke with irony. 'His father is dead!'

'What? What are you saying, Peter? You yourself made the disclosure. You are the one who said Michael was Barney's father!'

'I know, I know,' admitted Peter, lowering his tone and giving way to defeat.

'Then?' asked Father curiously.

'Father, and I say this at my own peril, I have documentary evidence to verify the death.'

Father was changed. His curiosity deepened, tightening his brow. *How could this be, alive and dead at the one time?*

Peter raised a hand to halt Father's next question. He then stepped aside to a file cabinet where he rummaged and found a single-page document. Without hesitation he came to Father's side and placed the page squarely before him. Peter then moved to an open window to gain himself space.

Father's eyes were agog when he read:

CERTIFICATE OF DEATH

Name and occupation of
deceased}

Thomas Simpson, Farrier/
Prospector

Date and place of Death}

25/6/1877, Palmer River Gold
Field

Sex and Age}

Male, 44 years (approx.)

Cause of Death}

Accidental fall

Informant—name and
occupation}

Nugget Hayes, Venturer/
Prospector

When and Where Buried}

27/6/1877, Maytown, Queensland

Witness to the Burial}

Nugget Hayes, Venturer/
Prospector

Place and Date of Birth}

Sydney, Australia, date unknown

How long in Australian Colony/
Colonies}

Since birth

Religion}

Unknown

Place of Marriage and to Whom}

Sydney, Bess James

Children of the Marriage}

Barnabas Simpson

Registrar of Deaths, Maytown, Queensland
L.F. Kieff. 28/6/1877

Father was amazed rather than shocked as the realisation took hold. The death certificate was a sham, a falsification that, undoubtedly, had been contrived by Peter. Its purpose was also clear: with Tom Simpson officially deceased on paper the file would be destined for the archives and the manhunt would be no more.

Both men kept their distance until Father invited Peter to return from the window with the simple words, 'I understand.'

Peter sat again then explained how, only last month, he had arranged for the death of a little known miner to be substituted for that of Tom Simpson's. 'If the secret's kept, it will never be proved otherwise,' he said. 'This bloodless piece of paper guarantees Tom's freedom if confidentiality is kept.'

'And Barney?' asked Father.

Peter took the certificate between his fingers, folded it, then handed it back. 'Take this copy, Father. Talk to young Simpson and impress on him that his father's life depends upon the secret being kept. And of the girl, tell Simpson ...'

Father listened further as Peter, once again, cussed Barney and demanded his immediate departure. Father said little more and excused himself at the first opportunity.

He found Prudence in the accounts office of the hotel and was quick to hand her the death certificate. Prue read the contents carefully then turned Father's way. Mutual grins told of their approval.

'We must go and tell Laura,' said Prue feeling euphoric.

'Where is she?' asked Father.

'Resting in her room.'

Father was slightly hesitant at entering a young lady's bedroom but, once there, with Laura and Prue perched on the bedside and he standing before them, he found it as natural as sharing dinner around a dining table. Laura cried at being told the news, not sobs of dismay but clear tears of joy. 'It's providence,' she exclaimed, pressing the paper to her chest. 'The Lord has answered our prayers. Thank you, Lord,' and she led the way with the three bowing in prayer. Everything was perfect. Laura's patience, together with all her personal care and preparation, had come to fruition. Her exhilaration was shared by Prue and Father when, after praying, they instinctively held hands and danced a jig. Round and round they went till, suddenly, Laura struck upon a magnificent thought: 'Barney!' she cried, 'I must tell Barney!' and off she raced.

On telling Barney the last remnants of his estrangement were tossed aside. He clutched Laura, saluting her with kisses and hugs. When she was able Laura remarked, 'You'll never have to sleep in the feed shed again. You can stay with me tonight and we can sail tomorrow.' She added, 'I've already made a tentative booking on the *Fair Trader*. It sails at eleven in the morning.'

Laura was so excited that she then hurried off, as fast as her condition would allow, to tell Father of their decision and the sailing arrangements.

CHAPTER 41

Father O'Gorman rose at daybreak, washed and dressed hastily, then by the gathering light saddled Jack Straw. He rode to the Britfield's home, found Peter by the stables and told him of Barney's planned departure. He then expressed his primary concern which was Barney leaving without prior unification with his father. They discussed this together with other questions that might be raised if Michael's past was made known: Would Abbey's upset be inflamed further? Might Barney decide to stay in Cooktown? Could it be kept secret from the townspeople? As for Michael, who was already on his way to work at the police camp, would it be possible to persuade him to a reunion and, if so, did time permit before the *Fair Trader* sailed at eleven? Both men were encouraged by the prospect of a meeting and agreed when Father said, 'It would be best if we made a clean breast of it.' Having reached agreement Father mounted Jack Straw and trotted off towards the police camp.

Now that Michael's past would be revealed to Abbey it was imperative that Peter speak to her first. He also wanted to discuss her pregnancy but not divulge his knowledge of her affair with Barney Simpson. He once again recalled part of the diary entry: *I have sought the warmth of another. Only briefly but with lasting consequences. Please be accepting when the signs become apparent.*

After breakfast he went to her bedroom and was met with gloom. The drapes were closed, the reflection in the mirror dull and the bed linen crumpled and cold. Abbey sat alone at the duchesse and took no notice. To break the silence Peter crossed the room and opened the drapes at the French windows. A bolt of light shafted through, lighting his uniform, the carpet and the edge of the duchesse. A spill of softer light settled on Abbey's white night dress and the brush in her lap. The brightness roused Abbey and she lifted her head, acknowledging Peter's presence. He moved to her side and, unsure how he would be received, began by saying, 'Abbey, I have some important things to talk about.' Abbey shifted her gaze to the open windows.

'For too long we haven't been close to each other. Remember the old days when we built castles in the sand under the chestnut tree at Dunleigh? Jessie the old nurse maid who refereed our squabbles? She was such a righteous woman, always shaping things the best she could to make us happy. Such a wise old soul. I can remember her saying, 'Peter, of all the things in life, family is the most important.'

Abbey turned his way and looked at him, anticipating what he would say next.

Peter followed her cue and got to the point. 'It's about the entry you made in my diary,' he said quietly.

At hearing the words Abbey burst into tears and held her head in her hands. She then exclaimed, 'It's Barney Simpson, the lad from the Cavalier Hotel. He's the father of my baby! He's the father but doesn't know!' She almost shrieked the last words then lowered her head and hands to her lap in shame.

Peter moved close and placed his hands on her shoulders. 'Sis, Sis,' he said using an old term of endearment, one he had not spoken since leaving England, 'don't do this to yourself. Things will work out ...'

Abbey's sobbing gradually dwindled to a whimper, allowing her to hear.

To another call of 'Sis' she lifted her head and saw Peter's reflection in the mirror.

Peter then asked caringly, 'How do you know that it's young Simpson?'

Abbey steadied her gaze on Peter's reflection and replied, 'He's the only one. It can't be anyone else. Michael's not up to it and hasn't been since Juliette was born. Her arrival shocked him somehow and it's never been a full event since.'

Peter held Abbey's shoulders more firmly then asked, 'It's possible you could have conceived to Michael, isn't it?'

'Yes,' she stammered, 'but it's unlikely.'

'Nevertheless you agree that it's possible?'

'Yes.'

'Then it's best that we presume this to be the case and not make mention to anybody else.'

Abbey nodded in agreement and laid her head back against him.

Peter then, in exchange for Abbey's confession, disclosed a secret that was equally stunning. 'What would you say, Sis, if I told you that young Simpson was related to Michael?' Abbey remained mute with disbelief. 'I wasn't going to tell you but, given the situation, it's inevitable that you will find out.'

Peter hesitated till confident of his voice. He then told of Michael's true identity, his relationship to Barney, his misdeed, his means of hiding and the falsified death certificate. He also told of Barney's knowledge of the situation and named the others who knew. He then told of Barney's association with Laura and their plans for Brisbane. He finished by saying, 'Sis, you haven't been the only one at fault. We're all due for a reprimand one way or another.'

It was all so strange to Abbey, particularly that the others had also been holding secrets which, in their own way, were as excessive as her own. Best of all for Abbey was Peter's acceptance. After waiting momentarily he confirmed his care by taking the brush from her lap and brushing her hair while whispering words that were long overdue.

As Father jogged towards the police camp he passed a patrol heading the other way with pack horses in tow. Some gave him a knowing wave while others, not being acquainted, paid no particular attention to the old man wandering the track. At sighting the camp his mind switched to rehearsing how best to inform Michael of the news. Father hitched Jack Straw to the same tree as on the previous visit then walked towards the smithy shop. Michael almost pre-empted the importance of the visit when he met Father halfway and, with urgency in his voice, asked, 'What's the matter?'

Father smiled to allay his fear.

'It's early for you to visit,' added Michael still unconvinced for, since leaving Abbey earlier, an uneasiness had filled his thoughts; so much so that now at eight thirty the forge still lay cold. He had also given his native assistant leave to go fishing.

Father bypassed his usual rambling prelude. 'Michael, I have news that, at the least, will surprise you and may even upset you but news that, once sorted, will probably be the best you've ever heard!'

Michael remained mystified and anxious.

'Michael, it's with the blessing of the Lord's intervention that I've come to learn about your past and your son, Barney.' He quickly went on, 'Barney's in Cooktown!'

Michael was staggered. He thought the news would relate to Abbey's distress. Never had he imagined that Father would be the one to unveil his darkest secret.

Father rushed on, 'Don't worry, everything is under control. The authorities don't know anything of this. There's only a handful of us that know and it's held in the strictest confidence. Your past was first revealed when ...' Father outlined what he had been told of the murder charge, of Barney's arrival in Cooktown and the subsequent doings. 'Michael, the urgency is this: Barney's discovered your whereabouts. He was out here yesterday spying on you and—' Father was momentarily taken aback by the fright possessing Michael. 'And he's leaving this morning. He sails on the eleven o'clock tide and is taking his girl with him!'

'Why? Why leave so soon?' Michael managed to ask.

'It's at Peter's insistence. He has a grand plan that I can tell you about on the way to town. We'll have to hurry if we're to catch Barney before he sails!'

Michael tossed a saddle on his mount and girthed it quickly, ready to travel by the time Father had mounted Jack Straw. Jack Straw in his aged condition was unable to maintain more than a medium trot which, in a disguised way, was to the benefit. This pace allowed the men to talk as they went and provided enough time for Father to brief Michael with more detail. Michael was in a whirl, not knowing if everything of his escape had been undone or whether Father's plan would secure his future. Michael asked again of Peter's attitude, Abbey's probable reaction and, most importantly, Barney's wellbeing. At the Four Mile, that part of the road passing near the Templeman's residence, Father broached something most worrying. It would not wait. He must know before they arrived home. 'Michael,' he asked, puffing from the strain of riding, 'what of your marriage to Abbey, if you're still legally wed to Bess?'

Michael drew rein to steady his horse level with Father's but did not reply. The direct reference to Bess, Barney's mother, drew fresh pain to Michael's mind. In spite of all that Bess was, of all the whorishness in which she engaged, she still retained a place in his heart, a dear memory that three years of absence had not erased. He loved Abbey, yes, but always with Bess in her shadow. It was this conflict between a past and present love that held Michael's answer in abeyance.

A little further along the road Father prompted, 'I must know!'

Michael turned in his saddle, embraced Father with his gaze then explained, 'Father, I'm not guilty of bigamy. Bess and I were never married.'

Father was unable to hide his doubt. 'Is that true?'

'Yes, Father, it's the truth. And I add that if it had been my decision then we would have married and if I had my way we would still be together. I'm sorry, Father, but you asked and I'm telling you the truth.'

'What about when she knew she was expecting Barney?'

'Oh, that was even worse. She didn't want him. She's always thought of him as a burden. Bess had a dream that one day she would marry a man with money and position. That's all she's ever wanted.'

They spoke on, then digressed to talk about the reception they would receive from the Britfields, and upon approaching the house a whinny from Peter's stallion told that he was home.

The emotions of those involved intensified when Father and Michael stepped through the gateway, and more so as they walked the pathway to the steps where Peter was waiting. Father trailed behind Michael, allowing him to approach Peter on his own terms. No one was sure but the solemness on all their faces was lightened when Peter held forth a hand of friendship. Michael did likewise and they shook hands.

'Where's Abbey?' asked Michael anxiously when they broke the clasp.

'Inside.'

'Should I?'

Peter suggested otherwise, alluding to the necessity of their first having a talk. The nervousness which had claimed Michael upon being told all was still apparent: his cheeks pale, eyes anxious and posture rigid. Peter was in no way hostile. In fact, his greeting was marked by deep sincerity. Peter had finally reconciled himself with Michael; all of his past prejudices, those disapprovals and disappointments he had harboured, suddenly dissipated in the wake of this real crisis. Father joined the conversation but said little, allowing the other men to talk. There were no secrets. Each told the other, honestly and openly, the truth. There was a complete absence of animosity. No denials were made; not one recrimination was passed. Decency presided throughout. Every aspect but one was talked about. Peter was not asked nor did he divulge any mention of Barney's involvement with Abbey. Father noticed the ease which, after twenty minutes of talking, became apparent in Michael's manner. It was then that Michael excused himself and went to see Abbey.

Abbey was aware of their nearness. She had heard the horses whinnying and traces of their voices but chose to stay closeted in the bedroom. Suddenly, a lull in their conversation caused her to choke. It was now her turn. She was overcome with terror. *Never*, she thought, *will I survive this day!*

Michael found her, statue still, standing by the open windows, bathed in sunlight. Abbey was not sure what happened next. She recalled Michael coming to her and taking her tenderly into his arms. There were tears, that was certain. She remembered him sniffing. For how long they consoled one another she was unable to recall except that something of a serene bliss descended upon her. Whether it was spiritual care or simply relief she was unsure. When she opened her eyes to brave the outside world Michael's face was still beside hers with his greying hair cushioned against her cheek. The surrounds were the same, the soft carpet and full length curtains. Yet, amassed before Abbey was change. Her fear had gone. Her sense of being trapped was no more. No longer did she feel doomed. She realised that here, in her arms, was a loving and loyal man, a man with sufficient courage to stand by her side in this time of need. He was, truly, a man. What is more, this upset revealed the true nature of her love for Michael. Till now, through the muddle of emotions, she had never realized that her love for Michael was really that of a daughter for a father and not that of a wife for a husband. The revelation caused no dismay. On the contrary, the knowing hastened away any confusion, leaving her love in its pure form. This sudden self-discovery turned to tears. She hugged Michael dearly, kissing his wet cheeks and sobbing words of love.

For Michael, while the journey of his troubles was not yet at an end, he experienced the relief that comes from sharing. No longer did he have to suffer the deprivation of hiding from those dear and near.

They felt so secure in each other's arms that neither wished to let go. This embrace held them together for a few more minutes till Michael whispered, 'We better join the others. They'll be expecting us.'

Peter and Father felt relief when, as a unified couple, Abbey and Michael joined them on the verandah. While Father was overjoyed, he was equally concerned that time was running short if they were to meet with Barney before he sailed

CHAPTER 42

The coachman arrived at the Cavalier Hotel at ten o'clock. Barney and Laura left immediately for the wharf, holding hands and leaning against each other to the sway of the coach. Their high expectations excited their mood. Nothing seemed impossible. All things were within reach. All the dreams that had danced before Laura were coming to pass. Here, by her side, dressed in gentlemanly persuasion, was her man, charming and protective. Barney recalled the couple he had seen in the rickshaw on that first night ashore and felt proud that he now had his very own lassie by his side. Laura again squeezed Barney's hand then turned to press her lips to his. It mattered not who might spy them through the open coach windows. The shop fronts fell from sight, giving way to the esplanade and the adjoining walkway upon which Barney had first felt the spring of adventure on arrival at Cooktown. The tide, almost full and slightly awash, lapped the bank of the narrowing way to the dock. The horses halted of their own accord at the timber decking, whereupon the coachman alighted and helped Barney carry the weighty trunks to a nearby trolley. The *Fair Trader*, a clipper designed more for cargo than passenger travel, lay in wait, listing gently on the swell. Crewmen were busily securing the last of the cargo and attending the rigging. On being shown the tickets a steward whisked the loaded trolley up the gangway. Laura slipped her arms about Barney's waist and snuggled close. If the situation were any less real Laura might have been inclined to believe that all was just a fantasy. She tested the truth once again by bracing her lips against his. Bystanders worried them not. They were as free as the wind playing in their hair. The world was theirs. While they waited for the call to board Barney spoke of his dreams, spilling forth ideas that were decidedly ambitious. As he spoke he beheld Laura's moist lips and the caress of her gaze. It was all too joyous and he too wondered if life's experience could really be so kind. Laura understood the question asked by his look and confirmed it with another reassuring touch of her lips. She then said, 'Darling, it's true. You and I, off to make a start!' Barney responded by looking towards Mount Saunders on the north bank of the river. Laura let her interest follow Barney's to the mountain's steep slopes. Together they viewed the daring height, scaling in their minds the might of what could be, preparing themselves for the greatest adventure of their lives.

Prue had reflected while bathing and dressing, so much so that she was now running late. She was further delayed when she had to scramble to find a pair of sandals for Hornet. She bundled Hornet into the waiting coach, raised her hem to board then called to the driver to stop at Vanity Place to collect Cherie. Cherie boarded the moment the wheels stopped rolling then, with a word of haste to the driver, they drove to the wharf.

Hornet's attention drifted to a sailor who, high in the rigging of the *Fair Trader*, prepared to unfurl a sail. He jumped from the coach the moment it stopped, trotted ahead of Prue and Cherie, tripped on an uneven plank and cussed the sandals. Most of what was happening remained a mystery to Hornet. He had pieced together that Laura was somehow with child, that she and Barney were special friends and going away together; but apart from this he had no real concept of matrimony. He spoke to Laura and Barney till the others joined them. Their conversation centred on well wishes, writing letters and the like, until a brisk voice interrupted with the call, 'All aboard!' With that the sentiment that each held constrained was suddenly unleashed. Cherie put her arms about Laura and began to cry. Laura flushed then cried also. Their friendship, sealed over time, was paraded unashamedly amidst the tears and their words of endearment. Prue, though she tried, was unable to hide her affection. Her modesty fell aside when Laura turned her way. As a mother hugs a child, Prue clung to Laura, holding her hot cheek to Laura's for as long as discretion would allow. She then held Laura at arm's length to take one last look. Cherie, the girl who would be a wise choice in any man's mind, flung her arms about Barney in a kind of frolic then smacked a kiss squarely on his lips. Prue followed, but more modestly, pressing her lips tenderly to Barney's cheek. Her caring touch brought tears to his eyes. Hornet's greatest bewilderment was why Laura and Barney should decide to sail away at such short notice. He mustered enough courage to shake Barney's hand but his expression clearly showed the pain in his heart. He allowed Laura to squeeze him so tightly that he thought his ribs would crack. To these, their friends, Barney and Laura said a final goodbye then stepped to the gangway. Laura's dress, fitting and becoming, together with her matching shoes and hat, presented to the crew a lady of note.

No sooner were they at the hand rail of the clipper than Eli arrived, paying the cab driver handsomely with two florin pieces for pressing the horses so hard. He then ran along the wharf, bypassed those ashore with only a quick gesture, spoke smartly to the ticket steward, then boarded the ship. Both Laura and Barney were grateful for his arrival and devoted themselves to him while preparations were being made to cast off.

CHAPTER 43

Father's plan for a reunification with Barney before he departed had been frustrated by delays. He had risen early to allow time to visit Peter, ride to the police camp and return with Michael, speak further with Peter and maybe Abbey and, hopefully, they could all see Barney before he sailed. However, the twenty minute discussion with Peter and Michael had not been allowed for, then the time Michael spent with Abbey in the bedroom seemed forever. While he understood the importance of these meetings, he considered it imperative that Barney be included. Now, with them all assembled on the verandah and thirty minutes to sailing time Father decided to act. He stepped forward and said, 'Please, excuse. I must say, one and all, we really must hurry if we are to see Barney off?'

Peter quickly agreed.

'I will need to change,' observed Abbey hurrying away.

'Then hurry! Let's go!' exclaimed Peter, starting to his feet.

While Michael and Peter quickly gathered the carriage horses to harness, Abbey slipped into a day dress. Father opened the carriage gateway then continued counting the time. 'Sixteen minutes to go, fifteen minutes to go ...' When Abbey descended the steps on the ninth minute he shouted for her to hurry. The four greys, in pairs, baulked at the fluster, rearing and plunging, causing an annoying delay at the stables. Madeline, with Juliette in arms, watched from the verandah; little did she know the significance of the mission. The instant the last breeching strap was secured they all bustled aboard. Michael commanded the reins, flicking them sharply, tossing the steeds into an abrupt start. The team took fright, leaping forward and jolting the open carriage into motion. Father held his hat tightly upon his head. Abbey braced herself, clutching the railing with one hand while holding her stomach with the other. Peter knelt on the front carriage seat. With more flicks and a few sharp words the carriage sped through the gateway. Neither the horses nor Michael heeded the steep incline down the hill. Caution was lost in the gravel spraying from the flying hooves. Time was out. By Father's reckoning the last minute had just expired. The tug boat may well be taking the strain, hauling the *Fair Trader* to open water.

'Ha-chaa! Ha-chaa!' shouted Michael, fully aware of the finality of time. The carriage, bouncing and bucking, broadsided about the curves, sliding perilously close to the steep edge. Peter moved about, balancing the weight, trying to even the load to each wheel. They descended at a gallop, leaving behind a column of dust clearly seen from the town's centre.

'Ha-chaa! Ha-chaa ...' Michael continued shouting, eking everything he could from the team. Fresh clouds of dust floated with each turn of the wheels, billowing behind then ascending skywards. Froth turned to foam, showing against the dapples of the magnificent four. Sweat dribbled down their broad faces and heaving flanks. Shoulder to shoulder, head to tail and with manes afloat they flung their most into every stride.

The intersection at Charlotte Street was taken at a gallop, swinging to the right, drifting the carriage out to a precarious tilt. Fortunately, the horses lurched with the load to avoid capsizing. Michael could now see the pall of black smoke issuing from the stack of the steam tug under load. The *Fair Trader* was sailing! Michael became possessed. The street traffic moved aside, making way while witnessing his reckless driving. Of the purpose they knew nothing and no one was about to question the inspector. They galloped, fleeting by buildings and onlookers, racing to the wharf.

Crew members of the *Fair Trader* stood aloft in the rigging, lowering the furls from the yards, making ready for the sails to be sheeted to the wind. A group of passengers assembled at the stern could be seen waving goodbye.

The team pounded its way along the esplanade, bouncing echoes from the rocky hillside. At the immediate approach to the wharf the horses sensed danger and jibbed at the first plank. Michael rose to his feet, held the reins high then commanded the frightened horses forward with both word and touch. They listened, took one step, then another, breaking into a trot, clattering the carriage across the roughly hewn timbers till they halted at the wharf's end, with the water shimmering beneath the nostrils of the lead horses.

Eli, Prue, Cherie and Hornet ran after them the last few paces then crowded about Peter and the others when they stepped down. Prue instinctively sided with Abbey while Eli and Peter did likewise. Michael stepped forward to be alone while Hornet drew comfort by moving close to Father's side. The tug was about to set the *Fair Trader* adrift. The sailors, whose chants were still audible to those ashore, heaved at the lines, pulling the bellied sheets taut to the breeze. Their figures, like those of the passengers, were clearly visible.

Barney and Laura had seen all: the mad dash along lower Charlotte Street, the risky approach to the wharf's end and now the occupants as clear in view as they were to Barney in name. He spluttered to Laura, 'It's Dad, the one out front. It's him!' Of the others he cried, 'It's the Britfields, Abbey and Peter and Father!' Laura, who had been waving all this while, raised Barney's arm for him to start waving again. Utter disbelief, absolute amazement overtook Barney. His emotions, at breaking point, spilled over. He shouted to his father, identifying himself as Barney, his son. Laura joined too, waving wildly and tossing kisses. It was as a fever, uncontrollable and wholly consuming, a condition from which there could be no escape.

Michael was distraught. He cried. He shouted to his son, to the wind, caring not of any others. He begged, as best he could from that distance, for Barney to soon return, not to lose touch. In frustration he hammered a pylon with his open palms then renewed his cry for the return of his son. Everything of Michael was manifest before the eyes of his friends. All the deprivation and despair he had endured from that one incident in which he had been indecently provoked spilled forth. He was frantic, unable to undo that which had been done. He was stricken with the sickening thought that he might never see Barney again for he knew not Barney's intentions. He was blinded by the fear of not knowing.

As it had done before, the sea once again separated them. Barney, sobbing with want, held Michael in view for as long as possible but, gradually, the figure of his father became less clear till, finally, the small speck which he knew was his father faded altogether from sight. Michael, likewise, held his post, hoping that by some act of providence the ship would be turned around. He kept the ship within view till well after Barney became obscured, following the dwindling silhouette of the ship with his soul. When the *Fair Trader* turned southward and disappeared behind the headland of Grassy Hill, Abbey came forward with a pledge in her heart. She promised Michael that never again would he be left alone. At the same time, aboard ship, Laura comforted Barney with assurances that all would be well, that Michael was in good care.

Within a year of Barney and Laura leaving Cooktown they made contact with the Britfields, Peter Britfield and members of the O'Reilly family. Abbey responded and this, in turn, led to a regular exchange of letters. The letters conveyed information such as Laura giving birth to a healthy son, Barney starting his own farriery business, and that they were a happy family. On the Britfields' side they were able to tell that Abbey had given birth to me and named me William O'Reilly. Peter had left the police force and gone into partnership with Eli by buying James Mulligan's share of Mulligan's Trading. Michael had ceased being the farrier for the police and worked as a storeman for Mulligan's Trading. Most of Abbey's letters contained mention of Father O'Gorman. Those at the Cavalier Hotel sent their best wishes via Abbey. Barney and Laura were also very pleased to hear that Hornet had filled Barney's position at the hotel and that Peter had learned that Nicholas Hart was living on the Mossman River with his brother Dan. Barney wrote to his aunt Kate in Sydney, explaining the situation and advising that he would not be visiting because of the police.

After three years of letter writing Barney visited Cooktown and stayed with the Britfields for a month. The reunion was most successful with Barney spending much time alone with Michael. He also spent a lot of time with me. Michael was unaware of my true parentage but now, with a happy household, this was of no concern. Abbey confided to Barney that I was his child. Barney visited the

Cavalier a few times during his stay. Cherie had married and left the employ of the hotel. Prue was as busy as ever and Hornet now owned his first horse and cart. Billy was still around but showing his age.

Barney's next visit north was five years later. He again stayed with the Britfields. Peter still hadn't married and was resigned to life as a bachelor. The family had prospered since his last visit and now owned a stylish house on the side of Grassy Hill. Barney was pleased that I had taken an interest in horses and he showed me some of the finer points of horsemanship.

In subsequent years the flow of correspondence waned but the special occasions of Christmas and birthdays were still celebrated with cards and gifts. There were always letters enclosed and many of these letters still exist today.

In 1898 Mulligan's Trading was sold and the family moved to Cairns to live. Peter diarised the shift and an extract from his diary reads:

It is with some regret that Eli and I sold the business. However, Eli is of retirement age and he and Prue wish to enjoy the good years they have left. For me Cooktown has dealt a good hand. Abbey and Michael are happy to go. Most of our belongings have been forwarded to the new address. We sail tomorrow and I say 'Farewell Cooktown'.

Barney and Laura had another two sons and a daughter in the early years of their married life and eventually purchased a grazing property south of Ipswich in Queensland. They worked the cattle property and Barney continued shoeing horses to supplement the family income. The eldest lad became a surveyor and worked in the government service surveying pastoral properties while the other two sons stayed on the land. Their daughter married at age sixteen and had her first babe soon after.

Michael's health began to deteriorate after arriving in Cairns. His back problem gradually worsened till he became stooped and needed a stick to walk. The burden fell on Abbey to nurse him. For many years Peter worked as a part-time penciller for a local bookmaker. Juliette found her way to Sydney, married well and had two children. I stayed close and forged a career as a solicitor in Cairns and remained a bachelor.

Michael eventually passed away at Cairns in 1906. Family and friends attended the funeral. However, Barney had to travel by steamer and arrived some days late. His visit, with the death of Michael, made for an emotional stay.

Abbey and Peter remained in Cairns for the remainder of their lives. Peter passed away at age ninety, happy in the knowledge that Michael was never convicted of murder and that no one had ever found out that Barney's tampering with Archibald Hicksbury's sulky harness had caused his death. One year to the day after Peter's death Abbey passed away in her sleep and she too is at rest.

Barney and Laura retired on their family property. The family remained close knit, with thirteen grandchildren and some great grandchildren. Barney busied himself at the horse yards, still breaking in horses when in his seventies. The day Barney died was terrible. He was at the yards with two grandsons, roping a young horse, when he was struck by chest pain. The children ran shouting to Laura. She came running but on arriving at the yards found Barney dead in the yard with the rope still in his hand. Laura never fully recovered from the shock. Her first love had remained her lifelong love and now he was gone. She coped the best she could but those close to her knew that with the passing of Barney Laura would soon follow. Laura passed away within two years of Barney's death.

Thus was the closure of my father's life.

May he rest in peace.

William O'Reilly